Suddenly he wanted to run away more than ever, not to any formal goal like Australia or Brazil: just out of town. There was a streetcar line three blocks from his house. He could take it as far as it went, then walk. He could find something to do whenever he got far enough away. "My name is John—John Carter." Or, with a tightening in his throat, he wished that his father would come home and say heartily, "It's all right, son, I've talked to Caldwell," and magically, as it had been long ago in his childhood, it would be all right. But if he was young enough to hope for these escapes, he was old enough to know bitterly that they were impossible.

Allan Seager
"No Son, No Gun, No Streetcar"

"Were they pretty shocked?"

"Who?"

"The faculty. You know: all the ones who knew me, like the coaches I worked with. What did they say?"

"No one said much of anything. I think they were all surprised. I mean you were just about the last person anyone expected to be involved . . . like this. I'm afraid *I* was rather surprised, too," he added shyly, waiting.

But Flynn only snorted and looked out the window at the tower of the Administration Building, red brick against blue sky. At last he said: "I guess there *is* something wrong with me, Mr. Beckman, because I can't for the life of me see what business it is of anyone else what I do."

Gore Vidal
"The Zenner Trophy"

Robert Benard, a graduate of Yale University, lives and works in New York City. He is the author of *A Catholic Education* and the editor of *All Problems are Simple* And Other Stories, available in Laurel-Leaf editions.

In praise of ALL PROBLEMS ARE SIMPLE
And Other Stories
Nineteen Views of the College Years
"A fine collection of stories about college life, relationships, friendships, and discovery."—*School Library Journal*

QUANTITY SALES

Most Dell books are available at special quantity discounts when purchased in bulk by corporations, organizations, and special-interest groups. Custom imprinting or excerpting can also be done to fit special needs. For details write: Dell Publishing, 666 Fifth Avenue, New York, NY 10103. Attn.: Special Sales Department.

INDIVIDUAL SALES

Are there any Dell books you want but cannot find in your local stores? If so, you can order them directly from us. You can get any Dell book in print. Simply include the book's title, author, and ISBN number if you have it, along with a check or money order (no cash can be accepted) for the full retail price plus $2.00 to cover shipping and handling. Mail to: Dell Readers Service, P.O. Box 5057, Des Plaines, IL 60017.

Laurel-Leaf Library of American Literature

DO YOU LIKE IT HERE?

Edited by
Robert Benard

LAUREL-LEAF BOOKS bring together under a single imprint outstanding works of fiction and nonfiction particularly suitable for young adult readers, both in and out of the classroom. Charles F. Reasoner, Professor Emeritus of Children's Literature and Reading, New York University, is consultant to this series.

Published by
Dell Publishing
a division of
Bantam Doubleday Dell Publishing Group, Inc.
666 Fifth Avenue
New York, New York 10103

ISBN: 0-440-20435-6

RL: 7.2

Printed in the United States of America

September 1989

10 9 8 7 6 5 4 3 2 1

KRI

For his legerdemain in helping me compile this anthology I thank Gregg Mitchell; for her indefatigable help in assembling permissions, I thank Cary Fisher; and for his continuing seigneurial grace I thank my editor, George Nicholson.

CONTENTS

INTRODUCTION

The high school years, unveiling a maze of fresh possibilities, demand tentative stakeouts of independence, groping forays into the uncharted terrain of self-definition, painful yet exhilarating advances toward the goal of authentic identity.

In their incarnation of this necessary journey, these stories—by their revelatory beauty, meticulous detail, and moral generosity—transport the reader into their worlds and provide a set of maps, a series of guideposts, a list of ways into the future.

During this time of muscle-flexing, of testing limits, the grip of the past can be lethal: it cripples in "In History Audrey Touched Michael"; strangles speech in "Memorial Day"; impels a flight for survival in "The Hollow Boy" and an escape into morbid fancy in "The Liar" and "The Haunted Boy." But if its tense pressure can spur conformity and *self*-sacrifice, as in "First Love and Other Sorrows," it can also liberate—you can light out on your own—by instilling bravery, as in "The Other Way" and "Split Cherry Tree."

Successful stories are moral inquiries into the claims of authority. In high school, while still under its questionable thumb, officially children but prey to the same volatile crises and ennobling yearnings of any adult, the keen calibration of value constitutes education. Youth is all of life writ large, but things seem more intense, ordeals cut deeper, problems seem more intractable because they are unprecedented, lacking the ballast and detachment that experience provides. In "A Lesson in History" the teacher brutally tries to crush his student's spirit; in "The Zenner Trophy" he secretly envies Flynn's fierce integrity while conspiring in its punishment. But in "No Son, No Gun, No Streetcar" the voice of authority is redemptive, urging courage.

Clinging furiously to the past betrays fear of the future: difference seems dangerous. But whether its form is racial, class, or sexual, fear toxified into prejudice has sure antidotes: knowledge and love. These stories show the galvanizing effect of resistance, the refusal to recoil before freedom.

The wrenching power of love is also dramatized: romantic love haunts a lifetime in "The Other Times" and bursts out of the blue in "Mary Pride"; its sudden ending induces shock in "Sixteen" and unsuspected resilience in "Ten Indians."

All these stories underscore that finding yourself requires the freedom that can be quickened only by knowledge. To make yourself *from* something *into* something is the human vocation, one that exacts burdens of resistance and daring, but that earns the honor of triumphant dignity.

You Can't Tell a Man by the Song He Sings

by Philip Roth

It was in a freshman high school class called "Occupations" that, fifteen years ago, I first met the ex-con, Alberto Pelagutti. The first week my new classmates and I were given "a battery of tests" designed to reveal our skills, deficiencies, tendencies, and psyches. At the end of the week, Mr. Russo, the Occupations teacher, would add the skills, subtract the deficiencies, and tell us what jobs best suited our talents; it was all mysterious but scientific. I remember we first took a "Preference Test": "Which would you prefer to do, this, that, or the other thing . . ." Albie Pelagutti sat one seat behind me and to my left, and while this first day of high school I strolled happily through the test, examining ancient fossils here, defending criminals there, Albie, like the inside of Vesuvius, rose, fell, pitched, tossed, and swelled in his chair. When he finally made a decision, he made it. You could hear his pencil drive the *x* into the column opposite the activity in which he thought it wisest to prefer to engage. His agony reinforced the legend that had preceded him: he was seventeen; had just left Jamesburg Reformatory; this was his third high school, his third freshman year; but now—I heard another *x* driven home—he had decided "to go straight."

Halfway through the hour Mr. Russo left the room. "I'm going for a drink," he said. Russo was forever at pains to let us know what a square-shooter he was and that, unlike other teachers we might have had, he would not go out the front door of the classroom to sneak around to the back door and observe how responsible we were. And sure enough, when he returned after going for a drink, his lips were wet; when he came back from the men's room, you could smell the soap on his hands. "Take your time, boys," he said, and the door swung shut behind him.

His black wing-tip shoes beat down the marble corridor and five thick fingers dug into my shoulder. I turned around; it was Pelagutti. "What?" I said. "Number twenty-six," Pelagutti said, "What's the answer?" I gave him the truth: "Anything." Pelagutti rose halfway over his desk and glared at me. He was a hippopotamus, big, black, and smelly; his short sleeves squeezed tight around his monstrous arms as though they were taking his own blood pressure—which at that moment was sky-bound: "What's the answer!" Menaced, I flipped back three pages in my question booklet and reread number twenty-six. "Which would you prefer to do: (1) Attend a World Trade Convention. (2) Pick cherries. (3) Stay with and read to a sick friend. (4) Tinker with automobile engines." I looked blank-faced back to Albie, and shrugged my shoulders. "It doesn't matter—there's no right answer. Anything." He almost rocketed out of his seat. "Don't give me that crap! What's the answer!" Strange heads popped up all over the room—thin-eyed glances, hissing lips, shaming grins—and I realized that any minute Russo, wet-lipped, might come back and my first day in high school I would be caught cheating. I looked again at number twenty-six; then back to Albie; and then propelled—as I always was towards him—by anger, pity, fear, love, vengeance, and an instinct for irony that was at the time delicate as a mallet, I whispered, "Stay and read to a sick friend." The volcano subsided, and Albie and I had met.

We became friends. He remained at my elbow throughout the testing, then throughout lunch, then after school. I learned that Albie, as a youth, had done all the things I, under direction, had not: he had eaten hamburgers in strange diners; he had gone out after cold showers, wet-haired, into winter weather; he had been cruel to animals; he had trafficked with whores; he had stolen, he had been caught, and he had paid. But now he told me, as I unwrapped my lunch in the candy store across from school, "Now I'm through crappin' around. I'm gettin' an education. I'm gonna—" and I think he picked up the figure from a movie musical he had seen the previous afternoon while the rest of us were in English class—"I'm gonna put my best foot forward." The following week when Russo read the results of the testing it appeared that Albie's feet were not only moving forward but finding strange, wonderful paths. Russo sat at his desk, piles of tests stacked before him like ammunition, charts and diagrams mounted huge on either side, and delivered our destinies. Albie and I were going to be lawyers.

Of all that Albie confessed to me that first week, one fact in particular fastened on my brain: I soon forgot the town in Sicily where he was born; the occupation of his father (he either made ice or delivered it); the year and model of the cars he had stolen. I did not forget though that Albie had apparently been the star of the Jamesburg Reformatory baseball team. When I was selected by the gym teacher, Mr. Hopper, to captain one of my gym class's softball teams (we played softball until the World Series was over, then switched to touch football), I knew that I had to get Pelagutti on my side. With those arms he could hit the ball a mile.

The day teams were to be selected Albie shuffled back and forth at my side, while in the locker room I changed into my gym uniform—jockstrap, khaki-colored shorts, T-shirt, sweat socks, and sneakers. Albie had already changed: beneath his khaki gym shorts he did not wear a support but retained his lavender undershorts; they hung down three inches below the outer shorts and looked like a long fancy hem. Instead of a T-shirt he wore a sleeveless undershirt; and beneath his high, tar-black sneakers he wore thin black silk socks with slender arrows embroidered up the sides. Naked he might, like some centuries-dead ancestor, have tossed lions to their death in the Colosseum; the outfit, though I didn't tell him, detracted from his dignity.

As we left the locker room and padded through the dark basement corridor and up onto the sunny September playing field, he talked continually, "I didn't play sports when I was a kid, but I played at Jamesburg and baseball came to me like nothing." I nodded my head. "What you think of Pete Reiser?" he asked. "He's a pretty good man," I said. "What you think of Tommy Henrich?" "I don't know," I answered, "he's dependable, I guess." As a Dodger fan I preferred Reiser to the Yankees' Henrich; and besides, my tastes have always been a bit baroque, and Reiser, who repeatedly bounced off outfield walls to save the day for Brooklyn, had won a special trophy in the Cooperstown of my heart. "Yeh," Albie said, "I like all them Yankees."

I didn't have a chance to ask Albie what he meant by that, for Mr. Hopper, bronzed, smiling, erect, was flipping a coin; I looked up, saw the glint in the sun, and I was calling "heads." It landed tails and the other captain had first choice. My heart flopped over when he looked at Albie's arms, but calmed when he passed on and chose first a tall, lean, first-baseman type. Immediately I said, "I'll take Pelagutti." You don't very often see smiles like the one that crossed Albie Pelagutti's face that moment: You would think I had paroled him from a life sentence.

The game began. I played shortstop—left-handed—and batted second; Albie was in center field and, at his wish, batted fourth. Their first man grounded out, me to the first baseman. The next batter hit a high, lofty fly ball to center field. The moment I saw Albie move after it I knew Tommy Henrich and Pete Reiser were only names to him; all he knew about baseball he'd boned up on the night before. While the ball hung in the air, Albie jumped up and down beneath it, his arms raised upward directly above his head; his wrists were glued together, and his two hands flapped open and closed like butterfly's wings, begging the ball toward them.

"C'mon," he was screaming to the sky, "c'mon you bastard . . ." And his legs bicycle-pumped up and down, up and down. I hope the moment of my death does not take as long as it did for that damn ball to drop. It hung, it hung, Albie cavorting beneath like a Holy Roller. And then it landed, smack into Albie's chest. The runner was rounding second and heading for third while Albie twirled all around, looking, his arms down now, stretched out, as though he were playing ring-around-a-rosy with two invisible children. "Behind you, Pelagutti!" I screamed. He stopped moving. "What?" he called back to me. I ran halfway out to center field. "Behind you—relay it!" And then, as the runner rounded third, I had to stand there defining "relay" to him.

At the end of the first half of the first inning we came to bat behind, 8-0—eight home runs, all relayed in too late by Pelagutti.

Out of a masochistic delight I must describe Albie at the plate: first, he *faced* the pitcher; then, when he swung at the ball—and he did, at every one—it was not to the side but down, as though he were driving a peg into the ground. Don't ask if he was right-handed or left-handed. I don't know.

While we changed out of our gym uniforms I was silent. I boiled as I watched Pelagutti from the corner of my eye. He kicked off those crazy black sneakers and pulled his pink gaucho shirt on over his undershirt—there was still a red spot above the U front of the undershirt where the first fly ball had hit him. Without removing his gym shorts he stuck his feet into his gray trousers—I watched as he hoisted the trousers over the red splotches where ground balls had banged off his shins, past the red splotches where pitched balls had smacked his knee caps and thighs.

Finally I spoke. "Damn you, Pelagutti, you wouldn't know Pete Reiser if you fell over him!" He was stuffing his sneakers into his locker; he didn't answer. I was talking to his mountainous pink shirt back. "Where do you come off telling me you played for that prison team?" He mumbled something. "What?" I said. "I did," he grumbled. "Bullshit!" I said. He turned and, black-eyed, glared at me: "I did!" "That must've been some team!" I said. We did not speak as we left the locker room. As we passed the gym office on our way up to Occupations, Mr. Hopper looked up from his desk and winked at me. Then he motioned his head at Pelagutti to indicate that he knew I'd picked a lemon, but how could I have expected a bum like Pelagutti to be an All-American boy in the first place? Then Mr. Hopper turned his sun-lamped head back to his desk.

"Now," I said to Pelagutti as we turned at the second floor landing, "now I'm stuck with you for the rest of the term." He shuffled ahead of me without answering; his oxlike behind should have had a tail on it to flick the flies away—it infuriated me. "You goddamn liar!" I said.

He spun around as fast as an ox can. "You ain't stuck with nobody." We were at the top of the landing headed into the locker-lined corridor; the kids who were piling up the stairs behind stopped, listened. "No you ain't, you snot-ass!" And I saw five hairy knuckles coming right at my mouth. I moved, but not in time, and heard a crash inside the bridge of my nose. I felt my hips dip back, my legs and head come forward, and, curved like the letter *c,* I was swept fifteen feet backward before I felt cold marble beneath the palms of my hands. Albie stepped around me and into the Occupations room. Just then I looked up to see Mr. Russo's black wing-tip shoes enter the room. I'm almost sure he had seen Albie blast me but I'll never know. Nobody, including Albie and myself, ever mentioned it again. Perhaps it had been a mistake for me to call Albie a liar, but if he had starred at baseball, it was in some league I did not know.

By way of contrast I want to introduce Duke Scarpa, another ex-con who was with us that year. Neither Albie nor the Duke, incidentally, was a typical member of my high school community. Both lived at the other end of Newark, "down neck," and they had reached us only after the Board of Education had tried Albie at two other schools and the Duke at four. The Board hoped finally, like Marx, that the higher culture would absorb the lower.

Albie and Duke had no particular use for each other; where Albie had made up his mind to go straight, one always felt that the Duke, in his oily quietness, his boneless grace, was planning a job. Yet, though affection never lived between them, Duke wandered after Albie and me, aware, I suspect, that if Albie despised him it was because he was able to read his soul—and that such an associate was easier to abide than one who despises you because he does not know your soul at all. Where Albie was a hippopotamus, an ox, Duke was reptilian. Me? I don't know; it is easy to spot the animal in one's fellows.

During lunch hour, the Duke and I used to spar with each other in the hall outside the cafeteria. He did not know a hook from a jab and disliked having his dark skin roughened or his hair mussed; but he so delighted in moving, bobbing, coiling, and uncoiling, that I think he would have paid for the privilege of playing the serpent with me. He hypnotized me, the Duke; he pulled some slimy string inside me—where Albie Pelagutti sought and stretched a deeper and, I think, a nobler cord.

But I make Albie sound like peaches-and-cream. Let me tell you what he and I did to Mr. Russo.

Russo believed in his battery of tests as his immigrant parents (and Albie's, and maybe Albie himself) believed in papal infallibility. If the tests said Albie was going to be a lawyer then he was going to be a lawyer. As for Albie's past, it seemed only to increase Russo's devotion to the prophecy: he approached Albie with salvation in his eyes. In September, then, he gave Albie a biography to read, the life of Oliver Wendell Holmes; during October, once a week, he had the poor fellow speak impromptu before the class; in November he had him write a report on the Constitution, which I wrote; and then in December, the final indignity, he sent Albie and me (and two others who displayed a legal bent) to the Essex County Court House where we could see "real lawyers in action."

It was a cold, windy morning and as we flicked our cigarettes at the Lincoln statue on the courtyard plaza, and started up the long flight of white cement steps, Albie suddenly did an about-face and headed back across the plaza and out to Market Street. I called to him but he shouted back that he had seen it all before, and then he was not walking, but running towards the crowded downtown streets, pursued not by police, but by other days. It wasn't that he considered Russo an ass for having sent him to visit the Court House—Albie respected teachers too much for that; rather I think he felt Russo had tried to rub his nose in it.

No surprise, then, when the next day after gym Albie announced his assault on the Occupations teacher; it was the first crime he had planned since his decision to go straight back in September. He outlined the action to me and indicated that I should pass the details on to the other members of the class. As liaison between Albie and the well-behaved, healthy nonconvicts like myself who made up the rest of the class, I was stationed at the classroom door and as each member passed in I unfolded the plot into his ear: "As soon after ten-fifteen as Russo turns to the blackboard, you bend over to tie your shoelace." If a classmate looked back at me puzzled, I would motion to Pelagutti hulking over his desk; the puzzled expression would vanish and another accomplice would enter the room. The only one who gave me any trouble was the Duke. He listened to the plan and then scowled back at me with the look of a man who's got his own syndicate, and, in fact, has never even heard of yours.

Finally the bell rang; I closed the door behind me and moved noiselessly to my desk. I waited for the clock to move to a quarter after; it did; and then Russo turned to the board to write upon it the salary range of aluminum workers. I bent to tie my shoelaces—beneath all the desks I saw other upside-down grinning faces. To my left behind me I heard Albie hissing; his hands fumbled about his black silk socks, and the hiss grew and grew until it was a rush of Sicilian, muttered, spewed, vicious. The exchange was strictly between Russo and himself. I looked to the front of the classroom, my fingers knotting and unknotting my shoelaces, the blood pumping now to my face. I saw Russo's legs turn. What a sight he must have seen—where there had been twenty-five faces, now there was nothing. Just desks. "Okay," I heard Russo say, "okay." And then he gave a little clap with his hands. "That's enough now, fellas. The joke is over. Sit up." And then Albie's hiss traveled to all the blood-pinked ears below the desks; it rushed about us like a subterranean stream—"Stay down!"

While Russo asked us to get up we stayed down. And we did not sit up until Albie told us to; and then under his direction we were singing—

> Don't sit under the apple tree
> With anyone else but me,
> Anyone else but me,
> Anyone else but me,
> Oh, no, no, don't sit under the apple tree . . .

And then in time to the music we clapped. What a noise!

Mr. Russo stood motionless at the front of the class, listening, astonished. He wore a neatly pressed dark blue pin-striped suit, a tan tie with a collie's head in the center, and a tieclasp with the initials R.R. engraved upon it; he had on the black wing-tip shoes; they glittered. Russo, who believed in neatness, honesty, punctuality, planned destinies—who believed in the future, in Occupations! And next to me, behind me, inside me, all over me—Albie! We looked at each other, Albie and I, and my lungs split with joy: *"Don't sit under the apple tree—"* Albie's monotone boomed out, and then a thick liquid crooner's voice behind Albie bathed me in sound: it was the Duke's; he clapped to a tango beat.

Russo leaned for a moment against a visual aids chart—"Skilled Laborers: Salaries and Requirements"—and then scraped back his chair and plunged down into it, so far down it looked to have no bottom. He lowered his big head to the desk and his shoulders curled forward like the ends of wet paper; and that was when Albie pulled his coup. He stopped singing "Don't Sit Under the Apple Tree"; we all stopped. Russo looked up at the silence; his eyes black and baggy, he stared at our leader, Alberto Pelagutti. Slowly Russo began to shake his head from side to side: this was no Capone, this was a Garibaldi! Russo waited, I waited, we all waited. Albie slowly rose, and began to sing *"Oh, say can you see, by the dawn's early light, what so proudly we hailed—"* And we all stood and joined him. Tears sparkling on his long black lashes, Mr. Robert Russo dragged himself wearily up from his desk, beaten, and as the Pelagutti basso boomed disastrously behind me, I saw Russo's lips begin to move, *"the bombs bursting in air, gave proof—"* God, did we sing!

Albie left school in June of that year—he had passed only Occupations—but our comradeship, that strange vessel, was smashed to bits at noon one day a few months earlier. It was a lunch hour in March, the Duke and I were sparring in the hall outside the cafeteria, and Albie, who had been more hospitable to the Duke since the day his warm, liquid voice had joined the others—Albie had decided to act as our referee, jumping between us, separating our clinches, warning us about low blows, grabbing out for the Duke's droopy crotch, in general having a good time. I remember that the Duke and I were in a clinch; as I showered soft little punches to his kidneys he squirmed in my embrace. The sun shone through the window behind him, lighting up his hair like a nest of snakes. I fluttered his sides, he twisted, I breathed hard through my nose, my eyes registered on his snaky hair, and suddenly Albie wedged between and knocked us apart—the Duke plunged sideways, I plunged forward, and my fist crashed through the window that Scarpa had been using as his corner. Feet pounded; in a second a wisecracking, guiltless, chewing crowd was gathered around me, just me. Albie and the Duke were gone. I cursed them both, the honorless bastards! The crowd did not drift back to lunch until the head dietitian, a huge, varicose-veined matron in a laundry-stiff white uniform had written down my name and led me to the nurse's office to have the glass picked out of my knuckles. Later in the afternoon I was called for the first and only time to the office of Mr. Wendell, the Principal.

Fifteen years have passed since then and I do not know what has happened to Albie Pelagutti. If he is a gangster he was not one with notoriety or money enough for the Kefauver Committee to interest itself in several years ago. When the Crime Committee reached New Jersey I followed their investigations carefully but never did I read in the papers the name Alberto Pelagutti or even Duke Scarpa—though who can tell what name the Duke is known by now. I do know, however, what happened to the Occupations teacher, for when another Senate Committee swooped through the state a while back it was discovered that Robert Russo—among others—had been a Marxist while attending Montclair State Teachers' College circa 1935. Russo refused to answer some of the Committee's questions, and the Newark Board of Education met, chastised, and dismissed him. I read now and then in the Newark *News* that Civil Liberties Union attorneys are still trying to appeal his case, and I have even written a letter to the Board of Education swearing that if anything subversive was ever done to my character, it wasn't done by my ex-high school teacher, Russo; if he was a Communist I never knew it. I could not decide whether or not to include in the letter a report of the "Star-Spangled Banner" incident: Who knows what is and is not proof to the crotchety ladies and chainstore owners who sit and die on Boards of Education?

And if (to alter an Ancient's text) a man's history is his fate, who knows whether the Newark Board of Education will ever attend to a letter written to them by me. I mean, have fifteen years buried that afternoon I was called to see the Principal?

. . . He was a tall, distinguished gentleman and as I entered his office he rose and extended his hand. The same sun that an hour earlier had lit up snakes in the Duke's hair now slanted through Mr. Wendell's blinds and warmed his deep green carpet. "How do you do?" he said. "Yes," I answered, non sequiturly, and ducked my bandaged hand under my unbandaged hand. Graciously he said, "Sit down, won't you?" Frightened, unpracticed, I performed an aborted curtsy and sat. I watched Mr. Wendell go to his metal filing cabinet, slide one drawer open, and take from it a large white index card. He set the card on his desk and motioned me over so I might read what was typed on the card. At the top, in caps, was my whole name—last, first, and middle; below the name was a Roman numeral one, and beside it, "Fighting in corridor; broke window (3/19/42)." Already documented. And on a big card with plenty of space.

I returned to my chair and sat back as Mr. Wendell told me that the card would follow me through life. At first I listened, but as he talked on and on the drama went out of what he said, and my attention wandered to his filing cabinet. I began to imagine the cards inside, Albie's card and the Duke's, and then I understood—just short of forgiveness—why the two of them had zoomed off and left me to pay penance for the window by myself. Albie, you see, had always known about the filing cabinet and these index cards; I hadn't; and Russo, poor Russo, has only recently found out.

Mary Pride
by Sue Kaufman

He had been dressed and waiting for twenty minutes, and was sitting on the end of his carefully remade bed in the darkness, thinking that the whole thing was really quite funny, like a cartoon about an elopement, when the whistle finally came. Round, low, warble-pure on the first note, it lightly switched to a clean bobwhite cutoff—a startling sound for a girl to make, especially that one. He picked up the little canvas airline bag that held his swimming trunks and a towel, quickly stole down the uncarpeted stairs, and went out the door, managing to close it behind him without so much as a click. She stood under the streetlight, straddling a boy's bicycle, her brother's, he supposed. With one long look at her, dressed in worn jeans, a shirt, sneakers, a bandanna around her head, he stopped thinking there was anything funny. She wouldn't look that way for anyone else, he thought angrily, irrationally, and padded noiselessly up the driveway to the garage.

Blindly entering the gassy darkness, he groped past rusted garden furniture, a lawn mower, a stack of old M.D. license plates until his fingers closed over the cold handlebars. Carefully he edged the bike out past the coupe's left fender and wheeled it to the front of the house. As he came up, she reached into a brown paper shopping bag hanging off her handlebars and took out a lumpy towel. "It keeps smacking my knees when I pedal," she explained loudly, ignoring the fact that it was just a little past five in the morning and everyone on the block was sleeping. "Can I put it in your basket?" He nodded, then inexplicably dropped the towel; it exploded on the damp sidewalk, a red bathing suit, a cap of pudgy red rubber flowers, a container of Toujours Moi talcum rolling out. She dropped her bike with a tinny clatter and stooped to pick up her swimming things, flipping them all back into the towel, jelly-roll fashion, then jamming it into his basket atop the canvas bag. "We'll use my shopping bags for the flowers. I brought four," she said, louder than ever, and went and remounted the boy's bicycle with movements that made him blink.

"Where are we going?" he asked, doggedly whispering.

"The bay. Dodie Finch and Greely Smith are meeting us there," she called, and set off. As he followed, David glanced uneasily up and down the block of ugly-tidy houses, certain that curious eyes were peeping from behind the pulled shades and billowing curtains, and equally certain she had intentionally, perversely wished to draw them. She's really crazy, he thought, knowing very well she had insisted on picking him up because she was ashamed of her own street, her own house; too dumb not to guess that he, just like every other boy in the three top grades of Willett High School, knew exactly where she lived. In fact he, like many others, often purposely used that rundown little street on his way into the village to run an errand for his mother, just to be able to pass the dingy stucco house where she lived with her mother, younger brother, and hopeless drunk of a father, and to let his mind, for soothing seconds, make the plunge from glaring daylight to suave soft dark.

As they turned onto the deserted boulevard, the sky above the streetlamps seemed a lighter gray. It was five-fifteen on what promised to be a fine clear day in June, ground mist aside. Which meant the bunting-trimmed tables could be set up on the school lawn, under the dipping willows, and mothers in straw and flower hats, fathers in light suits could pleasantly mill about, drinking orange punch out of paper cups and exchanging mutual congratulations.

It was the dawn of Willett's graduation day, the day on which he, David Thorne, and by some miracle she, Mary Pride, would graduate from Willett High School. Though no one quite knew why or when they had originated, an elaborate set of traditions had become attached to the events of this day. Always, for as long as anyone could remember, an escutcheon had stood on the auditorium platform where the graduating class sat trembling and perspiring in their white dresses and dark suits, a shield fashioned from flowers, bearing a blue *W* and the class numerals in cornflow-

ers on a white ground of daisies. Strangely enough, it was the
particular job of the graduating class to rise before dawn (on this
one day they ought to have been allowed the sleep of the just) and,
on bicycles (cars were taboo), to forage in the empty fields and
back lots of Willett for the flowers used in the shield.

Since hundreds of flowers were needed, the absolute minimum
was one bag of flowers per senior; two were hoped for. Once found,
the flowers were carried back to the school and dumped on the
grass in back of the gymnasium, a place where the more artistic
members of the junior class sat waiting, ready to begin weaving
them into a wire frame. Released, the seniors slowly convened at
Jim's Diner in the village. After eating a large breakfast, and after
waiting out a short token interval for digestion, they proceeded to a
small bathing beach on the inlet. There, in lockers still dank with
winter, they changed into bathing suits; giggling, covered with
goose bumps, they then ventured out onto the dock and after much
shoving and hanging back, plunged shrieking and howling into the
still chilly waters of the bay, unwillingly performing the ritual
which had become a sort of baptism for the graduation that afternoon.

David, who had decided long in advance that the whole set of
customs was stupid and childish, was now angrily certain of it as
he cycled down an asphalt road slick as tar from mist and dew.
Though for the first time in his life he was alone with Mary Pride
—a situation he had efficiently dealt with many times in his imagination—he couldn't think of anything but how cold he was without a sweater, how queasy he felt without breakfast, and how
frightened he suddenly was; riding along, he found he couldn't
remember one word of the valedictory address he had to give that
afternoon. At the moment it would have soothed him to see the
work of a practical joker in his being given Mary Pride as a part-
ner, but he knew very well that poor old Mr. Buckley had done the
pairing, and knew, better than anyone, that even had one of his
classmates done it, there was just no joke. True, Mary Pride was
what she was and, true, he was the valedictorian, one of the most
brilliant students Willett High School had seen in many years, but
he was not by a long shot the classic grind, the pimply bespectacled
scapegoat who is terrified of girls and is the constant butt of his

schoolmates' jokes. He didn't have pimples, he didn't wear glasses. He was tall, went out for sports, and was attractive enough to have always had all the friends and girls he could want. If he didn't want many, if he carefully limited the number of these, it was not out of any bookish sense of superiority but out of almost neurotic hypersensitivity about his father. Oh, he was the doctor's son all right, but with a difference. Like Mary Pride's father, his father drank, but unlike Mary Pride's father, who had started out as a bartender, his father had destroyed a practice which had once encompassed five counties, had disgraced a noble profession, to say nothing of what he had done to his wife, his son. Yet, strangely, David could not hate him. He was just horribly ashamed, in a coldly intellectualized way, of such massive human failure, and now, as he rode along behind Mary Pride, he could not help being struck by the irony of it all, bitterly thinking: If nothing else, we have *them* in common.

With a sudden mechanical click the streetlights went off, leaving the morning hanging shades lighter about them. Everything was coated with moisture; there was a steady *drip-a-drip* from the thick tangles of foliage clumped on either side of the road and from the tall old maples and elms that branched out over the street. His English bike was well over six years old, but David had taken care of it, just as he took care of all the personal possessions that so rarely came his way, and it was good as new. He rode easily, almost effortlessly, while up ahead Mary Pride was almost doubled over with the job of pedaling her brother's old balloon-tire bike. He had seen she was grimly determined to stay in the lead, and he let her, accepting the fact that she resented being paired off with him and didn't even want to ride alongside him. This was not because there was someone else she would rather have been with, or ought to have been with—a girl like that didn't have steady boyfriends; no one wanted the doubtful honor of it—but simply because she disliked him intensely, having mistaken his reluctance to venture even a casual "hi" or "good morning" for pure priggish snobbery.

If she only knew, thought David, suddenly relaxed enough to let his mind drift in this direction. As he had ridden along, his speech had completely come back to him, and he was so relieved he almost began to enjoy the predawn dampness, the strangeness of being out at that unlikely hour. Against his will he found himself staring at Mary Pride's back, unable to keep from noticing the way the thin strained shirting clearly outlined the straps and band of her brassiere, the suggestive way the worn brown leather seat fitted her full bottom. And then, in spite of everything—the hour, the surroundings—he felt it all beginning, the sludgy thickening of throat and tongue, the tensing of muscles in calves and forearms, the strange fumy lechery rising, burning in his chest. Like many sluttish girls—or, at least, girls with sluttish reputations—she roused frighteningly powerful and conflicting emotions: a pure, almost uncontainable lust, along with the brutal need to inflict humiliation, pain. It was this that had kept David away from her, had kept him from making his try like the others. Though, like the others, he despised her, it was just because he despised her that he could not take advantage of what she was. Concerned for her, he was even more concerned for himself; he just didn't think he'd be able to handle the crushing load of self-loathing that was bound to come later, when he had finished with her, in whatever way.

As a result, he steered clear of her in the flesh and let himself meet her only in his mind, constructing lurid little daydreams from what he had heard stated as facts. For the stories about the poor girl were endless, and though David doubted that they were all true, they had the same powerful ability to goad and rouse that her person did, and just by saying some of them over to oneself one could experience a certain intense pleasure—without guilt. And so David let himself go now as he bicycled along in the raw morning air, let his mind swarm and fill with violent images while he softly repeated, like some profane litany, key phrases and words from the things he had heard.

Suddenly, without warning, Mary Pride pulled over to the side of the road, and he shot past her, braking his bike with a grinding squeak. When he turned he saw that she had already left her bicycle on the curbstone and had started on tiptoe across someone's lawn, her target a large flower bed which began on the left side of the house's front steps and ended against a tall privet hedge. Like the rule which forbade the use of cars, another stated that no one, under any circumstances, was to pick flowers from the private gardens in the town. Honor-bound honor student that he was, David smoldered with disgust and hatred as he watched her trample through the bed and greedily pick the flowers, and he began to glance almost hopefully up at the lead-framed windows where the blinds remained tightly closed. She finally came to dump the wet blue flowers into his wicker bicycle basket and smiled up into his furious face. He blushed, almost choking on his anger, and said hoarsely, "There are laws against trespassing."

"Oh, laws," she said with a scornful little laugh, and, her pale eyes full of contempt for all the laws she had knowingly, willfully, gladly broken, she went and remounted her bicycle.

Murder in his heart, David fell in behind her once again. Soon, with an abrupt turnoff, they left the main boulevard, and, passing through an open wooden gate, entered the intricate network of back roads that eventually led, like a maze, to the bay. Here asphalt gave way to dirt; trees arched and tangled in thick meshes overhead; houses, larger, statelier, sat far back on gently graded slopes, half hidden by tall ivy-covered walls or high hedges, reached by long winding gravel drives. As he followed her sure lead, David smiled to himself, taking a sanctimonious pleasure in noting the way she knew each devious turnoff, each new rutted road, until they suddenly passed an ugly yellow stucco wall, higher than the rest, topped with crude iron spikes, and his nasty smile vanished. In fact, he almost squirmed on his bicycle seat as he remembered being parked against that wall, remembered the glare of the flashlight that had thrust through the rolled-down window of his father's coupe and mercilessly exposed him, lipstick-smirched, struggling upward on the seat (the unbuttoned girl wisely stayed down), while a harsh Scottish-caretaker voice ordered him to get a move on before the cops were called. With a roar of the motor and a scrunch of tires on loose dirt, he *had* gotten a move on and had not been back in the two months since. But now, forced to let up on Mary Pride, unable to take cover in self-righteous deceit, David began to use her, found he could not keep from wondering what it would be like when she was beside one in a car parked under fragrant maples, the *tick-a-crick* of leaves, the soft chirrup of crickets, and the slow turning of bodies the only sounds in the dark.

Under a dazzling impact of red-gold light his mind stopped short. Dead ahead the sun was rising over the water, a red ball which burned through thinning mists; to the left and right of the road low grassy hills rolled away and glistened, covered with such a profusion of buttercups, daisies, dandelions, and cornflowers that David's heart began to race. The sun cast a heavy orange-yellow glaze on everything, thickly coating the crude little shacks that stood down near the water, ugly lean-tos which the fishermen used for their equipment. Between the shacks, rowboats lay on their sides in the sand, looking like big exhausted fish washed up by the tide. Not another living soul was about.

Mary Pride had already pulled her bike up into the grass on the right side of the road and sat in the roadbed unlacing her red sneakers. She set them carefully by the bicycle, rose, and without so much as a glance back at him, slipped the shopping bags off the handlebars and waded barefoot into the deep tangled grasses. When she got as far as a large oak halfway up the slope, she unceremoniously sat down on the grassless patch under its boughs, took a pack of cigarettes from her shirt pocket, and lit one. To his great annoyance, her utter indifference stung him, made him feel foolish. He left his bike on the grass near hers and resentfully plunged into the high wet grass, hating the way the bottoms of his khaki pants immediately became drenched and stuck to his ankles. When he reached the place where she sat, lordly as Robin Hood, under the spreading tree, she turned up her pale-blue eyes and for an unnerving moment just stared at him. Then, wordlessly, she held out the pack of cigarettes, with a book of matches neatly tucked down into the cellophane wrapper. After he lit one, he awkwardly dropped down into the dirt at her side. For several minutes they sat in almost hostile silence while twin elastic threads of smoke rose tautly to the boughs overhead, then broke into curly tangles when they hit the leaves. "Why'nt you roll up your pants?" she said suddenly. "And take off your sneakers. They'll only get all wet and sloshy."

Shrugging (but also maddeningly flushing), he rolled the soggy pants halfway up his calves but left his sneakers on; he had always been secretly ashamed of his long, bony, bumpy-toed feet. "Where do you suppose the others are?" he asked, not because he cared, but because he knew she did.

To his surprise she looked bored. "The easiest way to get here is from around the other side," she said, irritating him by her assumption that he would not know this part of town. She stood up. "I think we each ought to get one of a kind," she said as she handed him two paper bags. "One daisy and one cornflower apiece —don't you?"

He nodded and swallowed hard, forced to look away from the face suspended above him: several yellow snails of pinned-flat curls had worked their way out of the edges of her Paisley scarf; without its usual frame of carefully streaked hair, without the color lent by lipstick and powder, her face seemed strange—larger, pale, almost plain—and yet a blunted look of honesty and health and cleanliness shone out of those flat freckled planes, a look that took him unawares and deeply moved him, coming from where it did. Confused, he watched her stride purposefully away up the slope, then suddenly stop and begin to snatch at daisies, and he wondered if it was the cigarette that made him feel so lightheaded. He reluctantly rose and ambled out onto the hill. He veered off at an angle to the place where she worked and kept his distance from clumps of shiny three-pronged leaves he thought might be poison ivy. The thatchy abundance of flowers excited him, and soon he was wholly absorbed in the mechanics of picking the white flowers with furry gold centers, liking the way the hollow tubes of stems broke cleanly between his fingers, even liking the sticky milky substance they left. Methodically, as rhythmically as a field hand, he bent and picked, bent and picked, and he slowly filled one of the bags, astonished when he finally found himself on the crown of the hill, the sun suddenly hot and strong on his back and hands.

"Hey. How're you doing?" she called from somewhere close in back of him. He turned and found her less than twenty feet away, her face red and perspired, her ankles and wrists stuck with bits of wet leaves and grasses. For a long minute they stared warily at each other above the heads of the flowers. Then, simultaneously, they burst into laughter. "Both mine are filled," she said, coming to peer into the one bag he had almost finished. "Lord, but you're slow. I'll help you do the cornflowers. It's getting too hot."

Side by side, they slowly worked their way back down the hill, filling his second bag with the last of the cornflowers. Their grasping hands made rippy-plucky sounds as they closed quickly, almost in unison, over the brittle stems of the blue-starred flowers, which had a faint iodoform smell that David liked. By the time they were near the bicycles the bag was brimming. Mary Pride was left with a fistful of flowers and no place to put them. "Use my bicycle basket," David began, then stopped, perplexed by the look of horror that was slowly puckering her face. Holding her hand straight out in front of her, she slowly uncurled her fingers one by one; together they looked into the glistening, leaf-stained palm, where, mangled among the tangled stems, a large furry yellow and black bumblebee writhed and buzzed in agony. "Oh, no," she whispered, with a sharp little insuck of breath. "Please," she repeated, turning her back. *You* step on it, David. I'm barefoot." For the span of a second, David listened to the tortured buzzing. Then he took one heavy step forward and savagely ground his rubber heel into the dirt. He felt sick to his stomach. "Okay," he said.

She turned back, paler than ever. "I didn't mean to," she said like a child.

"It could have stung you," he said stupidly, feeling something terrible happening in his chest.

"No. I don't think bumbles do."

He didn't correct her. He just stood there, all hands and feet and neck, suddenly helplessly in love with her. "My sneakers are sloshy," he finally said.

"Take them off," she said simply.

Without a thought for his bumpy bony feet, he did. Setting the sneakers at the roadside to dry out in the sun, he looked at his wristwatch. It was six-thirty, and though there was still no sign of the others, he was reluctant even to mention them. "How would you like to take a ride in one of those boats?"

"Do you think we could?"

"I don't see why not," said he, the observer of rules, the guardian of private property. "Nobody's around. And it's not as if we were stealing it—"

Though she saw their earlier roles reversed, she permitted herself only a faint mischievous smile. She held out her hand, and he took it, pleased by the innocent way her fingers lightly curled in his, by the feeling of sun-warmed dirt under his bare soles. As they drew near the water, a gummy salt smell, thick as broth, rose from the broken shells littering the sand. The sun, climbing rapidly, had burned away the mist. When they walked out onto the sand, a big gull flapped from behind one of the weathered shacks and lit on the still water, sending out concentric rings of ripples.

Unable to bear the heat, David stripped off his damp shirt and laid it out on one of the boats, completely unself-conscious until he turned and saw that Mary Pride was staring at him, frankly curious—and surprised. He almost laughed aloud. Instead, acutely aware of himself, proud of his flat-muscled hairless chest, he quietly asked her to give him a hand with one of the boats. Together they easily turned and lifted one of the old shells, carrying it down and setting it in the shallow water, leaving one corner still resting on the sand. David picked up the oars that had fallen out and, fitting them into the rusted locks, handed her in. When she was seated, he shoved them off with a thrust of one long leg, and the boat slid out along the glassy top of the water. He decided to let it glide by itself, and drew in the oars, folding them across each other in back of him like big wooden grasshopper wings. The sun, shining directly down and reflecting off the slick water top, blinded them. But slowly, as though to oblige them, the boat eased around all by itself, and the sun was no longer in their eyes. It was then that they saw them—six of them—scattered across a grassy rise a quarter of a mile down the curving shore; on the road just below, the hood of a blue sedan iridescently glittered.

Going cold, David dully stared at the car, which belonged to Greely Smith's father, and he wondered about his own tenacity—stupidity, really: everyone else broke rules and got away with it; why did he feel so compelled to obey them?

He did not want to look directly at Mary Pride, did not want to see her reaction. But suddenly one of the figures on the hill straightened up, and after staring intently out at them began waving, calling, "—ary? —ary?, and David had to look at her. She sat very still, neat nostrils flaring. When the call came again she swore softly, and turning away, reached into her shirt pocket for the pack of cigarettes. Wordlessly shaking out two, she lit one for David and handed it to him. He put it, warm and moist from her pale mouth, into his own, but nothing in him stirred; like the mists, all his dank thoughts had burned away, dried up in the sun. Shifting so that he could no longer see the others on the shore, he stared at her. Her kerchief had come so loose she had finally snatched it off; she sat peacefully, unvain, faintly squinting, almost ugly with the light harshly striking her face and Medusa curls snaking all over her head.

"Are you happy about college? About getting in where you wanted?" she asked, breaking the long silence, shyly turning away to trail a finger in the water.

"Yes," he said flatly.

"Are you going to be a doctor too?" she went on innocently, but all the same he blushed, feeling the deep touchy ache that any mention, direct or indirect, of his father brought.

"No. Not a doctor."

"Well, what then?" she persisted clumsily.

"I don't know," he said, sounding curt and irritable, but actually just wanting to end this conversation which could only lead them to her own plans, to her future without college, which at best would contain a job in some village store and a marriage, if she was lucky, to some local fireman or policeman or gas-station attendant.

"I'm going to secretarial school," she announced, as though having read his mind. She looked almost angry, her face red, lips primly compressed. "A good one. In New York."

"That's fine," he said, too loudly. "Good secretarial jobs can lead to all sorts of things. You start that way—and who knows?"

"Yes. Who knows?" she said, her eyes like blue enamel buttons. Then, with a teasing smile, she gripped the gunwale to her right and slipped agilely over the side of the boat, leaving it gently drumming from side to side. She had somehow managed to do this without wetting her head. She laughed up at him as he peered down with stupefaction; then turned and gave several ploppy paddle strokes which carried her a few feet away. "What d'you think you're doing? You crazy?" he demanded, but, ignoring him, she splashed about in a listless circle, finally coming back to the boat. " 'S cold," she gasped breathlessly, laughing still.

"What did you expect?" he muttered, furious at her for making him furious. Stonily he watched while she gave a sudden puzzled grimace and went under, then swore aloud. She was willing to play games even at the expense of her hair, carefully washed and put up for the graduation and the dance that night. Almost beginning to hate her all over again, he watched her head break through the stirred-up water. " 'S a cramp," she spluttered, rolling forward like a seal, and through the clear green water he could see her, right under the surface, frantically doing something to one of her legs. For an eternal moment David, a fair swimmer, sat and unwillingly considered the lucid, icy water. Then he sprang to life, dropping prayerfully to his knees in the center of the boat. When she surfaced he leaned far out, grabbing hold of a cold and slippery wrist, and the boat gave a violent tipping lurch. "Steady," he said, more to the boat than to her, and drawing her in close, got hold of the other arm. Locked in a chill and viselike embrace, limbs working together, as synchronized as lovers', they slowly, between them, managed to ease her into the boat.

Eyes closed, she sank back into the bow of the boat. David stared disbelievingly at her heaving chest, quickly, guiltily looking away as she opened her eyes. "Felt like tangled rubber bands," she explained between breaths and experimentally moved her right leg. "Thank you."

Remembering his reluctance to jump into the water after her, he couldn't speak.

"I said, thank you, David," she repeated, louder now that her breathing was less labored, and, sitting up straight, stared challengingly into his eyes.

"For what?" he mumbled, hot-faced, and reached around in back of him to fit the oars into the locks.

When the boat gritted into the sandy shore the others were waiting. For a moment they just stood there, the girls tittering and shifting, the boys silent, tensely staring; the wet shirt clung to Mary Pride's torso, defining her deep breasts as explicitly as classic drapery in a museum. Incurious eyes flickered over David, helping her out; someone finally came forward with a shielding towel. At once, like nubile handmaidens, the girls closed ranks about Mary Pride, making hushing little gull sounds. From the boys there came low rumblings: "Bike on the car—" "Scratch the hood—" "I'll ride it to her house—" Dazed, David beached the boat, helped by Greely Smith, whom he heartily loathed, and who softly said, "Hey," winking as David buttoned his shirt back on over his bare chest.

The boys dispersed, one heading for Mary Pride's bicycle, the other two starting toward the shiny blue car. The girls were leading Mary Pride toward the road when she suddenly stopped in her tracks and, shaking herself free of them, turned. "David?" she called clearly, imperiously. "David Thorne!"

He blushed as he paused in the roadbed.

"You all right?" she asked; behind her, two of the girls exchanged a poking nudge.

"Sure," he said.

"I am too," she said, softer, as though they were suddenly alone. "I'm only going home to change into dry clothes. I'll be at the diner. Will you?"

Blinking, but not from the sunlight, David stared. For in her eyes was the whole summer ahead, the summer before he left for school, the last summer he ever intended to spend in this town. A summer of leaf-scented lanes, warm night sands, soft damp grasses, a glad and limitless giving of which he couldn't partake. He stared, appalled, at his future, at himself, met much too soon, longing to cry out and protest at what he saw. Oh, what kind of cripple *was* a person, so bound by honor and tied by self-esteem they could not move, could neither take in hatred nor love since each asked too high a price.

"David?" she said, uncertain, growing hurt, the girls behind her grinning now.

"Sure, I'll be there," he said lightly, committed. "Hurry and change—I'll save you a seat."

The Hollow Boy

by Hortense Calisher

When I was in high school, my best friend for almost a year was another boy of about the same age by the name of Werner Hauser, who disappeared from his home one night and never came back. I am reminded of him indirectly sometimes, in a place like Luchow's or Cavanagh's or Hans Jaeger's, when I am waited on by one of those rachitic-looking German waiters with narrow features, faded hair, and bad teeth, who serve one with an omniscience verging on contempt. Then I wonder whether Mr. Hauser, Werner's father, ever got his own restaurant. I am never reminded directly of Werner by anybody, because I haven't the slightest idea what he may have become, wherever he is. As for Mrs. Hauser, Werner's mother —she was in a class by herself. I've never met anybody at all like her, and I don't expect to.

Although Werner and I went to the same high school, like all the boys in the neighborhood except the dummies who had to go to trade school or the smart alecks who were picked for Townsend Harris, we were really friends because both our families had back apartments in the same house on Hamilton Terrace, a street which angled up a hill off Broadway and had nothing else very terrace-like about it, except that its five-story tan apartment buildings had no store fronts on the ground floors. Nowadays that part of Washington Heights is almost all Puerto Rican, but in those days nobody in particular lived around there. My parents had moved there supposedly because it was a little nearer to their jobs in the Seventh Avenue garment district than the Bronx had been—my father worked in the fur district on Twenty-eighth Street, and my mother still got work as a finisher when the season was on—but actually they had come on the insistence of my Aunt Luba, who lived nearby—a sister of my mother's, of whom she was exceptionally fond and could not go a day without seeing.

When Luba talked about the Heights being higher-class than the Bronx, my parents got very annoyed. Like a lot of the garment workers of that day they were members of the Socialist Labor Party, although they no longer worked very hard at it. Occasionally, still, of an evening, after my father had gotten all worked up playing the violin with two or three of his cronies in the chamber music sessions that he loved, there would be a vibrant discussion over the cold cuts, with my mother, flushed and gay, putting in a sharp retort now and then as she handed round the wine; then too my older sister had been named after Ibsen's Nora—which sounded pretty damn funny with a name like Rosenbloom—and of course nobody in the family ever went to a synagogue. That's about all their radicalism had amounted to. My younger sister was named Carol.

The Hausers had been in the building for a month when we moved in on the regular moving day, October first; later a neighbor told my mother that they had gotten September rent-free as a month's concession on a year's lease—a practice which only became common in the next few years of the depression, and, as I heard my mother say, a neater trick than the Rosenblooms would ever think of. Shortly after they came, a sign was put up to the left of the house entrance—Mrs. Hauser had argued down the landlord on this too. The sign said *Erna Hauser. Weddings. Receptions. Parties,* and maybe the landlord was mollified after he saw it. It was black enamel and gold leaf under glass, and about twice the size of the dentist's. When I got to know Werner, at the time of those first frank questions with which boys place one another, he told me that ever since he and his mother had been sent for to come from Germany five years before, the family had been living in Yorkville in a furnished "housekeeping" room slightly larger than the one Mr. Hauser had occupied during the eight years he had been in the United States alone. Now Mrs. Hauser would have her own kitchen and a place to receive her clientele, mostly ladies from the well-to-do Jewish families of the upper West Side, for whom she had hitherto "helped out" at parties and dinners in their homes. From now on she would no longer "help out"—she would cater.

Most of what I learned about Werner, though, I didn't learn from Werner. He would answer a question readily enough, but very precisely, very much within the limits of the question, and no over-tones thrown in. I guess I learned about him because he was my friend, by sucking it out of the air the way kids do, during the times I was in his house before he was forbidden to hang around with me, and during the dozens of times before and after, when he sneaked up to our place. He was at our place as often as he could get away.

Up there, a casual visitor might have taken him for one of the family, since he was blond and short-featured, like my mother and me. He was a head taller than me, though, with a good build on him that was surprising if you had already seen his father's sunken, nutcracker face and bent-kneed waiter's shuffle. It wasn't that he had the special quiet of the very stupid or the very smart, or that he had any language difficulty; he spoke English as well as I did and got mostly nineties at school, where he made no bones about plugging hard and was held up as an example because he had only been in the country five years. It was just that he had almost no informal conversation. Because of this I never felt very close to him, even when we talked sex or smoked on the sly, and sometimes I had an uneasy feeling because I couldn't tell whether he was stupid or smart. I suppose we were friends mostly out of conve-nience, the way boys in a neighborhood are. Our apartments partly faced each other at opposite sides of the small circular rear court of the building; by opening his bedroom window and our dining-room window we could shout to each other to come over, or to meet out in front. I could, that is, although my mother used to grumble about acting up like riffraff. He was not allowed to; once, even before the edict, I saw the window shut down hard on his shoul-ders by someone from behind. After the edict we used to raise the windows very slightly and whistle. Even then, I never felt really close to him until the day after he was gone.

Saturday mornings, when I was that age, seemed to have a spe-cial glow; surely there must have been rainy ones, but I remember them all in a powerful golden light, spattered with the gabble of the vegetable men as they sparred with women at the open stalls out-side their stores, and ringing with the loud, pre-Sunday clang of

the ash cans as the garbage collectors hoisted them into the trucks
and the trucks moved on in a warm smell of settling ash. It was a
Saturday morning when I first went up to the Hausers', to see if
Werner could get off to take the Dyckman Ferry with me for a hike
along the Palisades. I already knew that he helped his mother with
deliveries evenings and afternoons after school, but I had not yet
learned how prescribed all his hours were. The hall door of the
Hauser apartment was open a crack; through it came a yeasty
current as strong as a bakery's. I flicked the bell.

"Come," said a firm, nasal voice. Or perhaps the word was
"Komm." I was never to hear Mrs. Hauser speak English except
once, when Werner and I, who had not heard her come in, walked
through the parlor where she was dealing with a lady who had
come about a daughter's wedding. That was the occasion at which
I saw her smile—at the lady—a fixed grimace which dusted lightly
over the neat surface of her face like the powdered sugar she shook
over her coffee cakes.

I walked in, almost directly into the kitchen. It was very like
ours, small and badly lighted, but it had two stoves. Rows of copper molds and pans of all shapes hung on the walls. One graduated
row was all of *Bund* pans, like one my mother had, but it was the
first time I had seen utensils of copper, or seen them hung on walls.
Supplies, everything was in rows; nothing wandered or went askew
in that kitchen; even its choke-sweet odor had no domestic vagary
about it, but clamped the room in a hot, professional pall. Werner
and his mother, bent over opposite ends of a cloth-covered table,
were carefully stretching at a large plaque of strudel dough which
almost covered its surface. Both of them glanced up briefly and
bent their heads again; the making of strudel is the most intense
and delicate of operations, in which the last stretching of the
dough, already rolled and pulled to tissue thinness, is done on the
backs of the hands, and balances on an instinctive, feathery tension. I held my breath and watched. Luba and my mother made
strudel about once a year, in an atmosphere of confused merriment
and operatic anguish when the dough broke. As I watched, red
crept up on Werner's face.

Almost opposite me, Mrs. Hauser bent and rose, angularly deft,
but without grace. I had expected some meaty-armed *Hausfrau*

trundling an ample bosom smeared with flour; here was the virginal silhouette of a governess, black and busked—a dressmaker's form collared in lace. From the side, her face had a thin economy, a handsomeness that had meagered and was further strained by the sparse hair spicked back in a pale bun.

Suddenly she straightened. The paste had reached the edges of the cloth; in a few whisked motions it was dabbed with butter, filled, rolled, cut, and done. She brushed her hands together, blew on the spotless front of her dress, and faced me. She was not handsome at all. Her nose, blunt-ended, came out too far to meet one, her eyes protruded slightly with a lashless, committed stare, and the coin-shaped mouth was too near the nose. She wore no makeup, and her face had the triumphant neatness of the woman who does not; next to it Luba's and my mother's would have looked vital, but messy. Her skin was too bloodless though, and her lips and the nails of her floured hands were tinged with lavender, almost stone-colored, as if she suffered from some attenuation of the heart.

Werner mumbled out my first name, and I mumbled back my errand.

Mrs. Hauser, holding her hands lightly in front of her, still gave me her stare, but it was to Werner that she spoke at last.

"Sag ihm nein," she said, and turning on her heel, she left the room, still holding away from her dress the hands with the stone-colored nails.

After that, I knew enough not to go to Werner's unless he asked me to, usually on evenings when his father was on night duty in the restaurant where he worked, and Mrs. Hauser had an engagement, or on Sundays, when she had an especially fancy wedding and Mr. Hauser, dressed in his waiter's garb, went along to help her serve.

I never got used to the way their apartment looked, compared with the way it smelled. When there was no cooking going on, and the hot fumes had a chance to separate and wander, then it was filled, furnished with enticing suggestions of cinnamon, vanilla, and anise, and the wonderful, warm caraway scent of little pastries stuffed with hot forcemeat—a specialty of Mrs. Hauser's, of which her customers could never get enough. Standing outside the door, I

used to think it smelled the way the house in *Hansel and Gretel*
looked, in the opera to which my parents had taken me years
before—a house from whose cornices and lintels one might break
off a piece and find one's mouth full of marzipan, an aerie promising happy troupes of children feasting within, in a blissful forever
of maraschino and Nesselrode.

Actually, the four dim rooms, curtainless except for the blinds
which the landlord supplied—one yellow, one dark green to a window—had an almost incredible lack of traces of personal occu-
pancy, even after one knew that the Hausers never thought of the
place as anything but temporary. It was furnished with a bleak
minimum of tables and chairs like those in hired halls. Mrs.
Hauser had procured everything from a restaurant supply house,
all except the beds, which were little more than cots, and wore
hard white cotton spreads of the kind seen in hotels. Here, in the
bedrooms, some of the second-hand surfaces were protected with
doilies, on which a few European family photographs had been
placed. Years later, when I was staying in the luxurious house of a
family which had managed to keep on its servants in the old-fashioned way, stumbling inadvertently into the servants' wing, one
morning, I came upon a room that reminded me instantly of the
Hausers', although even its dresser had a homely clutter of tawdry
jewelry, dime-store boxes, and letters.

Even so, when Werner and I hung around awhile in his room, we
never sat on the drill-neat bed. Usually we sat on the floor and
leaned back against the bed. Except for the times we did our homework together, we either just talked or exchanged the contents of
our pockets, for it was the kind of house in which there was simply
nothing to do. Once or twice we smoked cigarettes there, carefully
airing the room and chewing soda-mints afterward. I supplied both
the cigarettes and the soda-mints, since it was an understood thing
that Werner never had any money of his own; the considerable
work he did for his mother was "for the business." The rows of
cakes, frilled cookies, and tiny *quenelles* that we sometimes passed,
going through the kitchen, were for the business too. I never got
anything to eat there.

Usually, after we had been there a short while, Werner, wrig-
gling his shoulders sheepishly, would say, "Let's go up to your

place," or I would invite him up. I knew why Werner liked to be there, of course, why he could not keep from coming even after Mrs. Hauser had forbidden it. It may sound naïve to say so in this day and age, but we were an awfully happy family. We really were. And I never realized it more strongly than during the times I used to watch Werner Hauser up there.

I guess the best way I can explain the kind of family we were is to say that, although I was the only nonmusical one in a family that practically lived for music, I never felt criticized or left out. My father, although he tired quickly because of a shoulder broken when he was a boy and never properly healed, was the best musician, with faultless pitch and a concertmeister's memory for repertoire. Nora played the cello with a beautiful tone, although she wouldn't work for accuracy, and Carol could already play several wind instruments; it was a sight to watch that stringy kid of ten pursing her lips and worrying prissily about her "embouchure." Both Luba and my mother had had excellent training in piano, and sang even better than they played, although Luba would never concede to my father that she occasionally flatted. My mother, contrarily, tended to sing sharp, which so fitted her mock-acid ways that my father made endless plays on words about it. "Someday," he would add, striking his forehead with his fist, "I am going to find a woman who sings exactly in the middle; then I will steal the company's payroll, and take her to live at The Breakers in Atlantic City!"

"Mir nix, dir nix," my mother would answer. "And what kind of music would be at The Breakers?"

"A string quartet," Luba would shout, "with a visiting accordion for the weekends!" Then the three of them would pound each other in laughter over the latest "visiting accordion" who had been to our house. All kinds of people were attracted to our house, many of whom had no conception of the professional quality of the music they heard there, and were forever introducing a protégé whom they had touted beforehand. Whenever these turned out to be violinists who had never heard of the Beethoven Quartets, or pianists who had progressed as far as a bravura rendition of the *Revolutionary Etude,* our secret name for them was "a visiting accordion." Not even Carol was ever rude to any of these though;

the musical part of the evening simply ended rather earlier than usual, and dissolved into that welter of sociable eating and talking which we all loved.

When I say I wasn't musical, I don't mean I didn't know music or love it—no one in that family could help it—I could reproduce it and identify it quite accurately in my head, but I just couldn't make it with my hands or my voice. It had long ago been settled upon that I was the historian, the listener, the critic. "Ask Mr. Huneker here," my father would say, pointing to me with a smile (or Mr. Gilman, or Mr. Downes, according to whatever commentator he had been reading). Sometimes, when in reading new music the group achieved a dissonance that harrowed him, he would turn on me: "We should all be like this one—Paganini today—Hoffman tomorrow—and all safe upstairs in the head." But the teasing took me in; it never left me out. That's what happened to Werner at our house. They took him in too.

We had our bad times of course. Often my father's suppertime accounts of his day on Seventh Avenue, usually reported with a deft, comedian's touch, turned to bitter invective, or were not forthcoming at all. Then we knew that the mood in which he regretted a life spent among values he despised had stolen over him, or else the money question was coming up again, and we ate in silence. Luba and my mother quarreled with the violence of people who differ and cannot live without one another; their cleavages and reunions followed a regular pattern, each stage of which pervaded the house as recognizably as what was simmering on the stove. My sister Nora, eighteen and beautiful, was having trouble with both these contingencies; each month, just before her monthly, she filled the house with a richly alternating brooding and hysteria that set us all to slamming doors and leaving the house. A saint couldn't have lived with it. And Carol and I bickered, and had our pint-size troubles too.

I can see how we must have seemed to Werner though. No matter what was going on, our house had a kind of ruddiness and satisfaction about it. Partly its attraction was because there *was* always something going on. If anyone had asked me about the state of my innards in regard to my family, I guess I would have said that I felt full. Not full of life, or happiness, or riches, or any of those tiddly phrases. Just chock full. I would have said this, most likely, because, as I watched Werner hanging, reticent but dogged, to the edge of our family, watched him being stuffed by my mother, twitted by my father, saw him almost court being ignored by Nora and annoyed by Carol, I had the awful but persistent fancy that he must be absolutely hollow inside. Literally hollow, I mean. I could see them, his insides—as bleak as the apartment where his parents were either oppressively absent or oppressively around, and scattered with a few rag-tag doilies of feeling that had almost no reason to be there. There would be nothing inside him to make a feeling out of, unless it were the strong, tidal perfume of the goodies that were meant for the business.

One evening at the beginning of that summer, Werner was with us when my father scooped us all up and took us to the concert at the Stadium, only a few minutes' walk from home. We went often to those concerts, although, as everyone knows, open-air music can rarely have the finish of the concert hall. But there is something infinitely arresting, almost pathetic, in music heard in the open air. It is not only the sight of thousands of ordinary faces, tranced and quiet in a celebration of the unreal. It is because the music, even while it is clogged and drowned now and then by the rusty noises of the world outside the wall, is not contaminated by them; even while it states that beauty and the world are irreconcilable, it persists in a frail suggestion that the beauty abides.

Werner, at his first concert, sat straight-backed on one of the straw mats my father had rented for us, taking in the fragments of talk milling around us, with the alertness of a person at a dinner who watches how his neighbor selects his silver. During the first half, when an ambulance siren, combined with the grinding of the trolleys on Amsterdam Avenue, clouded over a pianissimo, he winced carefully, like some of those around him. But during the second half, which ended with the Beethoven Fifth, when a dirigible stealing overhead drew a thousand faces cupped upward, Werner, staring straight ahead with a sleepy, drained look, did not join them.

As we all walked down the hill afterward, Carol began whistling the Andante. As she came to that wonderful breakthrough in the sixteenth measure, Werner took it up in a low, hesitant, but pure whistle, and completed it. Carol stopped whistling, her mouth open, and my father turned his head. No one said anything though, and we kept on walking down the hill. Suddenly Werner whistled again, the repetition of that theme, twenty-three bars from the end, when, instead of descending to the A flat, it rises at last to the G.

My father stopped in his tracks. "You play, Werner?"

Werner shook his head.

"Somebody plays at your house?"

"Nein," said Werner. I don't think he realized that he had said it in German.

"How is it you know music?"

Werner rubbed his hand across his eyes. When he spoke, he sounded as if he were translating. "I did not know that I know it," he said.

In the next few weeks Werner came with us almost every time we went. I didn't know where he got the money, but he paid his own way. Once, when he hadn't come to go with us, we met him afterward, loitering at the exit we usually took, and he joined us on the walk home. I think he must have been listening from outside the Stadium wall.

He always listened with a ravenous lack of preference. Once he turned to me at the intermission and said with awe, "I could hear them both together. The themes. At the *same* time." When I spoke sophomorically of what I didn't like, he used to look at me with pity, although at the end of a concert which closed with the "Venusberg," he turned to me, bewildered, and said. "It *is* possible not to like it." I laughed, but I did feel pretty comfortable with him just then. I always hated those triangles in the "Venusberg."

Then, one time, he did not come around for over a week, and when I saw him in the street he was definitely avoiding me. I thought of asking why he was sore at me, but then I thought: The hell with it. Anyway, that Sunday morning, as my father and I started out for a walk on Riverside Drive, we met Werner and his mother in the elevator. Mrs. Hauser carried some packages and Werner had two large cartons which he had rested on the floor. It was a tight squeeze, but the two of us got in, and after the door closed my father succeeded in raising his hat to Mrs. Hauser, but got no acknowledgment. My father replaced his hat on his fan-shaped wedge of salt-and-pepper hair. He chewed his lips back and forth thoughtfully under his large, mournful nose, but said nothing. When the door opened, we had to get out first. They passed ahead of us quickly, but not before we heard what Mrs. Hauser muttered to Werner. *"Was hab' ich gesagt?"* she said. *"Sie sind Juden!"*

Anybody who knows Yiddish can understand quite a lot of German too. My father and I walked a long way that day, not on the upper Drive, where the Sunday strollers were, but on those little paths, punctuated with iron street lamps but with a weak hint of country lane about them, where the city petered out into the river. We walked along, not saying much of anything, all the way up to the lighthouse at Inspiration Point. Then we climbed the hill to Broadway, where my father stopped to buy some cold cuts and a cheese cake, and took the subway home. Once, when my father was paying my fare, he let his hand rest on my shoulder before he waved me ahead of him through the turnstile, and once he caught himself whistling something, looked at me quickly, and closed his mouth. I didn't have a chance to recognize what he whistled.

We were at the table eating when the doorbell rang. Carol ran to answer it; she was the kind of kid who was always darting to answer the phone or the door, although it was almost never for her. She came back to the table and flounced into her seat.

"It's Werner. He wants to see you. He won't come in."

I went to the door. He wasn't lounging against the door frame, the way he usually did. He was standing a couple of paces away from it.

"Please come for a walk," he said. He was looking at his shoes.

"Gee, whyn't you come in?" I said. "I'm dead."

"Please," he said, "I want you please to come for a walk."

I was practically finished eating anyway. I went back to the table, grabbed up a hard roll and some pastrami, and followed him downstairs.

Summer in the city affects me the same way as open air music. I guess it's because both of them have such a hard time. Even when the evening breeze smells of nothing but hot brick, you get the feeling that people are carrying around leaves in their hearts. Werner and I walked down to our usual spot on the river, to a low stone wall, which we jumped, over to a little collection of bushes and some grass, on the other side. It was an open enough spot, but it reacted on us more or less like a private cave; we never said much of anything till we got there. This time it was up to Werner to speak. I had the sandwich, so I finished that.

The electric signs across the river on the Jersey side were already busy. Werner's face was turned parallel with the river, so that it looked as if the sign that gave the time signal were paying out its letters right out of his mouth. THE TIME IS NOW . . . 8:01 . . . Ordinarily I would have called his attention to this effect and changed seats with him so he could see it happen to me, but I didn't. The sign jazzed out something about salad oil, and then paid out another minute.

Werner turned his head. "You heard . . . this morning in the elevator?"

I nodded.

"Your father heard too?"

I nodded again.

He pressed his knuckles against his teeth. His words came through them with a chewed sound. "It is because they are servants," he said.

"Who do you mean?"

"My father and mother."

"You mean . . . they don't like Jews because they have to work for them sometimes?"

"Maybe," said Werner, "but it is not what I mean."

"It's no disgrace, what anybody works at, over here." I wasn't sure I believed this, but it was what one was told. "Besides, they have the business."

Werner turned his back on me, his shoulders humped up against the Palisades. "Inside them, they are servants."

He turned back to face me, the words tumbling out with the torn confiding of the closemouthed. "They do not care about the *quality* of anything." His voice lingered on the word. He jerked his head at the Mazola sign. "Butter maybe, instead of lard. But only because it is good for the business."

"Everybody has something wrong with his family," I muttered. Werner folded his arms almost triumphantly and looked at me. "But we are not a family," he said.

I got up and walked around the little grass plot. The way he had spoken the word *quality* stayed with me; it popped into my mind the time in spring when he and I had been sitting near the same old stone wall and two scarlet tanagers lit on it and strutted for a minute against the blue. You aren't supposed to see tanagers in New York City. Sooner or later, though, you'll see almost everything in New York. You'll have almost every lousy kind of feeling too.

The river had a dark shine to it now. It smelled like a packing-house for fish, but it looked like the melted, dark eyes of a million girls.

"I wish we were going up to the country this year," I said. "I'd like to be there right now."

"I hate the country!" Werner said. "That's where they're going to have the restaurant. They have almost enough money now."

Then it all came out—in a rush. "Come on back," he said. "They're out. I want to show you something."

All the way up the hill he talked: how his mother had worked as a housekeeper for a rich merchant after his father had left for America; how he had always been the child in the basement, allowed to play neither with the town children nor the merchant's; how his mother would not agree to come over until his father had saved a certain sum, and then required that it be sent to her in dollars before she would sail. Then, in Yorkville, where they had only taken a larger room because the landlady insisted, they used to walk the garish streets sometimes, listening to the din from the cafés—*"Ist das nicht ein . . . ? Ja, das ist ein . . ."*— but never going in for a snack or a glass of beer. "We breathed quiet," I remember him saying, "so we would not have to use up too much air."

And always, everything was for the restaurant. At Christmas-time and birthdays they did not give each other presents, but bought copper pans, cutlery, equipment for the restaurant. They had their eye on an actual place, on a side road not too far from some of the fancy towns in Jersey; it was owned by a man whose wife was a cousin of Mrs. Hauser's. It already had a clientele of connoisseurs who came to eat slowly, to wait reverently in a waft of roasting coffee, for the *Perlhuhn* and the *Kaiser-Schmarren*. The cousins were smart—they knew that Americans would pay the best for the best, and even wait a little long for it, in order to be thought European. But they had let the place get seedy; they did not have enough discipline for the long, sluggish day before the customers arrived, and they had not learned that while the Americans might wait out of snobbishness, they would not do so because the owners were getting drunk in the kitchen. The Hausers would be smarter still. They would serve everything of the best, at a suitably stately pace for such quality, and they would not get drunk in the kitchen.

He stopped talking when we got to his door. The whole time, he hadn't raised his voice, but had talked on and on in a voice like shavings being rubbed together.

His room was dark and full of the cloying smell. He stood in front of the window, not turning the light on, and I saw that he was looking over at our place. I saw how it looked to him.

That was the summer radios first really came in. Almost everyone had one now. We hadn't got one yet, but one of Nora's boy friends had given her a small table model. There were a couple of them playing now at cross purposes, from different places on the court.

"Thursday nights they are broadcasting the concerts, did you know?" he said softly. "Sometimes someone tunes in on it, and I can hear, if I keep the window open. The echoes are bad . . . and all the other noises. Sometimes, of course, no one tunes it in."

I wondered what he had to show me, and why he did not turn on the light.

"Today was my birthday," he said. "I asked them for a radio, but of course I did not expect it. I am to get working papers. When they leave, I am to leave the high school."

He walked away from the window and turned on the light. The objects on the bed sprang into sharp black and white: the tie disposed on the starched shirt, which lay neatly between the black jacket and pants. That's what it was. It was a waiter's suit.

"Of course I did not expect it," he said. "I did not."

* * *

It was after this that Werner, when he whistled across the court, started using themes from here and there. Sometimes it was that last little mocking bit from *Till Eulenspiegel* when Till's feet kick, sometimes it was the Ho-yo-to-ho of the Valkyries, sometimes the horns from the "Waltz of the Flowers." It was always something we had heard at the Stadium, something we had heard together. When my father, to whom I had blabbed most of that evening with Werner, heard the whistle, his face would sometimes change red, as if he were holding his breath in anger against someone; then this would be displaced by the sunk, beaten look he sometimes brought home from Seventh Avenue, and he would shrug and turn away. He never said anything to Werner or to me.

The last night, the night it must have happened, was a Thursday a few weeks later. It was one of those humid nights when the rain just will not come, and even the hair on your head seems too much to carry around with you. We were all sitting in the dining room, brushing limply now and then at our foreheads. Nora was in one of her moods—the boy who had given her the radio had not phoned. She had it turned on and sat glowering in front of it, as if she might evoke him from it.

My father was standing at the window, looking up at the sky. The court had its usual noises, children crying, a couple of other radios, and the rumble from the streets. Once or twice some kid catcalled from a higher floor, and a light bulb exploded on the alley below.

My father leaned forward suddenly, and looked across the court, watching intently. Then he walked slowly over to the radio, stood in front of it a moment, and turned it on loud. We all looked at him in surprise. He didn't think much of the thing, and never monkeyed with it.

I looked across the court at Werner's window. I couldn't see into its shadows, but it was open. I thought of the look on his face when he met us outside the Stadium walls and of his voice saying, "Sometimes no one tunes it in." I would have whistled to him, but I couldn't have been heard over the music—*Scheherazade,* it was—which was sweeping out loud and strong into the uneasy air.

My mother whispered a reproach to my father, then took a side look at his face, and subsided. I glanced around at Carol, Nora, all of us sitting there joined together, and for some reason or other I felt sick. It's the weather, I thought, and wiped my forehead.

Then, in the square across the court, the blackness merged and moved. The window began to grind down. And then we heard Werner's voice, high and desperate, louder even than the plashing waves of the Princess's story—a long, loud wail.

"No! Please! Scheherazade is speaking!"

Then there were two figures at the window, and the window was flung up again. My mother clapped her hand against her face, ran over to the radio and turned it down low, and stood bent over with her back against it, her fist to her mouth. So it was that we heard Werner again, his words squeezed out, hoarse, but clear. *"Bitte, Mutter. Lass mich hören. Scheherazade spricht."*

Then the window came down.

The next evening the house was like a hive with what had happened. The Hausers had gone to the police. There had been one really personal thing in their house after all, and Werner had taken it with him. He had taken the whole of the cache in the wall safe, the whole ten thousand dollars for the restaurant.

The detectives came around to question me—two pleasant enough Dutch uncles who had some idea that Werner might have made a pact with me, or that I could give them some clues as to what had been going on inside him. I couldn't tell them much of use. I wasn't going to tell them to look over at the Stadium, either outside or in, although for years afterward I myself used to scan the crowds there. And I wasn't fool enough to try to explain to them what I had hardly figured out yet myself—that nature abhors the vacuums men shape, and sooner or later pushes the hollow in.

Mr. and Mrs. Hauser stayed on, and as far as anyone could tell, kept on with their usual routine. They were still there when we moved—Luba had decided the air was better in Hollis, Queens. During the months while we were still at Hamilton Terrace though, my father acquired an odd habit. If he happened to pass the open dining room window when our large new radio was playing, he was likely to pause there, and look out across the court. Sometimes he shut the sash down hard, and sometimes he let it be, but he always stood there for a time. I never decided whether the look on his face was guilty or proud. I knew well enough why he stood there though. For it was from our house that the music had come. It was from our window that Scheherazade spoke.

A Fight Between a White Boy and a Black Boy in the Dusk of a Fall Afternoon in Omaha, Nebraska

by Wright Morris

How did it start? If there is room for speculation, it lies in how to end it. Neither the white boy nor the black boy gives it further thought. They stand, braced off, in the cinder-covered schoolyard, in the shadow of the darkened, red-brick building. Eight or ten smaller boys circle the fighters, forming sides. A white boy observes the fight upside down as he hangs by his knees from the iron rail of the fence. A black girl pasting cutouts of pumpkins in the windows of the annex seems unconcerned. Fights are not so unusual. Halloween and pumpkins come but once a year.

At the start of the fight there was considerable jeering and exchange of formidable curses. The black boy was much better at this part of the quarrel and jeered the feebleness of his opponent's remarks. The white boy lacked even the words. His experience with taunts and scalding invective proved to be remarkably shallow. Twice the black boy dropped his arms as if they were useless against such a potato-mouthed, stupid adversary. Once he laughed, showing the coral roof of his mouth. In the shadow of the school little else stood out clearly for the white boy to strike at. The black boy did not have large whites to his eyes, or pearly white teeth. In the late afternoon light he made a poor target except for the shirt that stood out against the fence that closed in the school. He had rolled up the sleeves and opened the collar so that he could breathe easier and fight better. His black bare feet are the exact color of the cinder yard.

The white boy is a big, hulking fellow, large for his age. It is not clear what it might be, since he has been in the same grade for three years. The bottom board has been taken from the drawer of his desk to allow for his knees. Something said about that may have started the quarrel, or the way he likes to suck on toy train wheels. (He blows softly and wetly through the hole, the wheel at the front of his mouth.) But none of that is clear; all that is known is that he stands like a boxer, his head ducked low, his huge fists doubled before his face. He stands more frontally than sidewise, as if uncertain which fist to lead with. As a rule he wrestles. He would much rather wrestle than fight with his fists. Perhaps he refused to wrestle with a black boy, and *that* could be the problem. One never knows. Who ever knows for sure what starts a fight?

The black boy's age hardly matters and it doesn't show. All that shows clearly is his shirt and the way he stands. His head looks small because his shoulders are so wide. He has seen pictures of famous boxers and stands with his left arm stretched out before him as if approaching something in the darkness. His right arm, cocked, he holds as if his chest pained him. Both boys are hungry, scared, and waiting for the other one to give up.

The white boy is afraid of the other one's blackness, and the black boy hates and fears whiteness. Something of their mutual fear is now shared by those who are watching. One of the small black boys hoots like an Indian and takes off. One of the white boys has a pocketful of marbles he dips his hand into and rattles. This was distracting when the fight first started, and he was asked to take his hands out of his pockets. Now it eases the strain of the silence.

The need to take sides has also dwindled, and the watchers have gathered with the light behind them, out of their eyes. They say "Come on!" the way you say "sic 'em," not caring which dog. A pattern has emerged which the two fighters know, but it is not yet known to the watchers. Nobody is going to win. The dilemma is how nobody is going to lose. It has early been established that the black boy will hit the white boy on the head with a sound like splitting a melon—but it's the white boy who moves forward, the black boy who moves back. It isn't clear if the white boy, or any of the watchers, perceives the method in this tactic. Each step backward the black boy takes he is closer to home, and nearer to darkness.

In time they cross the cinder-covered yard to the narrow steps going down to the sidewalk. There the fight is delayed while a passing adult, a woman with a baby sitting up in its carriage, tells them to stop acting like children, and asks their names to inform their teachers. The black boy's name is Eustace Beecher. The white boy's name is Emil Hrdlic, or something like that. He's a real saphead, and not at all certain how it is spelled. When the woman leaves, they return to their fighting and go along the fronts of darkened houses. Dogs bark. Little dogs, especially, enjoy a good fight.

The black boy has changed his style of fighting so that his bleeding nose doesn't drip on his shirt. The white boy has switched around to give his cramped, cocked arm a rest. The black boy picks up support from the fact that he doesn't take advantage of this situation. One reason might be that his left eye is almost closed. When he stops to draw a shirtsleeve across his face, the white boy does not leap forward and strike him. It's a good fight. They have learned what they can do and what they can't do.

At the corner lit up by the bug-filled streetlamp they lose about half of their seven spectators. It's getting late and dark. You can smell the bread baking on the bakery draft. The light is better for the fighters now than the watchers, who see the two figures only in profile. It's not so easy anymore to see which one is black and which one is white. Sometimes the black boy, out of habit, takes a step backward, then has to hop forward to his proper position. The hand he thrusts out before him is limp at the wrist, as if he had just dropped something unpleasant. The white boy's shirt, once blue in color, shines like a slicker on his sweaty back. The untied laces of his shoes are broken from the way he is always stepping on them. He is the first to turn his head and check the time on the bakery clock.

Behind the black boy the street enters the Negro section. Down there, for two long blocks, there is no light. A gas streetlamp can be seen far at the end, the halo around it swimming with insects. One of the two remaining fight-watchers whistles shrilly, then enters the bakery to buy penny candy. There's a gum-ball machine that sometimes returns your penny, but it takes time, and you have to shake it.

The one spectator left to watch this fight stands revealed in the glow of the bakery window. One pocket is weighted with marbles; the buckles of his britches are below his knees. He watches the fighters edge into the darkness where the white shirt of the black boy is like an object levitated at a séance. Nothing else can be seen. Black boy and white boy are swallowed up. For a moment one can hear the shuffling feet of the white boy; then that, too, dissolves into darkness. The street is a tunnel with a lantern gleaming far at its end. The last fight-watcher stands as if paralyzed until the rumble of a passing car can be felt through the soles of his shoes, tingling the blood in his feet. Behind him the glow of the sunset reddens the sky. He goes toward it on the run, a racket of marbles, his eyes fixed on the FORD sign beyond the school buildings, where there is a hollow with a shack used by ice skaters under which he can crawl and peer out like a cat. When the streetlights cast more light he will go home.

Somewhere, still running, there is a white boy who saw all of this and will swear to it; otherwise, nothing of what he saw remains. The Negro section, the bakery on the corner, the red-brick school with one second-floor window (the one that opens out on the fire escape) outlined by the chalk dust where they slapped the erasers —all of that is gone, the earth leveled and displaced to accommodate the ramps of the new freeway. The cloverleaf approaches look great from the air. It saves the driving time of those headed east or west. Omaha is no longer the gateway to the West, but the plains remain, according to one traveler, a place where his wife still sleeps in the seat while he drives through the night.

1970

Memorial Day

by Peter Cameron

I am eating my grapefruit with a grapefruit spoon my mother bought last summer from a door-to-door salesman on a large three-wheeled bike. My mother and I were sitting on the front steps that day and we watched him glide down the street, into our driveway, and up our front walk. He opened his case on the handlebars, and it was full of fruit appliances: pineapple corers, melon ballers, watermelon seeders, orange-juice squeezers, and grapefruit spoons. My mother bought four of the spoons and the man pedaled himself out of our lives.

That was about a year ago. Since then a lot has changed, I think as I pry the grapefruit pulp away from the skin with the serrated edge of the spoon. Since then, my mother has remarried, my father has moved to California, and I have stopped talking. Actually, I talk quite a lot at school, but never at home. I have nothing to say to anyone here.

Across the table from me, drinking Postum, is my new stepfather. He wasn't here last year. I don't think he was anywhere last year. His name is Lonnie, and my mother met him at a Seth Speaks seminar. Seth is this guy without a body who speaks out of the mouth of this lady and tells you how to fix your life. Both Lonnie and my mother have fixed their lives. "One day at a time," my mother says every morning, smiling at Lonnie and then, less happily, at me.

Lonnie is only thirteen years older than I am; he is twenty-nine but looks about fourteen. When the three of us go out together, he is taken to be my brother.

"Listen to this," Lonnie says. Both Lonnie and my mother continue to talk to me, consult with me, and read things to me, in the hope that I will forget and speak. "If gypsy moths continue to destroy trees at their present rate, North America will become a desert incapable of supporting any life by the year 4000." Lonnie has a morbid sense of humor and delights in macabre newspaper fillers. Because he knows I won't answer, he doesn't glance up at me. He continues to stare at his paper and says, "Wow. Think of that."

I look out the window. My mother is sitting in an inflated rubber boat in the swimming pool, scrubbing the fiberglass walls with a stiff brush and Mr. Clean. They get stained during the winter. She does this every Memorial Day. We always open the pool this weekend, and she always blows up the yellow boat, puts on her Yankee hat so her hair won't turn orange, and paddles around the edge of the pool, leaving a trail of suds.

Last year, as she scrubbed, the diamond from her old engagement ring fell out and sank to the bottom of the pool. She was still married to my father, although they were planning to separate after a last "family vacation" in July. My mother shook the suds off her hand and raised it in front of her face, as if she were admiring a new ring. "Oh, Stephen!" she said. "I think I've lost my diamond."

"What?" I said. I still talked then.

"The diamond fell out of my ring. Look."

I got up from the chair I was sitting on and kneeled beside the pool. She held out her hand, the way women do in old movies when they expect it to be kissed. I looked down at her ring and she was right: the diamond was gone. The setting looked like an empty hand tightly grabbing nothing.

"Do you see it?" she asked, looking down into the pool. Because we had just taken the cover off, the water was murky. "It must be down there," she said. "Maybe if you dove in?" She looked at me with a nice, pleading look on her face. I took my shirt off. I felt her looking at my chest. There is no hair on my chest, and every time my mother sees it I know she checks to see if any has grown.

I dove into the pool. The water was so cold my head ached. I opened my eyes and swam quickly around the bottom. I felt like one of those Japanese pearl fishers. But I didn't see the diamond.

I surfaced and swam to the side. "I don't see it," I said. "I can't see anything. Where's the mask?"

"Oh, dear," my mother said. "Didn't we throw it away last year?"

"I forget," I said. I got out of the pool and stood shivering in the sun. Suddenly I got the idea that if I found the diamond maybe my parents wouldn't separate. I know it sounds ridiculous, but at that moment, standing with my arms crossed over my chest, watching my mother begin to cry in her inflatable boat—at that moment, the diamond sitting on the bottom of the pool took on a larger meaning, and I thought that if it was replaced in the tiny clutching hand of my mother's ring we might live happily ever after.

So I had my father drive me downtown, and I bought a diving mask at the five-and-ten, and when we got home I put it on—first spitting on the glass so it wouldn't fog—and dove into the water, and dove again and again, until I actually found the diamond, glittering in a mess of leaves and bloated inchworms at the bottom of the pool.

I throw my grapefruit rind away, and go outside and sit on the edge of the diving board with my feet in the water. My mother watches me for a second, probably deciding if it's worthwhile to say anything. Then she goes back to her scrubbing.

Later, I am sitting by the mailbox. Since I've stopped talking, I've written a lot of letters. I write to men in prisons, and I answer personal ads, claiming to be whatever it is the placer desires: "an elegant educated lady for afternoon pleasure," or a "GBM." The mail from prisons is the best: long letters about nothing, since it seems nothing is done in prison. A lot of remembering. A lot of bizarre requests: Send me a shoehorn. Send me an empty egg carton (arts and crafts?). Send me an electric toothbrush. I like writing letters to people I've never met.

Lonnie is planting geraniums he bought this morning in front of the A & P when he did the grocery shopping. Lonnie is very good about "doing his share." I am not about mine. Every night I wait with delicious anticipation for my mother to tell me to take out the garbage: "How many times do I have to tell you? Can't you just do it?"

Lonnie gets up and walks over to me, trowel in hand. He has on plaid Bermuda shorts and a Disney World T-shirt. If I talked, I'd ask him when he went to Disney World. But I can live without the information.

Lonnie flips the trowel at me and it slips like a knife into the ground a few inches from my leg. "Bingo!" Lonnie says. "Scare you?"

I think when a person stops talking people forget that he can still hear. Lonnie is always saying dumb things to me—things you'd only say to a deaf person or a baby.

"What a day," Lonnie says, as if to illustrate this point. He stretches out beside me, and I look at his long white legs. He has sneakers and white socks on. He never goes barefoot. He is too uptight to go barefoot. He would step on a piece of glass immediately. That is the kind of person Lonnie is.

The Captain Ice Cream truck rolls lazily down our street. Lonnie stands up and reaches in his pocket. "Would you like an ice pop?" he asks me, looking at his change.

I shake my head no. An ice pop? Where did he grow up—Kentucky?

Lonnie walks into the street and flags down the ice-cream truck as if it's not obvious what he's standing there for.

The truck slows down and the ice-cream man jumps out. It is a woman. "What can I get you?" she says, opening the freezer on the side of the truck. It's the old-fashioned kind of truck, with the ice cream hidden in its frozen depths. I always thought you needed to have incredibly long arms to be a good Captain Ice Cream person.

"Well, I'd like a nice ice pop," Lonnie says.

"A Twin Bullet?" suggests the woman. "What flavor?"

"Do you have cherry?" Lonnie asks.

"Sure," the woman says. "Cherry, grape, orange, lemon, cola, and tutti-frutti."

For a second I have a horrible feeling that Lonnie will want a tutti-frutti. "I'll have cherry," he says.

Lonnie comes back, peeling the sticky paper from his cherry Bullet. It's a bright pink color. The truck drives away. "Guess how much this cost," Lonnie says, sitting beside me on the grass. "Sixty cents. It's a good thing you didn't want one." He licks his fingers and then the ice stick. "Do you want a bite?" He holds it out toward me.

Lonnie is so patient and so sweet. It's just too bad he's such a nerd. I take a bite of his cherry Bullet.

"Good, huh?" Lonnie says. He watches me eat for a second, then takes a bite himself. He breaks the Bullet in half and eats it in a couple of huge bites. A little pink juice runs down his chin.

"What are you waiting for?" he asks. I nod toward the mailbox.

"It's Memorial Day," Lonnie says. "The mail doesn't come." He stands up and pulls the trowel out of the ground. I think of King Arthur. "There is no mail for anyone today," Lonnie says. "No matter how long you wait." He hands me his two Bullet sticks and returns to his geraniums.

I have this feeling, holding the stained wooden sticks, that I will keep them for a long time, and come across them one day, and remember this moment, incorrectly.

After the coals in the barbecue have melted into powder, the fire-flies come out. They hesitate in the air, as if stunned by dusk.

Lonnie and my mother are sitting beside the now clean pool, and I am sitting on the other side of the "natural forsythia fence" that is planted around it, watching the bats swoop from tree to tree, feeling the darkness clot all around me. I can hear Lonnie and my mother talking, but I can't make out what they are saying.

I love this time of day—early evening, early summer. It makes me want to cry. We always had a barbecue on Memorial Day with my father, and my mother cooked this year's hamburgers on her new barbecue, which Lonnie bought her for Mother's Day (she's old enough to be his mother, but she isn't, I would have said, if I talked), in the same dumb, cheerful way she cooked last year's. She has no sense of sanctity, or ritual. She would give Lonnie my father's clothes if my father had left any behind to give.

My mother walks toward me with the hose, then past me toward her garden, to spray her pea plants. "O.K.," she yells to Lonnie, who stands by the spigot. He turns the knob and then goes inside. The light in the kitchen snaps on.

My mother stands with one hand on her hip, the other raising and lowering the hose, throwing large fans of water over the garden. She used to bathe me every night, and I think of the peas hanging in their green skins, dripping. I lie with one ear on the cool grass, and I can hear the water drumming into the garden. It makes me sleepy.

Then I hear it stop, and I look up to see my mother walking toward me, the skin on her bare legs and arms glowing. She sits down beside me, and for a while she says nothing. I pretend I am asleep on the ground, although I know she knows I am awake.

Then she starts to talk, as I knew she would. My mother says, "You are breaking my heart." She says it as if it were literally true, as if her heart were actually breaking. "I just want you to know that," she says. "You're old enough to know that you are breaking my heart."

I sit up. I look at my mother's chest, as if I could see her heart breaking. She has on a polo shirt with a little blue whale on her left breast. I am afraid to look at her face.

We sit like that for a while, and darkness grows around us. When I open my mouth to speak, my mother uncoils her arm from her side and covers my mouth with her hand.

I look at her.

"Wait," she says. "Don't say anything yet."

I can feel her flesh against my lips. Her wrist smells of chlorine. The fireflies, lighting all around us, make me dizzy.

Sixteen[1]

BY MAUREEN DALY

It wasn't that I'd never skated with a boy be-fore. Don't be silly. I told you before I get around. But this was different.

Now don't get me wrong. I mean, I want you to understand from the beginning that I'm not really so dumb. I know what a girl should do and what she shouldn't. I get around. I read. I listen to the radio. And I have two older sisters. So you see, I know what the score is. I know it's smart to wear tweedish skirts and shaggy sweaters with the sleeves pushed up and pearls and ankle socks and saddle shoes that look as if they've seen the world. And I know that your hair should be long, almost to your shoulders, and sleek as a wet seal, just a little fluffed on the ends, and you should wear a campus hat or a dink or else a peasant hankie if you've that sort of face. Properly, a peasant hankie should make you think of edelweiss, mist and sunny mountains, yodeling and Swiss cheese. You know, that kind of peasant. Now, me, I never wear a hankie. It makes my face seem wide and Slavic and I look like a picture always in one of those magazine articles that run—"And Stalin says the future of Russia lies in its women. In its women who have tilled its soil, raised its children—" Well, anyway. I'm not exactly too small-town either. I read Winchell's column. You get to know what New York boy is that way about some pineapple princess on the West Coast and what Paradise pretty is currently the prettiest, and why someone, eventually, will play Scarlett O'Hara. It gives you that cosmopolitan feeling. And I know that anyone who orders a strawberry sundae in a drugstore instead of a lemon coke would probably be dumb enough to wear colored ankle socks with high-

[1] This story, *Sixteen*, received first prize in the Short Story Division of the 1938 Scholastic Awards. It is reprinted from *Scholastic*, by permission of the editors.

heeled pumps or use Evening in Paris with a tweed suit. But I'm sort of drifting. This isn't what I wanted to tell you. I just wanted to give you the general idea of how I'm not so dumb. It's important that you understand that.

You see, it was funny how I met him. It was a winter night like any other winter night. And I didn't have my Latin done, either. But the way the moon tinseled the twigs and silver-plated the snowdrifts, I just couldn't stay inside. The skating rink isn't far from our house,—you can make it in five minutes if the sidewalks aren't slippery,—so I went skating. I remember it took me a long time to get ready that night because I had to darn my skating socks first. I don't know why they always wear out so fast—just in the toes, too. Maybe it's because I have metal protectors on the toes of my skates. That probably *is* why. And then I brushed my hair— hard, so hard it clung to my hand and stood up around my head in a hazy halo.

My skates were hanging by the back door all nice and shiny, for I'd just gotten them for Christmas and they smelled so queer—just like fresh smoked ham. My dog walked with me as far as the corner. She's a red Chow, very polite and well-mannered, and she kept pretending it was me she liked when all the time I knew it was the ham smell. She panted along beside me and her hot breath made a frosty little balloon balancing on the end of her nose. My skates thumped me good-naturedly on my back as I walked and the night was breathlessly quiet and the stars winked down like a million flirting eyes. It was all so lovely.

It was all so lovely I ran most of the way and it was lucky the sidewalks had ashes on them or I'd have slipped surely. The ashes crunched like cracker-jack and I could feel their cindery shape through the thinness of my shoes. I always wear old shoes when I go skating.

I had to cut across someone's back garden to get to the rink and last summer's grass stuck through the thin ice, brown and discour- aged. Not many people came through this way and the crusted snow broke through the little hollows between corn stubbles frozen hard in the ground. I was out of breath when I got to the shanty— out of breath with running and with the loveliness of the night. Shanties are always such friendly places. The floor all hacked to wet splinters from skate runners and the wooden wall frescoed with symbols of dead romance. There was a smell of singed wool as someone got too near the glowing isinglass grin of the iron stove. Girls burst through the door laughing, with snow on their hair, and tripped over shoes scattered on the floor. A pimply-faced boy grabbed the hat from the frizzled head of an eighth-grade blonde and stuffed it into an empty galosh to prove his love and then hastily bent to examine his skate strap with innocent unconcern.

It didn't take me long to get my own skates on and I stuck my shoes under the bench—far back where they wouldn't get knocked around and would be easy to find when I wanted to go home. I walked out on my toes and the shiny runners of my new skates dug deep into the sodden floor.

It was snowing a little outside—quick, eager little Lux-like flakes that melted as soon as they touched your hand. I don't know where the snow came from for there were stars out. Or maybe the stars were in my eyes and I just kept seeing them every time I looked up into the darkness. I waited a moment. You know, to start to skate at a crowded rink is like jumping on a moving merry-go-round. The skaters go skimming round in a colored blur like gaudy painted horses and the shrill musical jabber reëchoes in the night from a hundred human calliopes. Once in, I went all right. At least after I found out exactly where that rough ice was. It was "round, round, jump the rut, round, round, round, jump the rut, round, round—"

And then he came. All of a sudden his arm was around my waist so warm and tight and he said very casually, "Mind if I skate with you?" and then he took my other hand. That's all there was to it. Just that and then we were skating. It wasn't that I'd never skated with a boy before. Don't be silly. I told you before I get around. But this was different. He was a smoothie! He was a big shot up at school and he went to all the big dances and he was the best dancer in town except Harold Wright, who didn't count because he'd been to college in New York for two years! Don't you see? This was different.

I can't remember what we talked about at first; I can't even remember if we talked at all. We just skated and skated and laughed every time we came to that rough spot and pretty soon we were laughing all the time at nothing at all. It was all so lovely.

Then we sat on the big snow bank at the edge of the rink and just watched. It was cold at first even with my skating pants on, sitting on that hard heap of snow, but pretty soon I got warm all over. He threw a handful of snow at me and it fell in a little white shower on my hair and he leaned over to brush it off. I held my breath. The night stood still.

The moon hung just over the warming shanty like a big quarter slice of muskmelon and the smoke from the pipe chimney floated up in a sooty fog. One by one the houses around the rink twinked out their lights and somebody's hound wailed a mournful apology to a star as he curled up for the night. It was all so lovely.

Then he sat up straight and said, "We'd better start home." Not "Shall I take you home?" or "Do you live far?" but "We'd better start home." See, that's how I know he wanted to take me home. Not because he *had* to but because he *wanted* to. He went to the shanty to get my shoes. "Black ones," I told him. "Same size as Garbo's." And he laughed again. He was still smiling when he came back and took off my skates and tied the wet skate strings in a soggy knot and put them over his shoulder. Then he held out his hand and I slid off the snow bank and brushed off the seat of my pants and we were ready.

It was snowing harder now. Big quiet flakes that clung to twiggy bushes and snuggled in little drifts against the tree trunks. The night was an etching in black and white. It was all so lovely I was sorry I lived only a few blocks away. He talked softly as we walked, as if every little word were a secret. "Did I like Wayne King, and did I plan to go to college next year and had I a cousin who lived in Appleton and knew his brother?" A very respectable Emily Post sort of conversation, and then finally "how nice I looked with snow in my hair and had I ever seen the moon so—close?" For the moon was following us as we walked and ducking playfully behind a chimney every time I turned to look at it. And then we were home.

The porch light was on. My mother always puts the porch light on when I go away at night. And we stood there a moment by the front steps and the snow turned pinkish in the glow of the colored light and a few feathery flakes settled on his hair. Then he took my skates and put them over my shoulder and said, "Good night now. I'll call you." "I'll call you," he said.

I went inside then and in a moment he was gone. I watched him from my window as he went down the street. He was whistling softly and I waited until the sound faded away so I couldn't tell if it was he or my heart whistling out there in the night. And then he was gone, completely gone.

I shivered. Somehow the darkness seemed changed. The stars were little hard chips of light far up in the sky and the moon stared down with a sullen yellow glare. The air was tense with sudden cold and a gust of wind swirled his footprints into white oblivion. Everything was quiet.

But he'd said, "I'll call you." That's what he said—"I'll call you." I couldn't sleep all night.

And that was last Thursday. Tonight is Tuesday. Tonight is Tuesday and my homework's done, and I darned some stockings that didn't really need it, and I worked a crossword puzzle, and I listened to the radio, and now I'm just sitting. I'm just sitting because I can't think of anything else to do. I can't think of anything, anything but snowflakes and ice skates and yellow moons and Thursday night. The telephone is sitting on the corner table with its old black face turned to the wall so I can't see its leer. I don't even jump when it rings any more. My heart still prays, but my mind just laughs. Outside the night is still, so still I think I'll go crazy, and the white snow's all dirtied and smoked into grayness and the wind is blowing the arc light so it throws weird, waving shadows from the trees onto the lawn—like thin, starved arms begging for I don't know what. And so I'm just sitting here and I'm not feeling anything; I'm not even sad, because all of a sudden I know. All of a sudden I know. I can sit here now forever and laugh and laugh and laugh while the tears run salty in the corners of my mouth. For all of a sudden I know, I know what the stars knew all the time—he'll never, never call—never.

A Southern Landscape

by Elizabeth Spencer

If you're like me and sometimes turn through the paper reading anything and everything because you're too lazy to get up and do what you ought to be doing, then you already know about my home town. There's a church there that has a gilded hand on the steeple, with the finger pointing to Heaven. The hand looks normal size, but it's really as big as a Ford car. At least, that's what they used to say in those little cartoon squares in the newspaper, full of sketches and exclamation points—"Strange As It Seems," "This Curious World," or Ripley's "Believe It or Not." Along with carnivorous tropical flowers, the Rosetta stone, and the cheerful information that the entire human race could be packed into a box a mile square and dumped into Grand Canyon, there it would be every so often, that old Presbyterian hand the size of a Ford car. It made me feel right in touch with the universe to see it in the paper —something it never did accomplish all by itself. I haven't seen anything about it recently, but then, Ford cars have got bigger, and, come to think of it, maybe they don't even print those cartoons any more. The name of the town, in case you're trying your best to remember and can't, is Port Claiborne, Mississippi. Not that I'm *from* there; I'm from *near* there.

Coming down the highway from Vicksburg, you come to Port Claiborne, and then to get to our house you turn off to the right on State Highway No. 202 and follow along the prettiest road. It's just about the way it always was—worn deep down like a tunnel and thick with shade in summer. In spring, it's so full of sweet heavy odors, they make you drunk, you can't think of anything—you feel you will faint or go right out of yourself. In fall, there is the rustle of leaves under your tires and the smell of them, all sad and Indian-like. Then in the winter, there are only dust and bare limbs, and mud when it rains, and everything is like an old dirt-dauber's nest up in the corner. Well, any season, you go twisting along this tunnel for a mile or so, then the road breaks down into a flat open run toward a wooden bridge that spans a swampy creek bottom. Tall trees grow up out of the bottom—willow and cypress, gum and sycamore—and there is a jungle of brush and vines—kudzu, Jackson vine, Spanish moss, grapevine, Virginia creeper, and honeysuckle—looping, climbing, and festooning the trees, and harboring every sort of snake and varmint underneath. The wooden bridge clatters when you cross, and down far below you can see water, lying still, not a good step wide. One bank is grassy and the other is a slant of ribbed white sand.

Then you're going to have to stop and ask somebody. Just say, "Can you tell me where to turn to get to the Summerall place?" Everybody knows us. Not that we *are* anybody—I don't mean that. It's just that we've been there forever. When you find the right road, you go right on up through a little wood of oaks, then across a field, across a cattle gap, and you're there. The house is nothing special, just a one-gable affair with a bay window and a front porch—the kind they built back around fifty or sixty years ago. The shrubs around the porch and the privet hedge around the bay window were all grown up too high the last time I was there. They ought to be kept trimmed down. The yard is a nice flat one, not much for growing grass but wonderful for shooting marbles. There were always two or three marble holes out near the pecan trees where I used to play with the colored children.

Benjy Hamilton swore he twisted his ankle in one of those same marble holes once when he came to pick me up for something my senior year in high school. For all I know, they're still there, but Benjy was more than likely drunk and so would hardly have needed a marble hole for an excuse to fall down. Once, before we got the cattle gap, he couldn't open the gate, and fell on the barbed wire trying to cross the fence. I had to pick him out, a thread at a time, he was so tangled up. Mama said, "What were you two doing out at the gate so long last night?" "Oh, nothing, just talking," I said. She thought for the longest time that Benjy Hamilton was the nicest boy that ever walked the earth. No matter how drunk he was, the presence of an innocent lady like Mama, who said *"Drink-*

ing?" in the same tone of voice she would have said *"Murder?"* would bring him around faster than any number of needle showers, massages, ice packs, prairie oysters, or quick dips in December off the northern bank of Lake Ontario. He would straighten up and smile and say, "You made any more peach pickle lately, Miss Sadie?" (He could even say "peach pickle.") And she'd say no, but that there was always some of the old for him whenever he wanted any. And he'd say that was just the sweetest thing he'd ever heard of, but she didn't know what she was promising—anything as good as her peach pickle ought to be guarded like gold. And she'd say, well, for most anybody else she'd think twice before she offered any. And he'd say, if only everybody was as sweet to him as she was. . . . And they'd go on together like that till you'd think that all creation had ground and wound itself down through the vistas of eternity to bring the two of them face to face for exchanging compliments over peach pickle. Then I would put my arm in his so it would look like he was helping me down the porch steps out of the reflexes of his gentlemanly upbringing, and off we'd go.

It didn't happen all the time, like I've made it sound. In fact, it was only a few times when I was in school that I went anywhere with Benjy Hamilton. Benjy isn't his name, either; it's Foster. I sometimes call him "Benjy" to myself, after a big overgrown thirty-three-year-old idiot in *The Sound and the Fury,* by William Faulkner. Not that Foster was so big or overgrown, or even thirty-three years old, back then; but he certainly did behave like an idiot.

I won this prize, see, for writing a paper on the siege of Vicksburg. It was for the United Daughters of the Confederacy's annual contest, and mine was judged the best in the state. So Foster Hamilton came all the way over to the schoolhouse and got me out of class—I felt terribly important—just to "interview" me. He had just graduated from the university and had a job on the paper in Port Claiborne—that was before he started work for the *Times-Picayune* in New Orleans. We went into an empty classroom and sat down.

He leaned over some blank sheets of coarse-grained paper and scribbled things down with a thick-leaded pencil. I was sitting in the next seat; it was a long bench divided by a number of writing arms, which was why they said that cheating was so prevalent in our school—you could just cheat without meaning to. They kept trying to raise the money for regular desks in every classroom, so as to improve morals. Anyway, I couldn't help seeing what he was writing down, so I said, " 'Marilee' is all one word, and with an 'i,' not a 'y.' 'Summerall' is spelled just like it sounds." "Are you a senior?" he asked. "Just a junior," I said. He wore horn-rimmed glasses; that was back before everybody wore them. I thought they looked unusual and very distinguished. Also, I had noticed his shoulders when he went over to let the window down. I thought they were distinguished, too, if a little bit bony. "What is your ambition?" he asked me. "I hope to go to college year after next," I said. "I intend to wait until my junior year in college to choose a career."

He kept looking down at his paper while he wrote, and when he finally looked up at me I was disappointed to see why he hadn't done it before. The reason was, he couldn't keep a straight face. It had happened before that people broke out laughing just when I was being my most earnest and sincere. It must have been what I said, because I don't think I *look* funny. I guess I don't look like much of any one thing. When I see myself in the mirror, no adjective springs right to mind, unless it's "average." I am medium height, I am average weight, I buy "natural"-colored face powder and "medium"-colored lipstick. But I must say for myself, before this goes too far, that every once in a great while I look Just Right. I've never found the combination for making this happen, and no amount of reading the make-up articles in the magazines they have at the beauty parlor will do any good. But sometimes it happens anyway, with no more than soap and water, powder, lipstick, and a damp hairbrush.

My interview took place in the spring, when we were practicing for the senior play every night. Though a junior, I was in it because they always got me, after the eighth grade, to take parts in things. Those of us that lived out in the country Mrs. Arrington would take back home in her car after rehearsal. One night, we went over from the school to get a Coca-Cola before the drugstore closed, and there was Foster Hamilton. He had done a real nice article— what Mama called a "write-up." It was when he was about to walk out that he noticed me and said, "Hey." I said "Hey" back, and since he just stood there, I said, "Thank you for the write-up in the paper."

"Oh, that's all right," he said, not really listening. He wasn't laughing this time. "Are you going home?" he said.

"We are after 'while," I said. "Mrs. Arrington takes us home in her car."

"Why don't you let me take you home?" he said. "It might—it might save Mrs. Arrington an extra trip."

"Well," I said, "I guess I could ask her."

So I went to Mrs. Arrington and said, "Mrs. Arrington, Foster Hamilton said he would be glad to drive me home." She hesitated so long that I put in, "He said it might save you an extra trip." So finally she said, "Well, all right, Marilee." She told Foster to drive carefully. I could tell she was uneasy, but then, my family were known as real good people, very strict, and of course she didn't want them to feel she hadn't done the right thing.

That was the most wonderful night. I'll never forget it. It was full of spring, all restlessness and sweet smells. It was radiant, it was warm, it was serene. It was all the things you want to call it, but no word would ever be the right one, nor any ten words, either. When we got close to our turnoff, after the bridge, I said, "The next road is ours," but Foster drove right on past. I knew where he was going. He was going to Windsor.

Windsor is this big colonial mansion built back before the Civil War. It burned down during the 1890s sometime, but there were still twenty-five or more Corinthian columns, standing on a big open space of ground that is a pasture now, with cows and mules and calves grazing in it. The columns are enormously high and you can see some of the iron grillwork railing for the second-story gallery clinging halfway up. Vines cling to the fluted white plaster surfaces, and in some places the plaster has crumbled away, showing the brick underneath. Little trees grow up out of the tops of columns, and chickens have their dust holes among the rubble. Just down the fall of the ground beyond the ruin, there are some Negro houses. A path goes down to them.

It is this ignorant way that the hand of Nature creeps back over Windsor that makes me afraid. I'd rather there'd be ghosts there, but there aren't. Just some old story about lost jewelry that every once in a while sends somebody poking around in all the trash. Still it is magnificent, and people have compared it to the Parthenon and so on and so on, and even if it makes me feel this undertone of horror, I'm always ready to go and look at it again. When all of it was standing, back in the old days, it was higher even than the columns, and had a cupola, too. You could see the cupola from the river, they say, and the story went that Mark Twain used it to steer by. I've read that book since, *Life on the Mississippi,* and it seems he used everything else to steer by, too—crawfish mounds, old rowboats stuck in the mud, the tassels on somebody's corn patch, and every stump and stob from New Orleans to Cairo, Illinois. But it does kind of connect you up with something to know that Windsor was there, too, like seeing the Presbyterian hand in the newspaper. Some people would say at this point, "Small world," but it isn't a small world. It's an enormous world, bigger than you can imagine, but it's all connected up. What Nature does to Windsor it does to everything, including you and me—there's the horror.

But that night with Foster Hamilton, I wasn't thinking any such doleful thoughts, and though Windsor can be a pretty scary-looking sight by moonlight, it didn't scare me then. I could have got right out of the car, alone, and walked all around among the columns, and whatever I heard walking away through the weeds would not have scared me, either. We sat there, Foster and I, and never said a word. Then, after some time, he turned the car around and took the road back. Before we got to my house, though, he stopped the car by the roadside and kissed me. He held my face up to his, but outside that he didn't touch me. I had never been kissed in any deliberate and accomplished way before, and driving out to Windsor in that accidental way, the whole sweetness of the spring night, the innocence and mystery of the two of us, made me think how simple life was and how easy it was to step into happiness, like walking into your own rightful house.

This frame of mind persisted for two whole days—enough to make a nuisance of itself. I kept thinking that Foster Hamilton would come sooner or later and tell me that he loved me, and I couldn't sleep for thinking about him in various ways, and I had no appetite, and nobody could get me to answer them. I half expected him at play practice or to come to the schoolhouse, and I began to wish he would hurry up and get it over with, when, after play practice on the second night, I saw him uptown, on the corner, with this blonde.

Mrs. Arrington was driving us home, and he and the blonde were standing on the street corner, just about to get in his car. I never saw that blonde before or since, but she is printed eternally on my mind, and to this good day if I'd run into her across the counter from me in the ten-cent store, whichever one of us is selling lipstick to the other one, I'd know her for sure because I saw her for one half of a second in the street light in Port Claiborne with Foster Hamilton. She wasn't any ordinary blonde, either— dyed hair was in it. I didn't know the term "feather-bed blond" in those days, or I guess I would have thought it. As it was, I didn't really think anything, or say anything, either, but whatever had been galloping along inside me for two solid days and nights came to a screeching halt. Somebody in the car said, being real funny, "Foster Hamilton's got him another girl friend." I just laughed. "Sure has," I said. "Oh, Mari-leee!" they all said, teasing me. I laughed and laughed.

I asked Foster once, a long time later, "Why didn't you come back after that night you drove me out to Windsor?"

He shook his head. "We'd have been married in two weeks," he said. "It scared me half to death."

"Then it's a mercy you didn't," I said. "It scares *me* half to death right now."

Things had changed between us, you realize, between that kiss and that conversation. What happened was—at least, the main thing that happened was—Foster asked me the next year to go to the high school senior dance with him, so I said all right.

I knew about Foster by then, and that his reputation was not of the best—that it was, in fact, about the worst our county had to offer. I knew he had an uncommon thirst and that on weekends he went helling about the countryside with a fellow that owned the local picture show and worked at a garage in the daytime. His name was A. P. Fortenberry, and he owned a new convertible in a sickening shade of bright maroon. The convertible was always dusty—though you could see A.P. in the garage every afternoon, during the slack hour, hosing it down on the wash rack—because he and Foster were out in it almost every night, harassing the countryside. They knew every bootlegger in a radius of forty miles. They knew girls that lived on the outskirts of towns and girls that didn't. I guess "uninhibited" was the word for A. P. Fortenberry, but whatever it was, I couldn't stand him. He called me into the garage one day—to have a word with me about Foster, he said—but when I got inside he backed me into the corner and started trying it on. "Funny little old girl," he kept saying. He rattled his words out real fast. "Funny little old girl." I slapped him as hard as I could, which was pretty hard, but that only seemed to stimulate him. I thought I'd never get away from him—I can't smell the inside of a garage to this good day without thinking about A. P. Fortenberry.

When Foster drove all the way out to see me one day soon after that—we didn't have a telephone in those days—I thought he'd come to apologize for A.P., and I'm not sure yet he didn't intend for me to understand that without saying anything about it. He certainly put himself out. He sat down and swapped a lot of Port Claiborne talk with Mama—just pleased her to death—and then he went out back with Daddy and looked at the chickens and the peach trees. He even had an opinion on growing peaches, though I reckon he'd given more thought to peach brandy than he'd ever given to orchards. He said when we were walking out to his car that he'd like to take me to the senior dance, so I said O.K. I was pleased; I had to admit it.

Even knowing everything I knew by then (I didn't tell Mama and Daddy), there was something kind of glamorous about Foster Hamilton. He came of a real good family, known for being aristocratic and smart; he had uncles who were college professors and big lawyers and doctors and things. His father had died when he was a babe in arms (tragedy), and he had perfect manners. He had perfect manners, that is, when he was sober, and it was not that he departed from them in any intentional way when he was drunk. Still, you couldn't exactly blame me for being disgusted when, after ten minutes of the dance, I discovered that his face was slightly green around the temples and that whereas he could dance fairly well, he could not stand up by himself at all. He teetered like a baby that has caught on to what walking is, and knows that now is the time to do it, but hasn't had quite enough practice.

"Foster," I whispered, "have you been drinking?"

"Been *drinking?*" he repeated. He looked at me with a sort of wonder, like the national president of the W.C.T.U. might if asked the same question. "It's so close in here," he complained.

It really wasn't that close yet, but it was going to be. The gym doors were open, so that people could walk outside in the night air whenever they wanted to. "Let's go outside," I said. Well, in my many anticipations I had foreseen Foster and me strolling about on the walks outside, me in my glimmering white sheer dress with the blue underskirt (Mama and I had worked for two weeks on that dress), and Foster with his nice broad aristocratic shoulders. Then, lo and behold, he had worn a white dinner jacket! There was never anybody in creation as proud as I was when I first walked into the senior dance that night with Foster Hamilton.

Pride goeth before a fall. The fall must be the one Foster took down the gully back of the boys' privy at the schoolhouse. I still don't know quite how he did it. When we went outside, he put me carefully in his car, helped to tuck in my skirts, and closed the door in the most polite way, and then I saw him heading toward the privy in his white jacket that was swaying like a lantern through the dark, and then he just wasn't there any more. After a while, I got worried that somebody would come out, like us, for air, so I got out and went to the outside wall of the privy and said, "Foster, are you all right?" I didn't get any answer, so I knocked politely on the wall and said, "Foster?" Then I looked around behind and all around, for I was standing very close to the edge of the gully that had eroded right up to the borders of the campus (somebody was always threatening that the whole schoolhouse was going to cave off into it before another school year went by), and there at the bottom of the gully Foster Hamilton was lying face down, like the slain in battle.

What I should have done, I should have walked right off and left him there till doomsday, or till somebody came along who would use him for a model in a statue to our glorious dead in the defense of Port Claiborne against Gen. Ulysses S. Grant in 1863. That battle was over in about ten minutes, too. But I had to consider how things would look—I had my pride, after all. So I took a look around, hiked up my skirts, and went down into the gully. When I shook Foster, he grunted and rolled over, but I couldn't get him up. I wasn't strong enough. Finally, I said, "Foster, Mama's here!" and he soared up like a Roman candle. I never saw anything like it. He walked straight up the side of the gully and gave me a hand up, too. Then I guided him over toward the car and he sat in the door and lighted a cigarette.

"Where is she?" he said.

"Who?" I said.

"Your mother," he said.

"Oh, I just said that, Foster. I had to get you up someway."

At that, his shoulders slumped down and he looked terribly depressed. "I didn't mean to do this, Marilee," he said. "I didn't have any idea it would hit me this way. I'm sure I'll be all right in a minute."

I don't think he ever did fully realize that he had fallen in the gully. "Get inside," I said, and shoved him over. There were one or two couples beginning to come outside and walk around. I squeezed in beside Foster and closed the door. Inside the gym, where the hot lights were, the music was blaring and beating away. We had got a real orchestra specially for that evening, all the way down from Vicksburg, and a brass-voiced girl was singing a 1930s song. I would have given anything to be in there with it rather than out in the dark with Foster Hamilton.

I got quite a frisky reputation out of that evening. Disappearing after ten minutes of the dance, seen snuggling out in the car, and gone completely by intermission. I drove us away. Foster wouldn't be convinced that anybody would think it at all peculiar if he reappeared inside the gym with red mud smeared all over his dinner jacket. I didn't know how to drive, but I did anyway. I'm convinced you can do anything when you have to—speak French, do a double back flip off a low diving board, play Rachmaninoff on the piano, or fly an airplane. Well, maybe not fly an airplane; it's too technical. Anyway, that's how I learned to drive a car, riding up and down the highway, holding off Foster with my elbow, marking time till midnight came and I could go home without anybody thinking anything out of the ordinary had happened.

When I got out of the car, I said, "Foster Hamilton, I never want to see you again as long as I live. And I hope you have a wreck on the way home."

Mama was awake, of course. She called out in the dark, "Did you have a good time, Marilee?"

"Oh yes, Ma'am," I said.

Then I went back to my shed-ceilinged room in the back wing, and cried and cried. And cried.

There was a good bit of traffic coming and going out to our house after that. A. P. Fortenberry came, all pallid and sober, with a tie on and a straw hat in his hand. Then A.P. and Foster came together. Then Foster came by himself.

The story went that Foster had stopped in the garage with A.P. for a drink before the dance, and instead of water in the drink, A.P. had filled it up with grain alcohol. I was asked to believe that he did this because, seeing Foster all dressed up, he got the idea that Foster was going to some family do, and he couldn't stand Foster's family, they were all so stuck-up. While Foster was draining the first glass, A.P. had got called out front to put some gas in a car, and while he was gone Foster took just a little tap more whiskey with another glassful of grain alcohol. A.P. wanted me to understand that Foster's condition that night had been all his fault, that instead of three or four ounces of whiskey, Foster had innocently put down eighteen ounces of sheer dynamite, and it was a miracle only to be surpassed by the resurrection of Jesus Christ that he had managed to drive out and get me, converse with Mama about peach pickle, and dance those famous ten minutes at all.

Well, I said I didn't know. I thought to myself I never heard of Foster Hamilton touching anything he even mistook for water.

All these conferences took place at the front gate. "I never saw a girl like you," Mama said. "Why don't you invite the boys to sit on the porch?"

"I'm not too crazy about A.P. Fortenberry," I said. "I don't think he's a very nice boy."

"Uh-*huh*," Mama said, and couldn't imagine what Foster Hamilton was doing running around with him, if he wasn't a nice boy. Mama, to this day, will not hear a word against Foster Hamilton.

I was still giving some thought to the whole matter that summer, sitting now on the front steps, now on the back steps, and now on the side steps, whichever was most in the shade, chewing on pieces of grass and thinking, when one day the mailman stopped in for a glass of Mama's cold buttermilk (it's famous) and told me that Foster and A.P. had had the most awful wreck. They had been up to Vicksburg, and coming home had collided with a whole carload of Negroes. The carnage was awful—so much blood on everybody you couldn't tell black from white. They were both going to live, though. Being so drunk, which in a way had caused the wreck, had also kept them relaxed enough to come out of it alive. I warned the mailman to leave out the drinking part when he told Mama, she thought Foster was such a nice boy.

The next time I saw Foster, he was out of the hospital and had a deep scar on his cheekbone like a sunken star. He looked handsomer and more distinguished than ever. I had gotten a scholarship to Millsaps College in Jackson, and was just about to leave. We had a couple of dates before I left, but things were not the same. We would go to the picture show and ride around afterward, having a conversation that went something like this:

"Marilee, why are you such a nice girl? You're about the only nice girl I know."

"I guess I never learned any different, so I can't help it. Will you teach me how to stop being a nice girl?"

"I certainly will not!" He looked to see how I meant it, and for a minute I thought the world was going to turn over, but it didn't.

"Why won't you, Foster?"

"You're too young. And your mama's a real sweet lady. And your daddy's too good a shot."

"Foster, why do you drink so much?"

"Marilee, I'm going to tell you the honest truth. I drink because I like to drink." He spoke with real conviction.

So I went on up to college in Jackson, where I went in for serious studies and made very good grades. Foster, in time, got a job on the paper in New Orleans, where, during off hours, or so I understood, he continued his investigation of the lower things in life and of the effects of alcohol upon the human system.

It is twenty years later now, and Foster Hamilton is down there yet.

Millions of things have happened; the war has come and gone. I live far away, and everything changes, almost every day. You can't even be sure the moon and stars are going to be the same the day after tomorrow night. So it has become more and more important to me to know that Windsor is still right where it always was, standing pure in its decay, and that the gilded hand on the Presbyterian church in Port Claiborne is still pointing to Heaven and not to Outer Space; and I earnestly feel, too, that Foster Hamilton should go right on drinking. There have got to be some things you can count on, would be an ordinary way to put it. I'd rather say that I feel the need of a land, of a sure terrain, of a sort of permanent landscape of the heart.

A Lesson in History

by James T. Farrell

SCENE: *The large classroom of the second-year class at Saint Stanislaus High School in Chicago. It is a spring afternoon in 1921. The stage is cut into two sections; the large classroom is the dominating one, and on the right is a small portion of the corridor outside. In the classroom, back, left, is a wall with windows, and the back is a long blackboard. The teacher's desk is against the wall, right, set on a dais in the center of the room. To the right of the desk is a wastepaper basket and a map that is rolled up like a shade, and to the left of the desk, lower right front, a swinging door that leads into the corridor. Facing the teacher's desk are the rows of seats, almost all filled except for a few in the back, and except for Danny O'Neill's seat, the fourth from the front in the center aisle.*

FATHER KRANZ: *(seated at desk and finishing the roll call):* Zivic?

ZIVIC *(student in rear far row):* Here.

FATHER KRANZ: *(as he talks there is a dragging quality in his voice):* Well, now, we'll begin the lesson. Of course, I know you've all recuperated from the effects of Friday. *(They laugh. Various students turn to look at Bart Daly, sitting in the second seat third row, and Marty Mulligan in first seat, fourth row.)* I know that you've all studied and come here prepared, perhaps even prepared to teach me a little history. *(Students all over are noticed trying furtively to steal quick looks into their textbooks.)* I can see Mulligan there suffering the throes of anxiety. Aren't you, Mulligan? *(Laughs.)*

MARTY: No, Father. *(More laughter.)*

FATHER KRANZ: What do you mean, *no,* Father?

MARTY *(smiling):* I mean, yes, Father.

SHEEHAN: Father, he means that he would rather have you ask somebody else.

FATHER KRANZ: All right, Sheehan. Since you're so quick with your tongue, I'll let you answer. *(The class laughs.)*

SHEEHAN: Father, I'd as soon remain silent.

MARTY MULLIGAN: Father, he's already got a charley horse in his tongue from talking.

FATHER KRANZ: Well, we'll exercise the charley horse out of your tongue. *(As Father Kranz says this, Danny O'Neill is first heard, then seen running to the door admitting to the classroom.)* Now, Sheehan. . . .

DANNY O'NEILL *(bursting breathlessly into the classroom):* I see that the cohorts are all here.

FATHER KRANZ: Yes, and the jackass has arrived.

TIM DOOLAN *(as the class laughs):* He's not a jackass, Father. He's a *jumentum*.

FATHER KRANZ: No, he's a jackass in both English and Latin. *(Again the class laughs.)* I think we've had enough humor, and now we'll go on with the lesson. *(Again there are attempts to sneak quick looks into the textbooks.)* And don't do your studying now. You should have done it over the weekend.

DANNY: Father, I'm in perfect agreement with you.

FATHER KRANZ: That's such a good start, O'Neill, that I'll give you more opportunity to show how much you agree with me. Don't get too anxious.

DANNY: There's no danger, Father.

FATHER KRANZ: Sheehan, what is the lesson for today?

SHEEHAN: History. *(Laughter.)*

FATHER KRANZ: Sheehan, how did you think up such an answer? Did you listen to me here last Friday?

SHEEHAN: Yes, Father.

FATHER KRANZ: And so you answer my question by saying that the lesson of the day is history.

SHEEHAN: Well, it is, only I was going to go on from there but. . . .

FATHER KRANZ: But what?

SHEEHAN: Well, all this horseplay *(he points around the room)* made me forget. *(Laughter.)*

AD LIB: Yeah!

       Try again, that ain't so good.

       You talking horseplay.

FATHER KRANZ: Quiet. Now, everybody will be so quiet for thirty seconds that we can hear a pin drop. Quiet. *(A strained quiet of from fifteen to thirty seconds.)* Now, Sheehan, has your memory been restored to you?

SHEEHAN: Well, Father, the lesson is. . . .

FATHER KRANZ *(marking on card before him)*: Sheehan, if I could give you a mark lower than zero for your brilliant recitation, I'd do so. You'll have to be satisfied with zero. But to make up for the fact that that is the best mark I can give you, why, you can stay after school at two-thirty and copy the lesson out of the book. Maybe that will help you to remember tomorrow.

SHEEHAN: Gee, Father, I tell you, I did study. I had it all right at the fingertips of my mind, but these distractions made me forget.

FATHER KRANZ: All I'm doing, Sheehan, is giving you something to do that will be an aid to your memory in the future.

SHEEHAN: Aw, gee, Father, I tell you, I did study.

FATHER KRANZ: And I'm going to help you to study more effectively.

SHEEHAN: But, Father. . . .

FATHER KRANZ: You'd better sit down now, Sheehan, before you begin to abuse my patience.

SHEEHAN: But, gee, Father, that's an awful penance to give me.

FATHER KRANZ: Come on, sit down now. *(He looks around the room.)* Mulligan, you look bright today.

MARTY: Looks are often deceiving, Father.

FATHER KRANZ: Well, we'll find out.

MARTY: No, Father.

FATHER KRANZ: What do you mean? No, Father, what?

MARTY: I mean no, Father, I don't feel bright.

FATHER KRANZ: You tell Sheehan and the rest of the class here what is the history lesson for the day.

MARTY: But if I do, Father, they'll know as much as I do.

DANNY O'NEILL: That won't be very much.

MARTY *(turning toward Danny as many laugh)*: Wise guy!

FATHER KRANZ: Sit down, Mulligan. You can stay in the jug with Sheehan.

MARTY: But, Father, I got basketball practice this afternoon.

FATHER KRANZ: The team won't miss you. And writing out your lesson might make your hands more limber.

MARTY: I don't think so. And, Father, I don't know what I did to get a penance.

FATHER KRANZ: I'm telling you what you're going to do.

MARTY: But that's not fair, Father.

FATHER KRANZ: Don't talk any more!

MARTY: But listen, Father. . . .

FATHER KRANZ: I told you, Mulligan, to keep still. Now do it, or I'll have to make you! *(He flushes with sudden anger.)* All right, O'Neill, you like to talk. Stand up!

DANNY *(rising):* Yes, Father.

FATHER KRANZ: What is the lesson today?

VOICE *(whispering):* Adrian the Fourth.

FATHER KRANZ: Hurry up!

DANNY: Adrian the Fourth.

FATHER KRANZ: Who was he?

DANNY *(there are whispering voices telling him, but he can't catch what they say):* King.

FATHER KRANZ: King of what?

DANNY: England.

FATHER KRANZ: Tell me, O'Neill, who told you that?

DANNY: The book.

FATHER KRANZ: I heard prompting all the way up here, so tell me who told you that?

DANNY: A lot of them.

FATHER KRANZ: Well, a lot of them are wrong. I think I'll let you keep company with Mulligan and Sheehan after school.

SHEEHAN: Couldn't you let somebody else take his place, Father?

DANNY: Yes, Father, I don't think I should stay with them if they don't want me.

FATHER KRANZ *(as he talks, a student in back seat, far row, is shooting spitballs around the room with the aid of a rubber band):* It's not what they want but what I'm telling you to do when the bell rings at two-thirty and good students like Daly, Shanley, Dawson, and Doylan can all go out.

DANNY: Well, of course, Father, if you insist, then I'll stay. *(Laughter.)*

FATHER KRANZ: I thought you would, O'Neill, you are very obliging. *(Laughter.)* Now, let's see. *(He looks around the room.)* We have such a bright bunch here. Doolan, you look as if you were awake this afternoon. Stand up.

MARTY *(as Doolan arises and Danny sits down):* Father, that's a mistake about him being awake.

FATHER KRANZ *(curtly):* Mulligan, if that penance I gave you isn't enough, there are other things I can give you. From now on, you can speak when I speak to you first.

CARRIGAN: I wouldn't let him speak either, Father. He hasn't got a nice voice.

FATHER KRANZ: Carrigan, how are your knees?

CARRIGAN: Well, Father, we had a retreat last week.

FATHER KRANZ: Good, that gave you a chance to practice them. Now we'll test them. For the rest of the class hour, kneel in the hallway outside the doorway. I'm getting tired of some of you fellows. *(Carrigan slowly, sulkily walks to the door.)* All right, Doolan.

TIM DOOLAN: Father, you know, I've been puzzled by a question I wanted to ask you.

FATHER KRANZ: Yes? *(Interrupted by laughter caused by Carrigan, who made a face as he went through the door to kneel in the hallway in view of the audience.)*

TIM DOOLAN: Yes, Father, I wanted to ask you the derivation of the name Adrian.

FATHER KRANZ: Are you interested in etymology, Doolan?

DOOLAN: Of course. *(Laughter.)* You see, Father, I was reading the lesson, and I got to wondering and asking myself, now where did this name come from?

FATHER KRANZ: You did? Good. Now, I want to ask you a question.

TIM DOOLAN: Honest, I did, Father.

FATHER KRANZ: I know. And, of course, Doolan, I appreciate such curiosity because I know how well most of my students here have studied the day's assignment. So I appreciate the curiosity you have shown. However, before I answer your question, I want to ask you something. Now, Doolan, will you tell the class what you read about Adrian the Fourth?

DOOLAN: Sure I will, Father. But first, could you tell me where the name came from?

FATHER KRANZ: Did the assignment you read for today say anything about the derivation of the name?

DOOLAN: No. It said. . . . *(He pauses.)* It said. . . .

DANNY: Father, I know what it was. He was so concerned worrying over etymology that he forgot everything else.

DOOLAN: Hey, Goof!

FATHER KRANZ: Did it say that too? Hey, Goof! What historical character said that, Doolan?

DOOLAN *(as there is laughter)*: Well, Father.

FATHER KRANZ: You told me that about Well, Father. Now, what else? *(Doolan stands in long and nervous silence; students around him furtively look in books; others shoot spitballs; and outside Carrigan gets off his knees and stands against door listening.)* Doolan, you'd better keep your friends company after school. *(Looks around classroom.)* Close your books, everybody!

SHANLEY *(raising his hand)*: Father, I know.

FATHER KRANZ *(to Shanley as Marty directs a contemptuous look at him.)*: I know you do, Shanley. I want to try to find out if some of the others know. Now, I wonder who else is as interested in etymology as Doolan. *(Catching Marty furtively starting to begin his penance.)* Mulligan, put that pencil and paper away, close your book, and do your penance after school.

SHEEHAN: He can't tell time, Father.

FATHER KRANZ: If you don't like the atmosphere of the room, Sheehan, you can join Carrigan outside.

SHEEHAN: Oh, I do, Father.

FATHER KRANZ: I'm glad you do, Sheehan. Thank you.

SHEEHAN: You're welcome, Father.

FATHER KRANZ: Smilga. *(He rises from his desk on dais.)*

SMILGA *(Rising as Father Kranz stands over Sheehan.)*: Yes, Fadder.

FATHER KRANZ *(taking off the black belt he wears around his middle over the brown habit of his order):* What was the Bull Laudabilitor? *(Hands go up and fingers snap from students who know the answer.)*

SHEEHAN: Father, that might hurt.

FATHER KRANZ *(hitting Sheehan several blows on the back as he speaks):* Did you hear the question? *(At this moment Danny O'Neill is hit by a spitball and turns and shakes his fist toward the rear of the room.)*

SMILGA: Yes, Fadder.

FATHER KRANZ: Well, do you know the answer?

SMILGA: Yes, Fadder.

FATHER KRANZ: Why don't you give it to me then?

SMILGA: Is dat what you wanted, Fadder? *(Laughter.)*

FATHER KRANZ: You don't think I wanted you to tell me who won the basketball game last Friday, do you? *(More laughter.)*

SMILGA *(speaking rapidly, and with an accent, and pronouncing his "th's" as "de"):* Well, de Bull Laudabilitor is supposed to have been a bull issued by de Pope, Adrian de Fourth, to de King of England to give the King of England right over Ireland.

FATHER KRANZ: The first one in the class I have called on who could answer a question. Thank you, Smilga. Now, Doolan, tell Sheehan whether or not this particular bull was really issued by the Pope.

SHEEHAN: Father, the bull was only bull anyway.

FATHER KRANZ: Shut up, Sheehan, unless you want some more wallops. If I didn't give you enough, I'll oblige you more satisfactorily a second time.

DANNY: Father, Sheehan ought to be able to talk all about bull. That's all he knows.

FATHER KRANZ: And O'Neill has spoken his last word of this class hour. *(He aimlessly wanders toward door, and Carrigan slips back to his knees.)* Tell us, Shanley. *(Faces class.)*

SHANLEY: It was a forgery, Father, composed after the death of Pope Adrian the Fourth.

FATHER KRANZ: Suppose it were not a forgery? What was the argument behind the theory that this bull was a true document, and what is the justification for this alleged grant on the part of Pope Adrian the Fourth?

SHANLEY: The Pope, as a feudal overlord over all of Christendom, would have had such a right to grant a fief, like Ireland, to the King of England as his vassal.

FATHER KRANZ: O'Neill, are you listening?

DANNY *(points to his closed lips):* Can I talk, Father? You said I should be silent for the rest of the hour. *(Laughter.)*

FATHER KRANZ: Stop the nonsense and answer my question.

DANNY: Yes, Father.

FATHER KRANZ: Well, thank you for your attention. Now, Daly, tell Mulligan who was the Holy Roman Emperor during the papacy of Pope Adrian the Fourth.

DALY *(rising):* Frederick Barbarossa.

FATHER KRANZ: Can you tell me anything about the relationships between the Pope and the Emperor?

DALY: Yes, Father.

MARTY *(turning to Sheehan and yelling loudly):* Cut it out.

SHEEHAN: Get me a pocket knife and I will.

FATHER KRANZ: What's ailing you scholars? *(Laughter.)*

SHEEHAN *(to Mulligan):* I want to cut it out for you since you asked me to. *(Laughter.)*

FATHER KRANZ: Mulligan, haven't you been assigned a sufficient penance?

MARTY: I didn't do anything. Sheehan was shooting spitballs at me.

SHEEHAN: Father, I wasn't, and he's maligning me.

FATHER KRANZ: Someday, you kids are going to abuse my patience beyond the limits of endurance.

SHEEHAN: And, Father, he's abusing mine. *(Points at Marty.)*

MARTY: Yes, and I'll abuse more than your patience.

FATHER KRANZ: Shut up, both of you! If you're looking for a fight, come and fight me.

DANNY: But, Father, why don't you pick on someone your own size. *(Laughter.)*

FATHER KRANZ: O'Neill, come up here and kneel in the front of the room. *(More laughter.)*

DANNY *(rising and walking forward):* Gee, I don't want to wear my pants out.

FATHER KRANZ *(meeting Danny before his own desk):* You talk too much. *(Slaps Danny's face. Danny tries to cover up and gets a second slap on the side of the face.)* Enough is enough from you kids. *(Turns to Daly, and Danny goes to kneel in a corner.)* All right, Daly.

DALY: Father, Frederick Barbarossa wanted to be coronated by the Pope as the Holy Roman Emperor. When he and the Pope met. . . .

FATHER KRANZ: That's enough, Daly. I see that you know your lesson. I think I shall find out some more from some of my other really bright boys and interested students. Rychewski.

STEVE RYCHEWSKI: Yes, Fadder.

FATHER KRANZ: Tell Mulligan what Daly was trying to say.

STEVE RYCHEWSKI: He was talking about de meeting of de Pope and Frederick Barbarossa.

FATHER KRANZ: Well, what about the meeting?

STEVE RYCHEWSKI *(after a long pause):* Why, Fadder, they met.

FATHER KRANZ: Are you sure they met?

STEVE RYCHEWSKI: Yes, Fadder.

FATHER KRANZ: How do you know? Why are you so sure they met?

STEVE RYCHEWSKI: Because I know dey did.

FATHER KRANZ: How do you know?

STEVE RYCHEWSKI *(after another long pause):* Daly said so, didn't he? *(Laughter.)*

FATHER KRANZ: Did you study your history assignment over the weekend?

STEVE RYCHEWSKI: I always study.

FATHER KRANZ: How do you study?

STEVE RYCHEWSKI: I read de lesson you tell us to.

FATHER KRANZ: And what do you learn?

STEVE RYCHEWSKI: Whatever de book says.

FATHER KRANZ: What book? Buffalo Bill, Nick Carter, what book? *(Laughter.)*

STEVE RYCHEWSKI: De history book.

FATHER KRANZ: What history book?

TIM DOOLAN: He doesn't know that one, Father.

FATHER KRANZ: Then he's as bright as you, isn't he?

TIM DOOLAN: He comes from my home town.

DANNY *(turning back toward class):* Father, where they come from, West Pullman, the sidewalks are taken in at nine o'clock.

FATHER KRANZ: Do I hear noises from monkeys or what?

MARTY: No, Father, that's only O'Neill.

FATHER KRANZ: I wonder now, Rychewski, do you really know what a history book is?

STEVE RYCHEWSKI: Yes, Fadder, de textbook.

FATHER KRANZ *(returning to desk and holding before the class the thick, green-bound history textbook):* Tell me honestly, Rychewski, did you ever see this book before?

STEVE RYCHEWSKI: Yes, Fadder.

FATHER KRANZ: Do you know what's inside of it?

SCHAEFFER: Father, it has big words inside of it.

MARTY: And pictures.

FATHER KRANZ: Now, don't you fellows tell him. Rychewski, what is inside this book?

STEVE RYCHEWSKI: History.

FATHER KRANZ: And what is history?

STEVE RYCHEWSKI: Well, Fadder, history is. . . .

FATHER KRANZ: Mulligan, see if you can redeem yourself by telling Rychewski what history is.

MARTY: History is the thing that keeps me in the jug and gives me writer's cramp.

FATHER KRANZ *(glares at Marty and then looks woefully at Steve Rychewski):* I'll tell you, Rychewski, and I'll tell the whole class what history is. Now, listen closely. History is something that I cannot under any circumstances, and no matter what methods I use, manage to teach to you numskulls.

STEVE RYCHEWSKI: Yes, Fadder.

FATHER KRANZ *(irritated):* Sit down and take a load off your brains. You can keep your comrades company after two-thirty.

STEVE RYCHEWSKI *(sitting down, smiling meekly and in a friendly way):* Yes, Fadder.

FATHER KRANZ: How many here studied today's lesson? *(All hands go up.)* How many of you here know the Ten Commandments? *(All hands again go up.)* How many of you know that one of the Ten Commandments forbids lying? *(All hands go up.)* Well,

I'll find out. Now, McDonald, answer me, at the risk of your im-
mortal soul.

MCDONALD *(reluctantly rising):* That's a big order, Father.

SCHAEFFER: Father, he spent the weekend studying how to comb
his hair with vaseline.

FATHER KRANZ: You never studied, did you, Schaeffer?

MCDONALD: Father, he's defaming me. *(Points to Schaeffer.)*

FATHER KRANZ: Well, now, don't you, in turn, go and defame
the memory of Pope Adrian the Fourth.

MCDONALD: Father, you can prevent me from doing that.

FATHER KRANZ: How?

MCDONALD: By not asking me any questions.

FATHER KRANZ: Good. Sit down, and stay after school, and do
the same penance as the others.

MARTY: We don't want him in our jug, Father.

FATHER KRANZ: What can I do about that?

MARTY: You can let me go, and keep him.

FATHER KRANZ: That would be unfair.

MARTY: But, Father. *(He is laughing and grinning and he looks
up at the priest.)* . . .

FATHER KRANZ *(interrupting Mulligan):* Shut up, I'm being too
lenient with you kids as it is.

SHEEHAN: Lenient?

FATHER KRANZ: Sheehan, you can speak when you're spoken to.

MARTY: Yeh, Sheehan, freeze your trap.

FATHER KRANZ: Mulligan, you're talking too much. Why didn't
you talk when I asked you to recite?

MARTY: I would have, but I didn't want to show the rest of the
class up.

DANNY *(turning around from his kneeling position):* Mulligan
doesn't think much of himself, does he?

MARTY: Shut up, Dope!

FATHER KRANZ: Mulligan, are you the teacher?

TIM DOOLAN: Thank Caesar's ghost that he isn't.

MARTY: If I was, Father, I wouldn't be so hard on a guy.

FATHER KRANZ: Mulligan, I'm tired of you.

MARTY: Father, you aren't any more tired than my hand will be
this afternoon.

FATHER KRANZ *(rising and walking toward Marty's desk):* Do you talk to hear your own voice, or what?

DANNY *(again turning):* To reveal his ignorance.

MARTY: That's enough from you, O'Neill. You're only a goof.

FATHER KRANZ: Shut up, O'Neill. *(Moving more rapidly toward Marty.)* Mulligan, was your opinion of O'Neill asked?

MARTY: You don't expect me to listen to him making cracks like that at me, do you?

FATHER KRANZ: Mulligan, who do you think you're talking to? *(The class, seeing that this time the priest has actually lost his temper, becomes suddenly tense. Marty looks up at the priest, his friendly grin suddenly turning into an expression of surprise.)* Answer me. *(Mulligan's expression becomes one of fear.)*

MARTY: What do you mean, Father? *(Father Kranz punches Marty's face. Marty covers up as the second blow lands.)*

FATHER KRANZ *(punching angrily):* Answer me. *(He continues punching as the curtain falls.)*

May Queen

by Mary Robison

"I see her skirt, Denise," Mickey said to his wife. "It's blue. I can't see her face because her head's lowered, but the two attendants with her are wearing gloves, right?"

He was standing on the hood of his new tan Lincoln Continental, in a parking space behind the crowds of parents outside St. Rose of Lima church, in Indianapolis. He had one hand over his eyebrows, explorer style, against the brilliant noonday sun. He was trying to see their daughter, Riva, who had been elected May Queen by her senior high-school class, and who was leading students from all the twelve grades in a procession around the school grounds.

"There's a guy with balloons over there," Mickey said.

Denise stood with the small of her back leaning against one of the car headlights. Around her there were a good three or four hundred people, scattered in the parking lot and on some of the school's athletic fields. They held mimeographed hymn sheets, loose bunches of garden flowers, little children's hands. Some of the women wore straw hats with wide brims and some of the men wore visored golf hats, against the sun, which was cutting and white, gleaming on car chrome and flattening the colors of clothes.

Mickey and Denise had been late getting started, and then Mickey had had trouble parking. "It's a damn good thing that the nuns picked Riva up this morning," Denise had said. "We'd have fritzed this whole thing."

Mickey moved cautiously along the hood of the Lincoln and jumped to the ground. "They're headed our way," he said. "They're past the elementary annex and rounding the backstops."

Denise said, "How does she look, Mick? Scared?"

"Sharp," Mickey said. "Right in step."

"I know," Denise said, clapping her hands. "I love that dress, if I do say so."

"I keep forgetting it was your handiwork," Mickey said.

Denise pushed her glasses up on her nose and made a mad face. Her glasses had lenses that magnified her eyes. "So is this, you forget," she said, pinching the bodice of her dress. She stood away so Mickey could admire her sleeveless green shift and the matching veil pinned in her shining gray hair.

After a while she said, "You know, three other parishes are having May processions today. I don't care. Ours is best. Ours is always the best, though I do like the all-men's choir at St. Catherine's."

"Mi-mi-mi," Mickey sang, and Denise elbowed him.

"Shhh," she said. "There they are."

"So grown up," Mickey said. "I ought to be hanged for leaving the movie camera at work Friday."

Altar boys with raised crucifixes headed the march, and behind them came a priest in a cassock and surplice, swinging a smoking bulb of incense. Riva came next, flanked by two boy attendants, who held the hem of her short cape. Beneath the cape Riva wore a blue bridesmaid's frock. She carried a tiny wreath of roses and fern on a satin pillow. Her face was lifted in the white light. Her throat moved as she sang the Ave Maria.

A family of redheads who were grouped ahead of Denise and Mickey turned around and grinned. Mickey wagged his head left and right. "Great!" he said.

Denise slipped a miniature bottle of spray perfume from her pocketbook. "One of us smells like dry-cleaning fluid," she said. She wet her wrists with the perfume. "Unless I'm reacting to the incense."

"It's me, I'm afraid," Mickey said. "This suit's been in storage nine months." He brought his coat sleeve to his face and sniffed. "Maybe not. I don't know. Who cares? Let's enjoy the damn ceremony."

The procession had moved into the church and most of the people went in, too. Mickey and Denise threaded quickly through the crowd to the church doors. Mickey took the handle of Denise's pocketbook and guided her skillfully, but when they got inside the church, all the pew seats had been taken. They stood in back, in the center aisle, directly in front of the tabernacle. Riva was way up in front, kneeling between her attendants at the altar railing. The children's choir began a hymn about the month of May and the mother of Christ.

When the hymn was over, a young boy all in white got up on a stool near the front of the church and sang alone. Riva and her attendants got off their knees and moved to the left of the altar, where a stepladder, draped in linen and hung with bouquets, had been positioned next to a statue of the Virgin Mary. The arms of the statue extended over a bay of burning candles in supplication.

Riva climbed the stepladder, still carrying the wreath on the satin pillow. She faced the church crowd and held the wreath high. Mickey and Denise grabbed hands. Riva's eyes were raised. She turned and began to place the wreath over the Virgin's head.

"Am I right?" a man standing next to Mickey said. "Her dress looks like it's caught fire."

"Dress is on fire!" someone said loudly. There was quiet, and then there was noise in the church. People half-stood in their pews. A young priest hurried to Riva. She was batting at her gown with the satin pillow. The fern wreath wheeled in the air. Her attendants pulled her down the steps of the ladder.

Mickey shouted, "Stop!" and ran for the altar. He pushed people out of the way. "I'm her dad," he said.

The priest had Riva by both shoulders, pressed against him. He folded her in the apron of his cassock, and a white flame broke under his arm.

"They *both* caught," a woman in front of Mickey said.

The priest smothered Riva's flaring skirt. He looked left and right and said, "Everybody stay back." Riva collapsed on the priest's arm and slid toward the floor.

Mickey vaulted over a velvet cord in front of the altar. He and the priest picked up Riva and between them carried her quickly across the altar and through a doorway that led into the sacristy.

An usher with a lily dangling from the lapel of his suit jacket came into the room with a folded canvas cot. "Put her here," he said. "Just a minute. Just one minute." He unfolded the cot, yanking at the stiff wooden legs. "There she goes," he said.

When they got Riva lying down, an older priest, in vestments, began sending people away from the room. Denise was allowed in. She helped Mickey cover Riva's charred dress with a blanket.

"That leg is burned," the first priest said. "Don't cover it up."

"I'm sorry," Denise said.

The two priests sat facing each other in metal chairs, as if they were playing a card game.

"We called for an ambulance, Father," the usher said to both of them.

"It doesn't look too terrible," Mickey said as he folded the burned skirt back and examined his daughter's leg. He glanced around at the priests. "I think we're going to be okay here," he said.

Riva was sobbing softly.

Denise stood at the base of the cot and clutched each of Riva's white slippers.

"Listen, sweetheart," Mickey said, "your parents are right here. It's just a little burn, you know. What they call first degree, maybe."

Riva said nothing.

"When this thing is over," Mickey said, "and you're taken care of—listen to me, now—we'll go up to Lake Erie, okay? You hear me? How about that? Some good friends of mine, Tad Austin and his wife—you never met them, Riva—have an A-frame on the water there. We can lie around and bake in the sun all day. There's an amusement park, and you'll be eighteen then. You'll be able to drink, if you want to."

The priests were looking at Mickey. He blotted perspiration from his forehead with his coat sleeve.

Denise said, "I'm surprised they are not here yet." Her glasses had fallen off and she was crying with her mouth open, still holding Riva's feet.

"Give them a little longer," one of the priests said.

"You know," Mickey said to Riva, "something else I just

thought of. Tad's wife will be at Erie some of the time. Remember how I told you about her? She's the one who went on television and won a convertible."

"Will you shut up?" Riva said.

No Son, No Gun, No Streetcar

by Allan Seager

He began to be afraid before he even left the telephone. The first thing Mr. Caldwell had said was, "William, would you like to go to the opera tonight?" and in the little time before the next words were spoken, he had been pleased, not that he knew anything about opera—he had never seen one—or that he liked music very much unless what the Mound City Blue Blowers played was music. His pleasure sprang from a sudden vision of next Sunday's "open house" where, since it was vacation, college football players would be lounging (and he could watch how they moved and listen avidly to their talk) and all the pretty girls would be home from school up North, and he could mention his visit to the opera with a proper negligence and ease. But the pleasure and the foretaste of his admirable nonchalance vanished with the next words Mr. Caldwell said: "I have two tickets for tonight. It's *Aïda.*"

The fear began when he grasped that Mr. Caldwell said that he had *two* tickets. His forehead prickled and the bones of his knees seemed to melt. If Mr. Caldwell had only two tickets, it meant that only they two were going to the opera. Mr. Caldwell wanted to see him, talk to him alone, and because Mr. Caldwell was a gentleman, this was the way he would pick to tell him everything had been discovered.

"Would you like to come, William?"

"Yes. Yes, sir. I sure would," he said wretchedly, unable to summon a refusal, even sure that he could not honorably refuse after what he had done.

"I'll pick you up about a quarter past eight."

"Yes, sir. Thank you, sir."

He hung up the receiver and walked away. His tennis racket, which had been leaning against the calf of his leg, fell flat on the floor. He did not even look at it. He went into the living room and stood for a minute looking around as if he had never seen it before. He sat down precisely on the edge of an armchair and began to bounce the tennis ball he had been holding in his hand all the while he had been talking on the phone. How had Mr. Caldwell found out?

She wouldn't have told. She wouldn't breathe a word because she loved him. She had given herself to him. She had said it in so many words, raising herself out of his embrace, her hair shining in the hot moonlight. "All right. I'll give myself to you." It had been like a play, almost suffocatingly dramatic. And she had, sure enough, right there in the swing where they had spent so many summer evenings talking, murmuring, kissing and drinking, spiked with his gin, the lemonade the maid brought out. And when it was over and the quiet that followed it was over, she had walked up and down nervously before him on the grass asking if he believed her *now,* if there were anything he dared accuse her of *now,* did he think she loved Seton Taylor or Battle McDonough if she would do this for *him?* All in a high tense whisper. And he, stunned by a pride he could not help mistake for love, had meekly agreed until he remembered he was a man now, had seized her and pulled her back to the swing. Because he was eighteen and did not guess that she at seventeen knew much more than he did, he accepted what seemed to be the marvelous truth that they were in love, and for the first time in a year of doubts he was sure that the Betas would take him next fall and he would make the freshman football team. Remembering this evening of his initiation, he was certain she would not have betrayed him to her father. She loved him far too much. She had proved it.

But Mr. Caldwell had found out. How?

At the violence of his next guess, his stomach fluttered and got hot and he let the tennis ball bounce by itself until it dribbled away under the sofa. Perhaps she was going to have a baby and in that fear and desperation she had told her family. At once the campus of the university, its colonnades, the rotunda, and the serpentine brick walls crumbled and vanished from the place in his mind where they had been fixed ever since he was fourteen. He foresaw himself sweating over a long table in an office above the Front

Street levee, picking up little wisps of cotton from the table and testing the length of its fiber between his fingers, his seersuckers covered with lint, working for a cotton broker for so much a week if a cotton broker would have him, never learning how to drink corn licker out of a Mason jar, never going to the Easter dances, never dodging and butting his way for any touchdowns at all, rather going home to a little apartment where there was not even a servant but only *she* and his squalling son. He surmised that this must have been what happened and, as sick and angry as he felt, a twinge of useless pity for her crossed his mind chased by his fear.

He could run away. He almost started from his chair at the thought of Brazil or Australia and how he would start for them before sundown, before the opera. He relaxed miserably. It would be wrong, and besides, he had—he laid it out on his palm—only three dollars and twenty-seven cents.

He lunged forward out of his chair and walked tiptoe through the house so as not to wake his mother, who was taking her nap. He could not possibly have explained to her why he had not gone to play tennis. From the kitchen he stepped into a narrow pantry where on the top shelf stood a dozen bottles of whisky, vermouth, and gin, his father's cellar, still forbidden him.

He took down a half-full bottle of bourbon. He lit a cigarette and laid it carefully on the edge of a shelf, ready to hand. He poured out half a water-glassful of the bourbon, looked at it, swishing it round in his glass, and, taking a deep breath, drank. Holding his breath, he stuck the cigarette in his mouth and drew on it. Then he let the breath, the smoke, and the burn of whisky all out together. As if his little theft had made a noise like thunder in the house, he raised his head and listened—there was no sound. He waited a few minutes until the saliva stopped springing in his mouth and drank the rest of the whisky in the glass with the same ritual. He went into the kitchen, drew half a glassful of water from the tap and poured it into the bottle. It was as full as before. He set it back in the same place on the top shelf, opened a can of coffee, took out a small handful, and munching it for his breath, he returned to the chair in the living room, feeling better. At least he had done something to help himself, something a man might do who was in trouble.

In the way anyone can turn his attention to his heartbeat, hear it and count it because it is there all the time, he began to think of what he knew he would have to do, what he had known all along he had to do, frame his reply when Mr. Caldwell accused him. His own great-grandfather had had a troop in Forrest's cavalry but he knew because *she* had told him that Mr. Caldwell's grandfather had commanded a regiment in the Army of Northern Virginia and had twice sat down to dinner with General Lee at houses in Fauquier County. These facts were not part of a dim traditional background. They were touchstones burning in his mind as if he and Mr. Caldwell bore like scars on their foreheads the devices of their forebears' military rank. Undoubtedly Mr. Caldwell was his superior—that was why he was doing it all so casually, making a social occasion out of it, taking him to the opera, in fact. It was a crushing disadvantage to be forced to oppose a man who kept the ghost of Lee behind him but he knew by all the imperatives of his upbringing that his answer had to match Mr. Caldwell's question in ease and courtesy, no matter how he suffered while he made it.

Suddenly he wanted to run away more than ever, not to any formal goal like Australia or Brazil: just out of town. There was a streetcar line three blocks from his house. He could take it as far as it went, then walk. He could find something to do whenever he got far enough away. "My name is John—John Carter." Or, with a tightening in his throat, he wished that his father would come home and say heartily, "It's all right, son. I've talked to Caldwell," and magically, as it had been long ago in his childhood, it would be all right. But if he was young enough to hope for these escapes, he was old enough to know bitterly that they were impossible. He would have to go to the opera with Mr. Caldwell.

At eight o'clock he was sitting in a wicker chair on his front porch, upright, a hand on each knee, a strained and unfamiliar posture, staring straight ahead of him. He was wearing a fresh white linen suit and a straw sailor hat with a band in his prep-school colors lay unregarded between his knees. At dinner-time his mother had insisted on giving him an aspirin because he looked sick. He still looked sick and the sweat ran down his face in two steady rills just in front of his ears. The fear that he would be unable to make a proper answer to Mr. Caldwell had made him unable to form one at all. He was not thinking of *her*—she was merely bait that had lured him prematurely into a trap he had hardly been aware of although he had friends who had been caught in the same one and he had laughed at them then, but he, he had not been ready, not amply warned, and it was unfair somehow.

The opera was a summer civic project put on by local music lovers. The singers wore rented, what William took to be medieval, costumes. Warily he followed the plot closely enough to be able to say something in reply to Mr. Caldwell's comments when they walked in the steaming crowd in the lobby between the acts, smoking and buying cold drinks of lemonade, but the music seemed less loud than the pulse in his ears and the antics of the singers in the field of distant light were like dolls! If people were going to sing, he thought, why didn't they stand still and sing? If they wanted to act, why didn't they act and say what they had to say, not sing it? But his attention was only a film on the surface of his fear and anxiety. He still did not know how he was going to answer Mr. Caldwell.

It was not until the fourth act that he began to think about the .45 revolver that his father had brought in from the farm out near Somerville several years before. It lay in the top drawer of Father's bureau where it would be handy if there were prowlers at night. Twice he had been allowed to shoot it, his father handing him a bullet each time, because men did not need hand-guns in this part of the country any more and instruction in their feel and use was a paternal foible of his father's, who wanted him to know it but knew he would not need to in the way he had to know how to handle a twelve-gauge shotgun on quail. But he did not think of his own twelve-gauge standing in its case in the corner of his closet because it was for his present purpose too messy. It was rather the muzzle of the .45, the ring of bluish steel surrounding the dark nothing, the symbol of what came out when you pulled the trigger. He did not suppose it would hurt much and you could pull the trigger with your thumb. He did not plan on leaving any note of explanation, and he kept pushing away the suspicion that kept obtruding —that it was cowardly—because it was complete. People knew he was in love with her; people would know he was dead. Eventually, later, his love might become the cause of his death, and they might call him a fool but they also would acknowledge him a gentleman. Right through the forehead.

There was a roar of applause. The singers were taking their bows and the audience was standing up to go. Mr. Caldwell was standing up to go. There was no reason to speak in the crowd leaving the auditorium but he knew the crisis was approaching and he had decided nothing. The streetcar, yellow and lumbering; the heat-sodden little apartment; and the .45 all whirled in his head like a dreadful pinwheel. They got into Mr. Caldwell's car. They drove for several blocks in silence and it was clear that Mr. Caldwell was getting ready to say something and looking for a place to say it. William's head ached and his mouth was dry. There was nothing that would save him now but luck and he had never passed three times in a crap game in his life.

Mr. Caldwell turned his car into a dark street full of homes with trees overhanging from both sides. As he had expected, Mr. Caldwell slowed down and stopped. The street light at the end of the block seemed far away and all the people who lived on the street had gone to bed. There was only the light on the dashboard and the occasional glare from a passing car. Mr. Caldwell said, "Cigarette, William?"

"Thank you, sir." He took one and lit it from the other's match.

"I've been wanting to talk to you for some time," Mr. Caldwell said.

"Yes, sir," he said. He cleared his throat.

"You've been seeing quite a lot of Emily."

"Yes, sir. I been seeing her."

"She's a pretty girl."

"She's beautiful." At least he could match him there and he thought it was true.

"I don't know what your plans are . . ." Mr. Caldwell let it fade away. In the light from the dash William could see him staring at the end of the cigarette in his hand.

He could not speak. There was nothing to say because he didn't know what his plans were, either.

Mr. Caldwell flicked the ash away. He seemed to be considering the best way to put it, consistent with his honor and the feelings of his opponent. He was about thirty-eight years old, well into middle age, and growing bald. He looked up straight ahead of him and began, "William, I married a beautiful woman."

"Yes, sir," he said, trying to give it sincerity. He could see that Mrs. Caldwell had been, once, long ago.

"I don't know whether you know the Delta. Your people come from Fayette County here in Tennessee. The Delta's a strange place, a wild, violent place, and Mrs. Caldwell was from down there, Greenville. She was very lovely. I saw her at all the dances. I still don't know how come she picked me when there were so many to pick from." Mr. Caldwell turned his head and looked at William. "There certainly was a lot to pick from. But I married her at nineteen. She was seventeen."

Mr. Caldwell stopped and William said, "Yes, sir."

"After our marriage it was necessary I go to work. I had gone to Virginia just one year, you understand, and then I had to go to work."

"Yes, sir."

"Don't do it, William."

"Don't do what, sir?"

"Don't get married now. I know you're in love with my daughter but don't marry her. Don't even try to marry her."

It was like being tipped up on a seesaw when you were a little kid, the rush of confidence. "Yes, sir?" he said.

Mr. Caldwell seemed to be scrunched down in the seat. He spoke in a cold precise voice. "Because I am now the treasurer of a wholesale grocery company. I have a fine home, a wife, and a beautiful daughter and listen, William, listen to me, boy, I would swap them all, bury them under the ground, tip 'em all in the river, if I could be an architect. That's what I wanted to be, an architect."

"Yes, sir."

"That's a terrible thing to say. I know it. It is the one last final way a man can be unfaithful, the way a woman never understands. Don't get married now. Go be an architect first. Then marry."

"Yes, sir. Thank *you,* sir. I won't ever say anything about this."

Mr. Caldwell turned and stared at him, gave a short barking laugh, flipped the key, started the car, and drove William home.

Do You Like It Here?

by John O'Hara

The door was open. The door had to be kept open during study period, so there was no knock, and Roberts was startled when a voice he knew and hated said, "Hey, Roberts. Wanted in Van Ness's office." The voice was Hughes'.

"What for?" said Roberts.

"Why don't you go and find out what for, Dopey?" said Hughes.

"Phooey on you," said Roberts.

"Phooey on *you,*" said Hughes, and left.

Roberts got up from the desk. He took off his eyeshade and put on a tie and coat. He left the light burning.

Van Ness's office, which was *en suite* with his bedroom, was on the ground floor of the dormitory, and on the way down Roberts wondered what he had done. It got so after a while, after going to so many schools, that you recognized the difference between being "wanted in Somebody's office" and "Somebody wants to see you." If a master wanted to see you on some minor matter, it didn't always mean that you had to go to his office; but if it was serious, they always said, "You're wanted in Somebody's office." That meant Somebody would be in his office, waiting for you, waiting specially for you. Roberts didn't know why this difference existed, but it did, all right. Well, all he could think of was that he had been smoking in the shower room, but Van Ness never paid much attention to that. Everybody smoked in the shower room, and Van Ness never did anything about it unless he just happened to catch you.

For minor offenses Van Ness would speak to you when he made his rounds of the rooms during study period. He would walk slowly down the corridor, looking in at each room to see that the proper occupant, and no one else, was there; and when he had something to bawl you out about, something unimportant, he would consult a list he carried, and he would stop in and bawl you out about it and tell you what punishment went with it. That was another detail that made the summons to the office a little scary.

Roberts knocked on Van Ness's half-open door and a voice said, "Come in."

Van Ness was sitting at his typewriter, which was on a small desk beside the large desk. He was in a swivel chair and when he saw Roberts he swung around, putting himself behind the larger desk, like a damn judge.

He had his pipe in his mouth and he seemed to look over the steel rims of his spectacles. The light caught his Phi Beta Kappa key, which momentarily gleamed as though it had diamonds in it.

"Hughes said you wanted me to report here," said Roberts.

"I did," said Van Ness. He took his pipe out of his mouth and began slowly to knock the bowl empty as he repeated, "I did." He finished emptying his pipe before he began to smoke. He took a long time about it, and Roberts, from his years of experience, recognized that as torture tactics. They always made you wait to scare you. It was sort of like the third degree. The horrible damn thing was that it always did scare you a little, even when you were used to it.

Van Ness leaned back in his chair and stared through his glasses at Roberts. He cleared his throat. "You can sit down," he said.

"Yes, sir," said Roberts. He sat down and again Van Ness made him wait.

"Roberts, you've been here now how long—five weeks?"

"A little over. About six."

"About six weeks," said Van Ness. "Since the seventh of January. Six weeks. Strange. Strange. Six weeks, and I really don't know a thing about you. Not much, at any rate. Roberts, tell me a little about yourself."

"How do you mean, Mister?"

"How do I mean? Well—about your life, before you decided to honor us with your presence. Where you came from, what you did, why you went to so many schools, so on."

"Well, I don't know."

"Oh, now. Now. Roberts. Don't let your natural modesty overcome the autobiographical urge. Shut the door."

Roberts got up and closed the door.

"Good," said Van Ness. "Now, proceed with this—uh—dossier. Give me the—huh—huh—*lowdown* on Roberts, Humphrey, Second Form, McAllister Memorial Hall, et cetera."

Roberts, Humphrey, sat down and felt the knot of his tie. "Well, I don't know. I was born at West Point, New York. My father was a first lieutenant then and he's a major now. My father and mother and I lived in a lot of places because he was in the Army and they transferred him. Is that the kind of stuff you want, Mister?"

"Proceed, proceed. I'll tell you when I want you to—uh—halt." Van Ness seemed to think that was funny, that "halt."

"Well, I didn't go to a regular school till I was ten. My mother got a divorce from my father and I went to school in San Francisco. I only stayed there a year because my mother got married again and we moved to Chicago, Illinois."

"Chicago, Illinois! Well, a little geography thrown in, eh, Roberts? Gratuitously. Thank you. Proceed."

"Well, so then we stayed there about two years and then we moved back East, and my stepfather is a certified public accountant and we moved around a lot."

"Peripatetic, eh, Roberts?"

"I guess so. I don't exactly know what that means." Roberts paused.

"Go on, go on."

"Well, so I just went to a lot of schools, some day and some boarding. All that's written down on my application blank here. I had to put it all down on account of my credits."

"Correct. A very imposing list it is, too, Roberts, a very imposing list. Ah, to travel as you have. Switzerland. How I've regretted not having gone to school in Switzerland. Did you like it there?"

"I was only there about three months. I liked it all right, I guess."

"And do you like it here, Roberts?"

"Sure."

"You do? You're sure of that? You wouldn't want to change anything?"

"Oh, I wouldn't say that, not about any school."

"Indeed," said Van Ness. "With your vast experience, naturally you would be quite an authority on matters educational. I suppose you have many theories as to the strength and weaknesses inherent in the modern educational systems."

"I don't know. I just—I don't know. Some schools are better than others. At least I like some better than others."

"Of course. Of course." Van Ness seemed to be thinking about something. He leaned back in his swivel chair and gazed at the ceiling. He put his hands in his pants pockets and then suddenly he leaned forward. The chair came down and Van Ness's belly was hard against the desk and his arm was stretched out on the desk, full length, fist closed.

"Roberts! Did you ever see this before? Answer me!" Van Ness's voice was hard. He opened his fist, and in it was a wristwatch.

Roberts looked down at the watch. "No, I don't think so," he said. He was glad to be able to say it truthfully.

Van Ness continued to hold out his hand, with the wristwatch lying in the palm. He held out his hand a long time, fifteen seconds at least, without saying anything. Then he turned his hand over and allowed the watch to slip onto the desk. He resumed his normal position in the chair. He picked up his pipe, slowly filled it, and lit it. He shook the match back and forth long after the flame had gone. He swung around a little in his chair and looked at the wall, away from Roberts. "As a boy I spent six years at this school. My brothers, my two brothers, went to this school. My *father* went to this school. I have a deep and abiding and lasting affection for this school. I have been a member of the faculty of this school for more than a decade. I like to think that I am part of this school, that in some small measure I have assisted in its progress. I like to think of it as more than a mere steppingstone to higher education. At this very moment there are in this school the sons of men who were my classmates. I have not been without my opportunities to take a post at this and that college or university, but I choose to remain here. Why? Why? Because I love this place. I love this place, Roberts. I cherish its traditions. I cherish its good name." He paused, and turned to Roberts. "Roberts, there is no room here for a thief!"

Roberts did not speak.

"There is no room here for a thief, I said!"

"Yes, sir."

Van Ness picked up the watch without looking at it. He held it a few inches above the desk. "This miserable watch was stolen last Friday afternoon, more than likely during the basketball game. As soon as the theft was reported to me I immediately instituted a search for it. My search was unsuccessful. Sometime Monday afternoon the watch was put here, here in my rooms. When I returned here after classes Monday afternoon, this watch was lying on my desk. Why? Because the comtemptible rat who stole it knew that I had instituted the search, and like the rat he is, he turned yellow and returned the watch to me. Whoever it is, he kept an entire dormitory under a loathsome suspicion. I say to you, I do not know who stole this watch or who returned it to my rooms. But by God, Roberts, I'm going to find out, if it's the last thing I do. If it's the last thing I do. That's all, Roberts. You may go." Van Ness sat back, almost breathless.

Roberts stood up. "I give you my word of honor, I—"

"I said you may go!" said Van Ness.

Roberts was not sure whether to leave the door open or to close it, but he did not ask. He left it open.

He went up the stairs to his room. He went in and took off his coat and tie, and sat on the bed. Over and over, first violently, then weakly, he said it, "The bastard, the dirty bastard."

1939

In History Audrey Touched Michael

by John Rolfe Gardiner

In 1950 Farmer Schey is still content with animal speed. Mostly he drives his mules just to arrive somewhere else. When developments appear south and west of the little town, Schey explores their new avenues and cul de sacs in his wagon, driving his team past houses with white pillars on streets that go nowhere.

Health and welfare agencies have heard the miseries of his wife. The county schools accept attendance and truancy of his children. When his third grader is caught smoking Schey drives his team to answer the complaint. While he confers, his wagon blocks buses in the driveway. He means to pull all the children out of school again.

"You have a big family," the principal says. "Why don't you let them get ahead?"

Schey relents, but with rules: "Don't send homework. And they don't get needle shots."

Miss Anders who has taught three Scheys and knows more are coming, has told colleagues in the faculty lounge that Audrey is different. Under uniform of hand-me-down she's comely. Her darting glances and smug grin answer the daily commotion of schoolyard and classroom, though she won't betray her people with a raised hand.

In Science Michael Hutchins sits one row behind and a little to the left of her. In History, right beside her, he's too close. In Science he can seem to be watching Miss Anders while catching Audrey's face at an angle and the way she arranges herself in her sweater when she shifts in her seat.

At recess today Audrey steals a lipstick from Miss Anders's purse and goes into the girls' room to use it. Half painted, she hears someone coming and has to throw the lipstick into a toilet stall.

Wandering onto the playground, she sees a boys' basketball game at one end of the outdoor court and a girls' game at the other. Someone steals the girls' ball and takes a long shot at the far basket, confusing the boys' game. The extra ball is kicked far across the playground. One of the girls screams. The others walk away laughing, and the boys' game expands to full court.

Audrey walks the length of the school building and enters the auditorium in back. The Hutchins boy is at the piano on the stage. He's making the keys move quickly, making a song. When he's finished she says, "Anyone could learn that," and Michael agrees, moved by the smudge above Audrey's lip and by the red applied accurately.

After school, Audrey climbs a ladder in the auditorium and through the janitor's hatch onto the flat graveled roof, where she hid with Rodney once to do something they can't do at home. From the roof you can watch small people from elementary and junior high transferring for the final ride home. She's missing a family reunion on Number 45 where Scheys are pushing their way to the back to a kind of reserved section.

Having missed her bus she climbs down and walks through the empty building to the front steps where the Hutchins boy is waiting for his ride. He doesn't do sports. His fingers could get hurt.

"I know what's in your satchel," she says. "It's music. The taxi takes you to your lesson."

"The taxi could take you home," Michael says, reaching in his pocket, making sure of a quarter.

"She lives on the river road," Michael tells the driver, who agrees to take her because it's on the way.

"I take from Miss Jett," Michael tells Audrey. "She makes you memorize."

"Your mother dresses you funny." Audrey says. His blue jeans have white laces in back like old fashioned sailors' pants. On the way home Audrey learns that an étude is something you practice, but says that after it's practiced it must be a song.

Rodney would be amazed, she says. A boy's nose became a red

fountain on the playground and Michael had seen Rodney Schey keep on punching it. "What shows when you move your fingers?" Audrey wants to know.

"Just a lot of things," Michael says. "This is where she gets out."

Audrey hopes she's late enough that her father's had time to think of something else. But brothers and sisters are coming out of the back room to see a whipping. Get back, Schey tells them; do they expect him to beat the only one trying to get an education? What did she learn today, he wants to know, and she tells him "everything through the first three presidents."

In History Audrey's hand touches Michael's arm and Michael pretends not to notice. In Science she turns to him but he's looking at the floor so she waits at recess by the piano. Audrey wants more music explained.

"That's Italian for slowly," Michael says.

She thinks the song looks too hard for her and besides it's got fractions.

"That's the time it's in," Michael says, but doesn't know how to explain it.

"You can't do fractions?" she asks.

Michael says he has to tell her something: she can't ride home with him anymore.

"Anyone can ride in the taxi," she says and to prove it, that afternoon she pays her own way.

In the car she reminds him he promised to teach her how to play *Heart and Soul* with two fingers. Michael has to hold Audrey's index fingers, one in each hand, while he explains there's just one note between them and then you move them like this. "I don't know what Rodney'd do if he found out you're teaching me music," Audrey says.

When she gets home the others want to know why she missed the bus again. It's none of their business, she says, but she'll be coming home late a lot of times. "Because someone's teaching me piano," she tells them. "He says I've got just the right hands for it."

In home room next morning Audrey's missing but Michael knows other Scheys are here. They stood in a group by the bus until it was time for the younger ones to transfer. In Math Audrey's still missing, but in the middle of the period Michael sees her walk past the door with a sister in junior high who doesn't belong here.

In Science she's back and Miss Anders tells the class something's missing again—something from her purse. In History Audrey's absent. Someone says, "She was absent from Math too. But she was here in Science."

Next week Michael watches closely for the movement of Scheys. They're hard to follow, appearing and disappearing, in the cafeteria, gymnasium, classrooms, and lavatories. Another brother has been cutting classes with Audrey and Rodney. Then Rodney gets suspended and Farmer Schey pulls all his children out. Michael starts practicing on the school piano again.

It's Audrey who returns first. She follows Michael through the hall at recess. "My mother had a piano once," she says. "A tiny one she got for Christmas." Michael has a hard piece to practice and can't talk now.

After school there isn't any way to keep her out of the taxi. If she has the money, she can ride. "I wasn't supposed to be here today," she says. "You didn't look for me on the roof." Michael says he doesn't even know where the ladder is. Audrey can't say what her father might do when she gets home.

Rodney's suspension is over and all the Scheys are back. In History Audrey isn't taking notice of Michael. A note from her mother says:

PLEASE LET AUDREY WEAR THE MITTENS

In Science there's a test but Audrey can't write with gloves on. She's excused to the girls' room and doesn't come back. Michael's foot taps and his pen leaks. With stained lips he whispers as he writes. Scheys are loose in the building. Between classes he hears a teacher say, "She *can't* take them off. I think it's contagious."

Next day, no Scheys. But everyone has heard what their old man did. He trapped the taxi against the wall in the Chain Food lot and rammed it with the back of his wagon until its radiator leaked.

For a whole week, no Scheys. Then suddenly they're back, recapturing bus seats. And Audrey is using her pencil again, though her hands stay under the desk when she's not writing.

Years after his mother's dream of a son's grand recital has been hammered into the loose, black nail of a carpenter's thumb, Michael thinks if Audrey could have been plucked from her family he might have climbed to the roof with her. He could at least have told her how sorry, how responsible, he felt for her bruised, swollen fingers.

But it was recess and Rodney was coming through the auditorium door with Audrey. She was pointing at Michael, then hanging back while Rodney came forward. Michael played faster, until his fingers moved without instruction, playing without a mistake for Rodney, who stood by the piano cleaning his fingernails. He clapped and whistled raucously when Michael finished, then disappeared again through the halls with his sister.

The Haunted Boy

by Carson McCullers

Hugh looked for his mother at the corner, but she was not in the yard. Sometimes she would be out fooling with the border of spring flowers—the candytuft, the sweet William, the lobelias (she had taught him the names)—but today the green front lawn with the borders of many-colored flowers was empty under the frail sunshine of the mid-April afternoon. Hugh raced up the sidewalk, and John followed him. They finished the front steps with two bounds, and the door slammed after them.

'Mamma!' Hugh called.

It was then, in the unanswering silence as they stood in the empty, wax-floored hall, that Hugh felt there was something wrong. There was no fire in the grate of the sitting room, and since he was used to the flicker of firelight during the cold months, the room on this first warm day seemed strangely naked and cheerless. Hugh shivered. He was glad John was there. The sun shone on a red piece in the flowered rug. Red-bright, red-dark, red-dead—Hugh sickened with a sudden chill remembrance of 'the other time.' The red darkened to a dizzy black.

'What's the matter, Brown?' John asked. 'You look so white.'

Hugh shook himself and put his hand to his forehead. 'Nothing. Let's go back to the kitchen.'

'I can't stay but just a minute,' John said. 'I'm obligated to sell those tickets. I have to eat and run.'

The kitchen, with the fresh checked towels and clean pans, was now the best room in the house. And on the enameled table there was a lemon pie that she had made. Assured by the everyday kitchen and the pie, Hugh stepped back into the hall and raised his face again to call upstairs.

'Mother! Oh, Mamma!'

Again there was no answer.

'My mother made this pie,' he said. Quickly, he found a knife and cut into the pie—to dispel the gathering sense of dread.

'Think you ought to cut it, Brown?'

'Sure thing, Laney.'

They called each other by their last names this spring, unless they happened to forget. To Hugh it seemed sporty and grown and somehow grand. Hugh liked John better than any other boy at school. John was two years older than Hugh, and compared to him the other boys seemed like a silly crowd of punks. John was the best student in the sophomore class, brainy but not the least bit a teacher's pet, and he was the best athlete too. Hugh was a freshman and didn't have so many friends that first year of high school —he had somehow cut himself off, because he was so afraid.

'Mamma always has me something nice for after school.' Hugh put a big piece of pie on a saucer for John—for Laney.

'This pie is certainly super.'

'The crust is made of crunched-up graham crackers instead of regular pie dough,' Hugh said, 'because pie dough is a lot of trouble. We think this graham-cracker pastry is just as good. Naturally, my mother can make regular pie dough if she wants to.'

Hugh could not keep still; he walked up and down the kitchen, eating the pie wedge he carried on the palm of his hand. His brown hair was mussed with nervous rakings, and his gentle gold-brown eyes were haunted with pained perplexity. John, who remained seated at the table, sensed Hugh's uneasiness and wrapped one gangling leg around the other.

'I'm really obligated to sell those Glee Club tickets.'

'Don't go. You have the whole afternoon.' He was afraid of the empty house. He needed John, he needed someone; most of all he needed to hear his mother's voice and know she was in the house with him. 'Maybe Mamma is taking a bath,' he said. 'I'll holler again.'

The answer to his third call too was silence.

'I guess your mother must have gone to the movie or gone shopping or something.'

'No,' Hugh said. 'She would have left a note. She always does when she's gone when I come home from school.'

'We haven't looked for a note,' John said. 'Maybe she left it under the door mat or somewhere in the living room.'

Hugh was inconsolable. 'No. She would have left it right under this pie. She knows I always run first to the kitchen.'

'Maybe she had a phone call or thought of something she suddenly wanted to do.'

'She *might* have,' he said. 'I remember she said to Daddy that one of these days she was going to buy herself some new clothes.' This flash of hope did not survive its expression. He pushed his hair back and started from the room. 'I guess I'd better go upstairs. I ought to go upstairs while you are here.'

He stood with his arm around the newel post; the smell of varnished stairs, the sight of the closed white bathroom door at the top revived again 'the other time.' He clung to the newel post, and his feet would not move to climb the stairs. The red turned again to whirling, sick dark. Hugh sat down. *Stick your head between your legs,* he ordered, remembering Scout first aid.

'Hugh,' John called. 'Hugh!'

The dizziness clearing, Hugh accepted a fresh chagrin—Laney was calling him by his ordinary first name; he thought he was a sissy about his mother, unworthy of being called by his last name in the grand, sporty way they used before. The dizziness cleared when he returned to the kitchen.

'Brown,' said John, and the chagrin disappeared. 'Does this establishment have anything pertaining to a cow? A white, fluid liquid. In French they call it *lait.* Here we call it plain old milk.'

The stupidity of shock lightened. 'Oh, Laney, I am a dope! Please excuse me. I clean forgot.' Hugh fetched the milk from the refrigerator and found two glasses. 'I didn't think. My mind was on something else.'

'I know,' John said. After a moment he asked in a calm voice, looking steadily at Hugh's eyes: 'Why are you so worried about your mother? Is she sick, Hugh?'

Hugh knew now that the first name was not a slight; it was because John was talking too serious to be sporty. He liked John better than any friend he had ever had. He felt more natural sitting across the kitchen table from John, somehow safer. As he looked into John's gray, peaceful eyes, the balm of affection soothed the dread.

John asked again, still steadily: 'Hugh, is your mother sick?'

Hugh could have answered no other boy. He had talked with no one about his mother, except his father, and even those intimacies had been rare, oblique. They could approach the subject only when they were occupied with something else, doing carpentry work or the two times they hunted in the woods together—or when they were cooking supper or washing dishes.

'She's not exactly sick,' he said, 'but Daddy and I have been worried about her. At least, we used to be worried for a while.'

John asked: 'Is it a kind of heart trouble?'

Hugh's voice was strained. 'Did you hear about that fight I had with that slob Clem Roberts? I scraped his slob face on the gravel walk and nearly killed him sure enough. He's still got scars or at least he did have a bandage on for two days. I had to stay in school every afternoon for a week. But I nearly killed him. I would have if Mr. Paxton hadn't come along and dragged me off.'

'I heard about it.'

'You know why I wanted to kill him?'

For a moment John's eyes flickered away.

Hugh tensed himself; his raw boy hands clutched the table edge; he took a deep, hoarse breath. 'That slob was telling everybody that my mother was in Milledgeville. He was spreading it around that my mother was crazy.'

'The dirty bastard.'

Hugh said in a clear, defeated voice, 'My mother *was* in Milledgeville. But that doesn't mean that she was crazy,' he added quickly. 'In that big State hospital, there are buildings for people who are crazy, and there are other buildings, for people who are just sick. Mamma was sick for a while. Daddy and me discussed it and decided that the hospital in Milledgeville was the place where there were the best doctors and she would get the best care. But she was the furtherest from crazy than anybody in the world. You know Mamma, John.' He said again 'I ought to go upstairs.'

John said: 'I have always thought that your mother is one of the nicest ladies in this town.'

'You see, Mamma had a peculiar thing happen, and afterward she was blue.'

Confession, the first deep-rooted words, opened the festered secrecy of the boy's heart, and he continued more rapidly, urgent and finding unforeseen relief.

'Last year my mother thought she was going to have a little baby. She talked it over with Daddy and me,' he said proudly. 'We wanted a girl. I was going to choose the name. We were so tickled. I hunted up all my old toys—my electric train and the tracks . . . I was going to name her Crystal—how does the name strike you for a girl? It reminds me of something bright and dainty.'

'Was the little baby born dead?'

Even with John, Hugh's ears turned hot; his cold hands touched them. 'No, it was what they call a tumor. That's what happened to my mother. They had to operate at the hospital here.' He was embarrassed and his voice was very low. 'Then she had something called change of life.' The words were terrible to Hugh. 'And afterward she was blue. Daddy said it was a shock to her nervous system. It's something that happens to ladies; she was just blue and run-down.'

Although there was no red, no red in the kitchen anywhere, Hugh was approaching 'the other time.'

'One day, she just sort of gave up—one day last fall.' Hugh's eyes were wide open and glaring: again he climbed the stairs and opened the bathroom door—he put his hand to his eyes to shut out the memory. 'She tried to—hurt herself. I found her when I came in from school.'

John reached out and carefully stroked Hugh's sweatered arm.

'Don't worry. A lot of people have to go to hospitals because they are run-down and blue. Could happen to anybody.'

'We had to put her in the hospital—the best hospital.' The recollection of those long, long months was stained with a dull loneliness, as cruel in its lasting unappeasement as 'the other time'—how long had it lasted? In the hospital Mamma could walk around and she always had on shoes.

John said carefully: 'This pie is certainly super.'

'My mother is a super cook. She cooks things like meat pie and salmon loaf—as well as steaks and hot dogs.'

'I hate to eat and run,' John said.

Hugh was so frightened of being left alone that he felt the alarm in his own loud heart.

'Don't go,' he urged. 'Let's talk for a little while.'

'Talk about what?'

Hugh could not tell him. Not even John Laney. He could tell no one of the empty house and the horror of the time before. 'Do you ever cry?' he asked John. 'I don't.'

'I do sometimes,' John admitted.

'I wish I had known you better when Mother was away. Daddy and me used to go hunting nearly every Saturday. We *lived* on quail and dove. I bet you would have liked that.' He added in a lower tone, 'On Sunday we went to the hospital.'

John said: 'It's a kind of a delicate proposition selling those tickets. A lot of people don't enjoy the High School Glee Club operettas. Unless they know someone in it personally, they'd rather stay home with a good TV show. A lot of people buy tickets on the basis of being public-spirited.'

'We're going to get a television set real soon.'

'I couldn't exist without television,' John said.

Hugh's voice was apologetic. 'Daddy wants to clean up the hospital bills first because as everybody knows sickness is a very expensive proposition. Then we'll get TV.'

John lifted his milk glass. 'Skoal,' he said. 'That's a Swedish word you say before you drink. A good-luck word.'

'You know so many foreign words and languages.'

'Not so many,' John said truthfully. 'Just "kaput" and "adios" and "skoal" and stuff we learn in French class. That's not much.'

'That's *beaucoup*,' said Hugh, and he felt witty and pleased with himself.

Suddenly the stored tension burst into physical activity. Hugh grabbed the basketball out on the porch and rushed into the back yard. He dribbled the ball several times and aimed at the goal his father had put up on his last birthday. When he missed he bounced the ball to John, who had come after him. It was good to be outdoors and the relief of natural play brought Hugh the first line of a poem. 'My heart is like a basketball.' Usually when a poem came to him he would lie sprawled on the living room floor, studying to hunt rhymes, his tongue working on the side of his mouth. His mother would call him Shelley-Poe when she stepped over him, and sometimes she would put her foot lightly on his behind. His mother always liked his poems; today the second line came quickly, like magic. He said it out loud to John: " 'My heart is like a basketball, bouncing with glee down the hall." How do you like that for the start of a poem?'

'Sounds kind of crazy to me,' John said. The he corrected himself hastily. 'I mean it sounds—odd. Odd, I meant.'

Hugh realized why John changed the word, and the elation of play and poems left him instantly. He caught the ball and stood with it cradled in his arms. The afternoon was golden and the wisteria vine on the porch was in full, unshattered bloom. The wisteria was like lavender waterfalls. The fresh breeze smelled of sun-warmed flowers. The sunlit sky was blue and cloudless. It was the first warm day of spring.

'I have to shove off,' John said.

'No!' Hugh's voice was desperate. 'Don't you want another piece of pie? I never heard of anybody eating just one piece of pie.'

He steered John into the house and this time he called only out of habit because he always called on coming in. 'Mother!' He was cold after the bright, sunny outdoors. He was cold not only because of the weather but because he was so scared.

'My mother has been home a month and every afternoon she's always here when I come home from school. Always, always.'

They stood in the kitchen looking at the lemon pie. And to Hugh the cut pie looked somehow—odd. As they stood motionless in the kitchen the silence was creepy and odd too.

'Doesn't this house seem quiet to you?'

'It's because you don't have television. We put on our TV at seven o'clock and it stays on all day and night until we go to bed. Whether anybody's in the living room or not. There're plays and skits and gags going on continually.'

'We have a radio, of course, and a vic.'

'But that's not the company of a good TV. You won't know when your mother is in the house or not when you get TV.'

Hugh didn't answer. Their footsteps sounded hollow in the hall.

He felt sick as he stood on the first step with his arm around the newel post. 'If you could just come upstairs for a minute——'

John's voice was suddenly impatient and loud. 'How many times have I told you I'm obligated to sell those tickets. You have to be public-spirited about things like Glee Clubs.'

'Just for a second—I have something important to show you upstairs.'

John did not ask what it was and Hugh sought desperately to name something important enough to get John upstairs. He said finally: 'I'm assembling a hi-fi machine. You have to know a lot about electronics—my father is helping me.'

But even when he spoke he knew John did not for a second believe the lie. Who would buy a hi-fi when they didn't have television? He hated John, as you hate people you have to need so badly. He had to say something more and he straightened his shoulders.

'I just want you to know how much I value your friendship. During these past months I had somehow cut myself off from people.'

'That's O.K., Brown. You oughtn't to be so sensitive because your mother was—where she was.'

John had his hand on the door and Hugh was trembling. 'I thought if you could come up for just a minute——'

John looked at him with anxious, puzzled eyes. Then he asked slowly: 'Is there something you are scared of upstairs?'

Hugh wanted to tell him everything. But he could not tell what his mother had done that September afternoon. It was too terrible and—odd. It was like something a *patient* would do, and not like his mother at all. Although his eyes were wild with terror and his body trembled he said: 'I'm not scared.'

'Well, so long. I'm sorry I have to go—but to be obligated is to be obligated.'

John closed the front door, and he was alone in the empty house. Nothing could save him now. Even if a whole crowd of boys were listening to TV in the living room, laughing at funny gags and jokes, it would still not help him. He had to go upstairs and find her. He sought courage from the last thing John had said, and repeated the words aloud: 'To be obligated is to be obligated.' But the words did not give him any of John's thoughtlessness and courage; they were creepy and strange in the silence.

He turned slowly to go upstairs. His heart was not like a basketball but like a fast, jazz drum, beating faster and faster as he climbed the stairs. His feet dragged as though he waded through knee-deep water and he held on to the banisters. The house looked odd, crazy. As he looked down at the ground-floor table with the vase of fresh spring flowers that too looked somehow peculiar. There was a mirror on the second floor and his own face startled him, so crazy did it seem to him. The initial of his high school sweater was backward and wrong in the reflection and his mouth was open like an asylum idiot. He shut his mouth and he looked better. Still the objects he saw—the table downstairs, the sofa upstairs—looked somehow cracked or jarred because of the dread in him, although they were the familiar things of everyday. He fastened his eyes on the closed door at the right of the stairs and the fast, jazz drum beat faster.

He opened the bathroom door and for a moment the dread that had haunted him all that afternoon made him see again the room as he had seen it 'the other time.' His mother lay on the floor and there was blood everywhere. His mother lay there dead and there was blood everywhere, on her slashed wrist, and a pool of blood had trickled to the bathtub and lay dammed there. Hugh touched the doorframe and steadied himself. Then the room settled and he realized this was not 'the other time.' The April sunlight brightened the clean white tiles. There was only bathroom brightness and the sunny window. He went to the bedroom and saw the empty bed with the rose-colored spread. The lady things were on the dresser. The room was as it always looked and nothing had happened . . . nothing had happened and he flung himself on the quilted rose bed and cried from relief and a strained, bleak tiredness that had lasted so long. The sobs jerked his whole body and quieted his jazz, fast heart.

Hugh had not cried all those months. He had not cried at 'the other time,' when he found his mother alone in that empty house with blood everywhere. He had not cried but he made a Scout mistake. He had first lifted his mother's heavy, bloody body before he tried to bandage her. He had not cried when he called his father.

He had not cried those few days when they were deciding what to do. He hadn't even cried when the doctor suggested Milledgeville, or when he and his father took her to the hospital in the car—although his father cried on the way home. He had not cried at the meals they made—steak every night for a whole month so that they felt steak was running out of their eyes, their ears; then they had switched to hot dogs, and ate them until hot dogs ran out of their ears, their eyes. They got in ruts of food and were messy about the kitchen, so that it was never nice except the Saturday the cleaning woman came. He did not cry those lonesome afternoons after he had the fight with Clem Roberts and felt the other boys were thinking queer things of his mother. He stayed at home in the messy kitchen, eating fig newtons or chocolate bars. Or he went to see a neighbor's television—Miss Richards, an old maid who saw old-maid shows. He had not cried when his father drank too much so that it took his appetite and Hugh had to eat alone. He had not even cried on those long, waiting Sundays when they went to Milledgeville and he twice saw a lady on a porch without any shoes on and talking to herself. A lady who was a patient and who struck at him with a horror he could not name. He did not cry when at first his mother would say: *Don't punish me by making me stay here. Let me go home.* He had not cried at the terrible words that haunted him—'change of life'—'crazy'—'Milledgeville'—he could not cry all during those long months strained with dullness and want and dread.

He still sobbed on the rose bedspread which was soft and cool against his wet cheeks. He was sobbing so loud that he did not hear the front door open, did not even hear his mother call or the footsteps on the stairs. He still sobbed when his mother touched him and burrowed his face hard in the spread. He even stiffened his legs and kicked his feet.

'Why, Loveyboy,' his mother said, calling him a long-ago child name. 'What's happened?'

He sobbed even louder, although his mother tried to turn his face to her. He wanted her to worry. He did not turn around until she had finally left the bed, and then he looked at her. She had on a different dress—blue silk it looked like in the pale spring light.

'Darling, what's happened?'

The terror of the afternoon was over, but he could not tell it to his mother. He could not tell her what he had feared, or explain the horror of things that were never there at all—but had once been there.

'Why did you do it?'

'The first warm day I just suddenly decided to buy myself some new clothes.'

But he was not talking about clothes; he was thinking about 'the other time' and the grudge that had started when he saw the blood and horror and felt *why did she do this to me*. He thought of the grudge against the mother he loved the most in the world. All those last, sad months the anger had bounced against the love with guilt between.

'I bought two dresses and two petticoats. How do you like them?'

'I hate them!' Hugh said angrily. 'Your slip is showing.'

She turned around twice and the petticoat showed terribly. 'It's supposed to show, goofy. It's the style.'

'I still don't like it.'

'I ate a sandwich at the tearoom with two cups of cocoa and then went to Mendel's. There were so many pretty things I couldn't seem to get away. I bought these two dresses and look, Hugh! The shoes!'

His mother went to the bed and switched on the light so he could see. The shoes were flat-heeled and *blue*—with diamond sparkles on the toes. He did not know how to criticize. 'They look more like evening shoes than things you wear on the street.'

'I have never owned any colored shoes before. I couldn't resist them.'

His mother sort of danced over toward the window, making the petticoat twirl under the new dress. Hugh had stopped crying now, but he was still angry.

'I don't like it because it makes you look like you're trying to seem young, and I bet you are forty years old.'

His mother stopped dancing and stood still at the window. Her face was suddenly quiet and sad. 'I'll be forty-three years old in June.'

He had hurt her and suddenly the anger vanished and there was only love. 'Mamma, I shouldn't have said that.'

'I realized when I was shopping that I hadn't been in a store for more than a year. Imagine!'

Hugh could not stand the sad quietness and the mother he loved so much. He could not stand his love or his mother's prettiness. He wiped the tears on the sleeve of his sweater and got up from the bed. 'I have never seen you so pretty, or a dress and slip so pretty.' He crouched down before his mother and touched the bright shoes. 'The shoes are really super.'

'I thought the minute I laid eyes on them that you would like them.' She pulled Hugh up and kissed him on the cheek. 'Now I've got lipstick on you.'

Hugh quoted a witty remark he had heard before as he scrubbed off the lipstick. 'It only shows I'm popular.'

'Hugh, why were you crying when I came in? Did something at school upset you?'

'It was only that when I came in and found you gone and no note or anything——"

'I forgot all about a note.'

'And all afternoon I felt—John Laney came in but he had to go sell Glee Club tickets. All afternoon I felt——'

'What? What was the matter?'

But he could not tell the mother he loved about the terror and the cause. He said at last: 'All afternoon I felt—odd.'

Afterward when his father came home he called Hugh to come out into the back yard with him. His father had a worried look—as though he spied a valuable tool Hugh had left outside. But there was no tool and the basketball was put back in its place on the back porch.

'Son,' his father said, 'there's something I want to tell you.'

'Yes, sir?'

'Your mother said that you had been crying this afternoon.' His father did not wait for him to explain. 'I just want us to have a close understanding with each other. Is there anything about school—or girls—or something that puzzles you? Why were you crying?'

Hugh looked back at the afternoon and already it was far away, distant as a peculiar view seen at the wrong end of a telescope.

'I don't know,' he said. 'I guess maybe I was somehow nervous.'

His father put his arm around his shoulder. 'Nobody can be nervous before they are sixteen years old. You have a long way to go.'

'I know.'

'I have never seen your mother look so well. She looks so gay and pretty, better than she's looked in years. Don't you realize that?'

'The slip—the petticoat is supposed to show. It's a new style.'

'Soon it will be summer,' his father said. 'And we'll go on picnics —the three of us.' The words brought an instant vision of glare on the yellow creek and the summer-leaved, adventurous woods. His father added: 'I came out here to tell you something else.'

'Yes, sir?'

'I just want you to know that I realize how fine you were all that bad time. How fine, how damn fine.'

His father was using a swear word as if he were talking to a grown man. His father was not a person to hand out compliments —always he was strict with report cards and tools left around. His father never praised him or used grown words or anything. Hugh felt his face grow hot and he touched it with his cold hands.

'I just wanted to tell you that, Son.' He shook Hugh by the shoulder. 'You'll be taller than your old man in a year or so.' Quickly his father went into the house, leaving Hugh to the sweet and unaccustomed aftermath of praise.

Hugh stood in the darkening yard after the sunset colors faded in the west and the wisteria was dark purple. The kitchen light was on and he saw his mother fixing dinner. He knew that something was finished; the terror was far from him now, also the anger that had bounced with love, the dread and guilt. Although he felt he would never cry again—or at least not until he was sixteen—in the brightness of his tears glistened the safe, lighted kitchen, now that he was no longer a haunted boy, now that he was glad somehow, and not afraid.

The Liar

by Tobias Wolff

My mother read everything except books. Advertisements on buses, entire menus as we ate, billboards; if it had no cover it interested her. So when she found a letter in my drawer that was not addressed to her she read it. "What difference does it make if James has nothing to hide?"—that was her thought. She stuffed the letter in the drawer when she finished it and walked from room to room in the big empty house, talking to herself. She took the letter out and read it again to get the facts straight. Then, without putting on her coat or locking the door, she went down the steps and headed for the church at the end of the street. No matter how angry and confused she might be, she always went to four o'clock Mass and now it was four o'clock.

It was a fine day, blue and cold and still, but Mother walked as though into a strong wind, bent forward at the waist with her feet hurrying behind in short, busy steps. My brother and sisters and I considered this walk of hers funny and we smirked at one another when she crossed in front of us to stir the fire, or water a plant. We didn't let her catch us at it. It would have puzzled her to think that there might be anything amusing about her. Her one concession to the fact of humor was an insincere, startling laugh. Strangers often stared at her.

While Mother waited for the priest, who was late, she prayed. She prayed in a familiar, orderly, firm way: first for her late husband, my father, then for her parents—also dead. She said a quick prayer for my father's parents (just touching base; she had disliked them) and finally for her children in order of their ages, ending with me. Mother did not consider originality a virtue and until my name came up her prayers were exactly the same as on any other day.

But when she came to me she spoke up boldly. "I thought he wasn't going to do it any more. Murphy said he was cured. What am I supposed to do now?" There was reproach in her tone. Mother put great hope in her notion that I was cured. She regarded my cure as an answer to her prayers and by way of thanksgiving sent a lot of money to the Thomasite Indian Mission, money she had been saving for a trip to Rome. She felt cheated and she let her feelings be known. When the priest came in Mother slid back on the seat and followed the Mass with concentration. After communion she began to worry again and went straight home without stopping to talk to Frances, the woman who always cornered Mother after Mass to tell about the awful things done to her by Communists, devil-worshipers, and Rosicrucians. Frances watched her go with narrowed eyes.

Once in the house, Mother took the letter from my drawer and brought it into the kitchen. She held it over the stove with her fingernails, looking away so that she would not be drawn into it again, and set it on fire. When it began to burn her fingers she dropped it in the sink and watched it blacken and flutter and close upon itself like a fist. Then she washed it down the drain and called Dr. Murphy.

The letter was to my friend Ralphy in Arizona. He used to live across the street from us but he had moved. Most of the letter was about a tour we, the junior class, had taken to Alcatraz. That was all right. What got Mother was the last paragraph where I said that she had been coughing up blood and the doctors weren't sure what was wrong with her, but that we were hoping for the best.

This wasn't true. Mother took pride in her physical condition, considered herself a horse: "I'm a regular horse," she would reply when people asked about her health. For several years now I had been saying unpleasant things that weren't true and this habit of mine irked Mother greatly, enough to persuade her to send me to Dr. Murphy, in whose office I was sitting when she burned the letter. Dr. Murphy was our family physician and had no training in psychoanalysis but he took an interest in "things of the mind," as he put it. He had treated me for appendicitis and tonsilitis and Mother thought that he could put the truth into me as easily as he

ook things out of me, a hope Dr. Murphy did not share. He was
asically interested in getting me to understand what I did, and
ately he had been moving toward the conclusion that I understood
what I did as well as I ever would.

Dr. Murphy listened to Mother's account of the letter, and what
he had done with it. He was curious about the wording I had used
and became irritated when Mother told him she had burned it.
"The point is," she said, "he was supposed to be cured and he's
not."

"Margaret, I never said he was cured."

"You certainly did. Why else would I have sent over a thousand
dollars to the Thomasite mission?"

"I said that he was responsible. That means that James knows
what he's doing, not that he's going to stop doing it."

"I'm sure you said he was cured."

"Never. To say that someone is cured you have to know what
health is. With this kind of thing that's impossible. What do you
mean by curing James, anyway?"

"You know."

"Tell me anyway."

"Getting him back to reality, what else?"

"Whose reality? Mine or yours?"

"Murphy, what are you talking about? James isn't crazy, he's a
liar."

"Well, you have a point there."

"What am I going to do with him?"

"I don't think there's much you can do. Be patient."

"I've been patient."

"If I were you, Margaret, I wouldn't make too much of this.
James doesn't steal, does he?"

"Of course not."

"Or beat people up or talk back."

"No."

"Then you have a lot to be thankful for."

"I don't think I can take any more of it. That business about
leukemia last summer. And now this."

"Eventually he'll outgrow it, I think."

"Murphy, he's sixteen years old. What if he doesn't outgrow it? What if he just gets better at it?"

Finally Mother saw that she wasn't going to get any satisfaction from Dr. Murphy, who kept reminding her of her blessings. She said something cutting to him and he said something pompous back and she hung up. Dr. Murphy stared at the receiver. "Hello," he said, then replaced it on the cradle. He ran his hand over his head, a habit remaining from a time when he had hair. To show that he was a good sport he often joked about his baldness, but I had the feeling that he regretted it deeply. Looking at me across the desk, he must have wished that he hadn't taken me on. Treating a friend's child was like investing a friend's money.

"I don't have to tell you who that was."

I nodded.

Dr. Murphy pushed his chair back and swiveled it around so he could look out the window behind him, which took up most of the wall. There were still a few sailboats out on the Bay, but they were all making for shore. A woolly gray fog had covered the bridge and was moving in fast. The water seemed calm from this far up, but when I looked closely I could see white flecks everywhere, so it must have been pretty choppy.

"I'm surprised at you," he said. "Leaving something like that lying around for her to find. If you really have to do these things you could at least be kind and do them discreetly. It's not easy for your mother, what with your father dead and all the others somewhere else."

"I know. I didn't mean for her to find it."

"Well." He tapped his pencil against his teeth. He was not convinced professionally, but personally he may have been. "I think you ought to go home now and straighten things out."

"I guess I'd better."

"Tell your mother I might stop by, either tonight or tomorrow. And James—don't underestimate her."

While my father was alive we usually went to Yosemite for three or four days during the summer. My mother would drive and Father would point out places of interest, meadows where boom towns once stood, hanging trees, rivers that were said to flow upstream at certain times. Or he read to us; he had that grownups' idea that children love Dickens and Sir Walter Scott. The four of us sat in the back seat with our faces composed, attentive, while our hands and feet pushed, pinched, stomped, goosed, prodded, dug, and kicked.

One night a bear came into our camp just after dinner. Mother had made a tuna casserole and it must have smelled to him like something worth dying for. He came into the camp while we were sitting around the fire and stood swaying back and forth. My brother Michael saw him first and elbowed me, then my sisters saw him and screamed. Mother and Father had their backs to him but Mother must have guessed what it was because she immediately said, "Don't scream like that. You might frighten him and there's no telling what he'll do. We'll just sing and he'll go away."

We sang "Row Row Row Your Boat" but the bear stayed. He circled us several times, rearing up now and then on his hind legs to stick his nose into the air. By the light of the fire I could see his doglike face and watch the muscles roll under his loose skin like rocks in a sack. We sang harder as he circled us, coming closer and closer. "All right," Mother said, "enough's enough." She stood abruptly. The bear stopped moving and watched her. "Beat it," Mother said. The bear sat down and looked from side to side. "Beat it," she said again, and leaned over and picked up a rock.

"Margaret, don't," my father said.

She threw the rock hard and hit the bear in the stomach. Even in the dim light I could see the dust rising from his fur. He grunted and stood to his full height. "See that?" Mother shouted: "He's filthy. Filthy!" One of my sisters giggled. Mother picked up another rock. "Please, Margaret," my father said. Just then the bear turned and shambled away. Mother pitched the rock after him. For the rest of the night he loitered around the camp until he found the tree where we had hung our food. He ate it all. The next day we drove back to the city. We could have bought more supplies in the valley, but Father wanted to go and would not give in to any argument. On the way home he tried to jolly everyone up by making jokes, but Michael and my sisters ignored him and looked stonily out the windows.

Things were never easy between my mother and me, but I didn't underestimate her. She underestimated me. When I was little she suspected me of delicacy, because I didn't like being thrown into the air, and because when I saw her and the others working themselves up for a roughhouse I found somewhere else to be. When they did drag me in I got hurt, a knee in the lip, a bent finger, a bloody nose, and this too Mother seemed to hold against me, as if I arranged my hurts to get out of playing.

Even things I did well got on her nerves. We all loved puns except Mother, who didn't get them, and next to my father I was the best in the family. My speciality was the Swifty—" 'You can bring the prisoner down,' said Tom condescendingly." Father encouraged me to perform at dinner, which must have been a trial for outsiders. Mother wasn't sure what was going on, but she didn't like it.

She suspected me in other ways. I couldn't go to the movies without her examining my pockets to make sure I had enough money to pay for the ticket. When I went away to camp she tore my pack apart in front of all the boys who were waiting in the bus outside the house. I would rather have gone without my sleeping bag and a few changes of underwear, which I had forgotten, than be made such a fool of. Her distrust was the thing that made me forgetful.

And she thought I was cold-hearted because of what happened the day my father died and later at his funeral. I didn't cry at my father's funeral, and showed signs of boredom during the eulogy, fiddling around with the hymnals. Mother put my hands into my lap and I left them there without moving them as though they were things I was holding for someone else. The effect was ironical and she resented it. We had a sort of reconciliation a few days later after I closed my eyes at school and refused to open them. When several teachers and then the principal failed to persuade me to look at them, or at some reward they claimed to be holding, I was handed over to the school nurse, who tried to pry the lids open and scratched one of them badly. My eye swelled up and I went rigid. The principal panicked and called Mother, who fetched me home. I wouldn't talk to her, or open my eyes, or bend, and they had to lay me on the back seat and when we reached the house Mother had to lift me up the steps one at a time. Then she put me on the couch and played the piano to me all afternoon. Finally I opened my eyes. We hugged each other and I wept. Mother did not really believe my tears, but she was willing to accept them because I had staged them for her benefit.

My lying separated us, too, and the fact that my promises not to lie any more seemed to mean nothing to me. Often my lies came back to her in embarrassing ways, people stopping her in the street and say how sorry they were to hear that ————. No one in the neighborhood enjoyed embarrassing Mother, and these situations stopped occurring once everybody got wise to me. There was no saving her from strangers, though. The summer after Father died I visited my uncle in Redding and when I got back I found to my surprise that Mother had come to meet my bus. I tried to slip away from the gentleman who had sat next to me but I couldn't shake him. When he saw Mother embrace me he came up and presented her with a card and told her to get in touch with him if things got any worse. She gave him his card back and told him to mind his own business. Later, on the way home, she made me repeat what I had said to the man. She shook her head. "It's not fair to people," she said, "telling them things like that. It confuses them." It seemed to me that Mother had confused the man, not I, but I didn't say so. I agreed with her that I shouldn't say such things and promised not to do it again, a promise I broke three hours later in conversation with a woman in the park.

It wasn't only the lies that disturbed Mother; it was their morbidity. This was the real issue between us, as it had been between her and my father. Mother did volunteer work at Children's Hospital and St. Anthony's Dining Hall, collected things for the St. Vincent de Paul Society. She was a lighter of candles. My brother and sisters took after her in this way. My father was a curser of the dark. And he loved to curse the dark. He was never more alive than when he was indignant about something. For this reason the most important act of the day for him was the reading of the evening paper.

Ours was a terrible paper, indifferent to the city that bought it, indifferent to medical discoveries—except for new kinds of gases that made your hands fall off when you sneezed—and indifferent to politics and art. Its business was outrage, horror, gruesome coincidence. When my father sat down in the living room with the paper Mother stayed in the kitchen and kept the children busy, all except me, because I was quiet and could be trusted to amuse myself. I amused myself by watching my father.

He sat with his knees spread, leaning forward, his eyes only inches from the print. As he read he nodded to himself. Sometimes he swore and threw the paper down and paced the room, then picked it up and began again. Over a period of time he developed the habit of reading aloud to me. He always started with the society section, which he called the parasite page. This column began to take on the character of a comic strip or a serial, with the same people showing up from one day to the next, blinking in chiffon, awkwardly holding their drinks for the sake of Peninsula orphans, grinning under sunglasses on the deck of a ski hut in the Sierras. The skiers really got his goat, probably because he couldn't understand them. The activity itself was inconceivable to him. When my sisters went to Lake Tahoe one winter weekend with some friends and came back excited about the beauty of the place, Father calmed them right down. "Snow," he said, "is overrated."

Then the news, or what passed in the paper for news: bodies unearthed in Scotland, former Nazis winning elections, rare animals slaughtered, misers expiring naked in freezing houses upon mattresses stuffed with thousands, millions; marrying priests, divorcing actresses, high-rolling oilmen building fantastic mausoleums in honor of a favorite horse, cannibalism. Through all this my father waded with a fixed and weary smile.

Mother encouraged him to take up causes, to join groups, but he would not. He was uncomfortable with people outside the family. He and my mother rarely went out, and rarely had people in, except on feast days and national holidays. Their guests were always the same, Dr. Murphy and his wife and several others whom they had known since childhood. Most of these people never saw each other outside our house and they didn't have much fun together. Father discharged his obligations as host by teasing everyone about stupid things they had said or done in the past and forcing them to laugh at themselves.

Though Father did not drink, he insisted on mixing cocktails for the guests. He would not serve straight drinks like rum-and-Coke or even Scotch-on-the-rocks, only drinks of his own devising. He gave them lawyerly names like "The Advocate," "The Hanging Judge," "The Ambulance Chaser," "The Mouthpiece," and described their concoction in detail. He told long, complicated stories in a near-whisper, making everyone lean in his direction, and repeated important lines; he also repeated the important lines in the stories my mother told, and corrected her when she got something wrong. When the guests came to the ends of their own stories he would point out the morals.

Dr. Murphy had several theories about Father, which he used to test on me in the course of our meetings. Dr. Murphy had by this time given up his glasses for contact lenses, and lost weight in the course of fasts which he undertook regularly. Even with his baldness he looked years younger than when he had come to the parties at our house. Certainly he did not look like my father's contemporary, which he was.

One of Dr. Murphy's theories was that Father had exhibited a classic trait of people who had been gifted children by taking an undemanding position in an uninteresting firm. "He was afraid of finding his limits," Dr. Murphy told me: "As long as he kept stamping papers and making out wills he could go on believing that he didn't *have* limits." Dr. Murphy's fascination with Father made me uneasy, and I felt traitorous listening to him. While he lived, my father would never have submitted himself for analysis; it seemed a betrayal to put him on the couch now that he was dead.

I did enjoy Dr. Murphy's recollections of Father as a child. He told me about something that happened when they were in the Boy Scouts. Their troop had been on a long hike and Father had fallen behind. Dr. Murphy and the others decided to ambush him as he came down the trail. They hid in the woods on each side and waited. But when Father walked into the trap none of them moved or made a sound and he strolled on without even knowing they were there. "He had the sweetest look on his face," Dr. Murphy said, "listening to the birds, smelling the flowers, just like Ferdinand the Bull." He also told me that my father's drinks tasted like medicine.

* * *

While I rode my bicycle home from Dr. Murphy's office Mother fretted. She felt terribly alone but she didn't call anyone because she also felt like a failure. My lying had that effect on her. She took it personally. At such times she did not think of my sisters, one happily married, the other doing brilliantly at Fordham. She did not think of my brother Michael, who had given up college to work with runaway children in Los Angeles. She thought of me. She thought that she had made a mess of her family.

Actually she managed the family well. While my father was dying upstairs she pulled us together. She made lists of chores and gave each of us a fair allowance. Bedtimes were adjusted and she stuck by them. She set regular hours for homework. Each child was made responsible for the next eldest, and I was given a dog. She told us frequently, predictably, that she loved us. At dinner we were each expected to contribute something, and after dinner she played the piano and tried to teach us to sing in harmony, which I could not do. Mother, who was an admirer of the Trapp family, considered this a character defect.

Our life together was more orderly, healthy, while Father was dying than it had been before. He had set us rules to follow, not much different really than the ones Mother gave us after he got sick, but he had administered them in a fickle way. Though we were supposed to get an allowance we always had to ask him for it and then he would give us too much because he enjoyed seeming magnanimous. Sometimes he punished us for no reason, because he was in a bad mood. He was apt to decide, as one of my sisters was going out to a dance, that she had better stay home and do something to improve herself. Or he would sweep us all up on a Wednesday night and take us ice-skating.

He changed after he learned about the cancer, and became more calm as the disease spread. He relaxed his teasing way with us, and from time to time it was possible to have a conversation with him which was not about the last thing that had made him angry. He stopped reading the paper and spent time at the window.

He and I became close. He taught me to play poker and sometimes helped me with my homework. But it wasn't his illness that drew us together. The reserve between us had begun to break down after the incident with the bear, during the drive home. Michael and my sisters were furious with him for making us leave early and wouldn't talk to him or look at him. He joked: though it had been a grisly experience we should grin and bear it—and so on. His joking seemed perverse to the others, but not to me. I had seen how terrified he was when the bear came into the camp. He had held himself so still that he had begun to tremble. When Mother started pitching rocks I thought he was going to bolt, really. I understood —I had been frightened too. The others took it as a lark after they got used to having the bear around, but for Father and me it got worse through the night. I was glad to be out of there, grateful to Father for getting me out. I saw that his jokes were how he held himself together. So I reached out to him with a joke: " 'There's a bear outside,' said Tom intently." The others turned cold looks on me. They thought I was sucking up. But Father smiled.

When I thought of other boys being close to their fathers I thought of them hunting together, tossing a ball back and forth, making birdhouses in the basement, and having long talks about girls, war, careers. Maybe the reason it took us so long to get close was that I had this idea. It kept getting in the way of what we really had, which was a shared fear.

Toward the end Father slept most of the time and I watched him. From below, sometimes, faintly, I heard Mother playing the piano. Occasionally he nodded off in his chair while I was reading to him; his bathrobe would fall open then, and I would see the long new scar on his stomach, red as blood against his white skin. His ribs all showed and his legs were like cables.

I once read in a biography of a great man that he "died well." I assume the writer meant that he kept his pain to himself, did not set off false alarms, and did not too much inconvenience those who were to stay behind. My father died well. His irritability gave way to something else, something like serenity. In the last days he became tender. It was as though he had been rehearsing the scene, that the anger of his life had been a kind of stage fright. He managed his audience—us—with an old trouper's sense of when to clown and when to stand on his dignity. We were all moved, and admired his courage, as he intended we should. He died downstairs in a shaft of late afternoon sunlight on New Year's Day, while I was reading to him. I was alone in the house and didn't know what to do. His body did not frighten me but immediately and sharply I missed my father. It seemed wrong to leave him sitting up and I tried to carry him upstairs to the bedroom but it was too hard, alone. So I called up my friend Ralphy across the street. When he came over and saw what I wanted him for he started crying but I made him help me anyway. A couple of hours later Mother got home and when I told her that Father was dead she ran upstairs, calling his name. A few minutes later she came back down. "Thank God," she said, "at least he died in bed." This seemed important to her and I didn't tell her otherwise. But that night Ralphy's parents called. They were, they said, shocked at what I had done and so was Mother when she heard the story, shocked and furious. Why? Because I had not told her the truth? Or because she had learned the truth, and could not go on believing that Father had died in bed? I really don't know.

"Mother," I said, coming into the living room, "I'm sorry about the letter. I really am."

She was arranging wood in the fireplace and did not look at me or speak for a moment. Finally she finished and straightened up and brushed her hands. She stepped back and looked at the fire she had laid. "That's all right," she said. "Not bad for a consumptive."

"Mother, I'm sorry."

"Sorry? Sorry you wrote it or sorry I found it?"

"I wasn't going to mail it. It was a sort of joke."

"Ha ha." She took up the whisk broom and swept bits of bark into the fireplace, then closed the drapes and settled on the couch. "Sit down," she said. She crossed her legs. "Listen, do I give you advice all the time?"

"Yes."

"I do?"

I nodded.

"Well, that doesn't make any difference. I'm supposed to. I'm your mother. I'm going to give you some more advice, for your own good. You don't have to make all these things up, James.

They'll happen anyway." She picked at the hem of her skirt. "Do you understand what I'm saying?"

"I think so."

"You're cheating yourself, that's what I'm trying to tell you. When you get to be my age you won't know anything at all about life. All you'll know is what you've made up."

I thought about that. It seemed logical.

She went on. "I think maybe you need to get out of yourself more. Think more about other people."

The doorbell rang.

"Go see who it is," Mother said. "We'll talk about this later."

It was Dr. Murphy. He and mother made their apologies and she insisted that he stay for dinner. I went to the kitchen to fetch ice for their drinks, and when I returned they were talking about me. I sat on the sofa and listened. Dr. Murphy was telling Mother not to worry. "James is a good boy," he said. "I've been thinking about my oldest, Terry. He's not really dishonest, you know, but he's not really honest either. I can't seem to reach him. At least James isn't furtive."

"No," Mother said, "he's never been furtive."

Dr. Murphy clasped his hands between his knees and stared at them. "Well, that's Terry. Furtive."

Before we sat down to dinner Mother said grace; Dr. Murphy bowed his head and closed his eyes and crossed himself at the end, though he had lost his faith in college. When he told me that, during one of our meetings, in just those words, I had the picture of a raincoat hanging by itself outside a dining hall. He drank a good deal of wine and persistently turned the conversation to the subject of his relationship with Terry. He admitted that he had come to dislike the boy. Then he mentioned several patients of his by name, some of them known to Mother and me, and said that he disliked them too. He used the word "dislike" with relish, like someone on a diet permitting himself a single potato chip. "I don't know what I've done wrong," he said abruptly, and with reference to no particular thing. "Then again maybe I haven't done anything wrong. I don't know what to think any more. Nobody does."

"I know what to think," Mother said.

"So does the solipsist. How can you prove to a solipsist that he's not creating the rest of us?"

This was one of Dr. Murphy's favorite riddles, and almost any pretext was sufficient for him to trot it out. He was a child with a card trick.

"Send him to bed without dinner," Mother said. "Let him create that."

Dr. Murphy suddenly turned to me. "Why do you do it?" he asked. It was a pure question, it had no object beyond the satisfaction of his curiosity. Mother looked at me and there was the same curiosity in her face.

"I don't know," I said, and that was the truth.

Dr. Murphy nodded, not because he had anticipated my answer but because he accepted it. "Is it fun?"

"No, it's not fun. I can't explain."

"Why is it all so sad?" Mother asked, "Why all the diseases?"

"Maybe," Dr. Murphy said, "sad things are more interesting."

"Not to me," Mother said.

"Not to me, either," I said. "It just comes out that way."

After dinner Dr. Murphy asked Mother to play the piano. He particularly wanted to sing "Come Home Abbie, the Light's on the Stair."

"That old thing," Mother said. She stood and folded her napkin deliberately and we followed her into the living room. Dr. Murphy stood behind her as she warmed up. Then they sang "Come Home Abbie, the Light's on the Stair," and I watched him stare down at Mother intently, as if he were trying to remember something. Her own eyes were closed. After that they sang "O Magnum Mysterium." They sang it in parts and I regretted that I had no voice, it sounded so good.

"Come on, James," Dr. Murphy said as Mother played the last chords. "These old tunes not good enough for you?"

"He just can't sing," Mother said.

When Dr. Murphy left, Mother lit the fire and made more coffee. She slouched down in the big chair, sticking her legs straight out and moving her feet back and forth. "That was fun," she said.

"Did you and Father ever do things like that?"

"A few times, when we were first going out. I don't think he really enjoyed it. He was like you."

I wondered if Mother and Father had had a good marriage. He admired her and liked to look at her; every night at dinner he had us move the candlesticks slightly to right and left of center so he could see her down the length of the table. And every evening when she set the table she put them in the center again. She didn't seem to miss him very much. But I wouldn't really have known if she did, and anyway I didn't miss him all that much myself, not the way I had. Most of the time I thought about other things.

"James?"

I waited.

"I've been thinking that you might like to go down and stay with Michael for a couple of weeks or so."

"What about school?"

"I'll talk to Father McSorley. He won't mind. Maybe this problem will take care of itself if you start thinking about other people."

"I do."

"I mean helping them, like Michael does. You don't have to go if you don't want to."

"It's fine with me. Really. I'd like to see Michael."

"I'm not trying to get rid of you."

"I know."

Mother stretched, then tucked her feet under her. She sipped noisily at her coffee. "What did that word mean that Murphy used? You know the one?"

"Paranoid? That's where somebody thinks everyone is out to get him. Like that woman who always grabs you after Mass—Frances."

"Not paranoid. Everyone knows what that means. Sol-something."

"Oh. Solipsist. A solipsist is someone who thinks he creates everything around him."

Mother nodded and blew on her coffee, then put it down without drinking from it. "I'd rather be paranoid. Do you really think Frances is?"

"Of course. No question about it."

"I mean really *sick?*"

"That's what paranoid *is,* is being sick. What do you think, Mother?"

"What are you so angry about?"

"I'm not angry." I lowered my voice. "I'm not angry. But you don't believe those stories of hers, do you?"

"Well, no, not exactly. I don't think she knows what she's saying, she just wants someone to listen. She probably lives all by herself in some little room. So she's paranoid. Think of that. And I had no idea. James, we should pray for her. Will you remember to do that?"

I nodded. I thought of Mother singing "O Magnum Mysterium" saying grace, praying with easy confidence, and it came to me that her imagination was superior to mine. She could imagine things as coming together, not falling apart. She looked at me and I shrank; I knew exactly what she was going to say. "Son," she said, "do you know how much I love you?"

The next afternoon I took the bus to Los Angeles. I looked forward to the trip, to the monotony of the road and the empty fields by the roadside. Mother walked with me down the long concourse. The station was crowded and oppressive. "Are you sure this is the right bus?" she asked at the loading platform.

"Yes."

"It looks so old."

"Mother—"

"All right." She pulled me against her and kissed me, then held me an extra second to show that her embrace was sincere, not just like everyone else's, never having realized that everyone else does the same thing. I boarded the bus and we waved at each other until it became embarrassing. Then Mother began checking through her handbag for something. When she had finished I stood and adjusted the luggage over my seat. I sat and we smiled at each other, waved when the driver gunned the engine, shrugged when he got up suddenly to count the passengers, waved again when he resumed his seat. As the bus pulled out my mother and I were looking at each other with plain relief.

I had boarded the wrong bus. This one was bound for Los Angeles but not by the express route. We stopped in San Mateo, Palo Alto, San Jose, Castroville. When we left Castroville it began to rain, hard; my window would not close all the way, and a thin stream of water ran down the wall onto my seat. To keep dry I had to stay away from the wall and lean forward. The rain fell harder. The engine of the bus sounded as though it were coming apart.

In Salinas the man sleeping beside me jumped up but before I had a chance to change seats his place was taken by an enormous woman in a print dress, carrying a shopping bag. She took possession of her seat and spilled over onto half of mine, backing me up to the wall. "That's a storm," she said loudly, then turned and looked at me. "Hungry?" Without waiting for an answer she dipped into her bag and pulled out a piece of chicken and thrust it at me. "Hey, by God," she hooted, "look at him go to town on that drumstick!" A few people turned and smiled. I smiled back around the bone and kept at it. I finished that piece and she handed me another, and then another. Then she started handing out chicken to the people in the seats near us.

Outside of San Luis Obispo the noise from the engine grew suddenly louder and just as suddenly there was no noise at all. The driver pulled off to the side of the road and got out, then got on again dripping wet. A few moments later he announced that the bus had broken down and they were sending another bus to pick us up. Someone asked how long that might take and the driver said he had no idea. "Keep your pants on!" shouted the woman next to me. "Anybody in a hurry to get to L.A. ought to have his head examined."

The wind was blowing hard around the bus, driving sheets of rain against the windows on both sides. The bus swayed gently. Outside the light was brown and thick. The woman next to me pumped all the people around us for their itineraries and said whether or not she had ever been where they were from or where they were going. "How about you?" She slapped my knee. "Pa ents own a chicken ranch? I hope so!" She laughed. I told her I w from San Francisco. "San Francisco, that's where my husband was stationed." She asked me what I did there and I told her I worked with refugees from Tibet.

"Is that right? What do you do with a bunch of Tibetans?"

"Seems like there's plenty of other places they could've gone," said a man in front of us. "Coming across the border like that. We don't go there."

"What do you do with a bunch of Tibetans?" the woman repeated.

"Try to find them jobs, locate housing, listen to their problems."

"You understand that kind of talk?"

"Yes."

"Speak it?"

"Pretty well. I was born and raised in Tibet. My parents were missionaries over there."

Everyone waited.

"They were killed when the Communists took over."

The big woman patted my arm.

"It's all right," I said.

"Why don't you say some of that Tibetan?"

"What would you like to hear?"

"Say 'The cow jumped over the moon.' " She watched me, smiling, and when I finished she looked at the others and shook her head. "That was pretty. Like music. Say some more."

"What?"

"Anything."

They bent toward me. The windows suddenly went blind with rain. The driver had fallen asleep and was snoring gently to the swaying of the bus. Outside the muddy light flickered to pale yellow, and far off there was thunder. The woman next to me leaned back and closed her eyes and then so did all the others as I sang to them in what was surely an ancient and holy tongue.

The Other Way

by Shirley Ann Grau

Sandra Lee was late. It was nearly five o'clock when she got off the school bus. She walked through the narrow alley along the side of her house and heard the hollow echo of her heels on the brick. The philodendrons which her grandmother insisted on growing in the six inches of soil by the high board fence brushed crinkled leaves against her face, and she ducked her head to avoid them.

I been doing this every day of my life, she thought, since I been old enough to walk. And how many times does that make it?

She liked to think of numbers. She always counted things. The walk now, it had two hundred and sixty-eight bricks. And then you were at the kitchen door. She climbed the worn wood steps, the ones her grandmother still scrubbed with brown soap every day, rain or shine, hot or cold. The way she had done ever since she was a young bride just moved into the house. The steps now were a silvery gray color, the veins of the wood standing up hard and clear, the surface rough and uneven like a washboard when you sat on it.

She went in, letting the screen bang shut behind her. She knew who would be there—the same people were always there each day when she came home from school. There was her mother, short and heavy, dark brown and frizzled-haired, with only light green eyes to show her white blood. She would be standing at the enamel-topped table under the window beginning to fix supper, staring out at the line of fluttering clothes that ran from the back porch to the back shed. There was her aunt Norris, sitting in her wheel chair, across her withered legs the endless balls of cord she used to crochet. She went very fast, the shiny little hook squirming about among the knotting thread. So fast that the finished product seemed to run smoothly off the tips of her black fingers. And there was the old lady, her grandmother. She would be at the wooden dining table, back in the dusky part of the room, reading the evening paper under the light of the overhead lamp, her gold-rimmed glasses sliding halfway down her nose. She had gotten those glasses from a lady she cooked for years ago, back when her children were still small; she found the glasses suited her fine and she had used them ever since. Now and then she would take them off, and stare at them, and you could tell that she was remembering back to those days when she was young.

Most likely too, they would be talking when Sandra Lee came in —the soft, muttered Cajun French. They always spoke it during the day when they were alone in the house. It was the only language her grandmother felt comfortable in. English came stiff and hard to her tongue, she said.

When Sandra Lee came, they stopped at once, for they would never speak French in front of her. She asked sometimes, but they only laughed and told her, "Layovers to catch meddlers, baby. No need for you to go talking the old folks' talk."

This was the same as every other evening. They stopped talking when they heard her foot on the step. They all looked up when she came through the door. Her mother asked: "How was school today?" and she answered, "Fine," and put her books down on the table beside her grandmother's paper.

Then her mother would tell her what to do: go to the grocery, or get the clothes in, or wash your hands and set the table.

Today her mother said: "I won't be needing any help. But you could put the hem in that dress I ripped for you this morning."

"Growing like a Jerusalem weed," Norris said, as her fingers went back to their contortions with the strip of steel and the cotton thread.

So Sandra Lee fetched the dress, and brought it back to the kitchen and threaded her needle and checked to see just how it was that her mother had basted the hem.

"Who'd you eat lunch with?" her mother asked.

"Some kids." She began sewing, quickly, deftly.

"Like who?"

"Well, Peggy and Amelie."

"What they have for lunch?"

"I didn't look."

"Lunch now," her grandmother said. "It used to be called dinner. When I was cooking we'd have four or five courses and never think anything of it. Excepting it was crawfish bisque. I guess I picked ten tons of crawfish in my day."

"If John and the boys got them," Norris said, "we could make some again this spring."

And then Sandra Lee said what she had been saving up to say all afternoon: "I'm not going back."

They stopped whatever they were doing. They all looked at her. She could feel them looking through her.

"I'm not going back to that school." She found she was speaking louder than she intended. "I'm going where I was last year."

In the little silence they could hear the rattle of dishes and the television set in the house next door.

Her mother said slowly: "What do I got to tell your father?"

Her grandmother said: "Jesus Lord!"

"I thought you liked it. I thought you was happy there," her mother said.

And Norris said: "Alberta's quitting, no?"

She knows everything, Sandra Lee thought. And she nodded.

"And you plain don't want to be the only little black chile in the school."

"God, God," her mother said, chopping onions on the wood board with a steady, practiced thumping.

Norris said: "Alberta's a silly little ass."

"She quit yesterday," Sandra Lee said. "She wasn't there today."

"Was they mean to you?" her grandmother said.

"Did somebody say something to you today?" her mother asked. "Was somebody mean to you?"

Sandra Lee shook her head and began stitching in the hem, slowly.

Norris smoothed the folds of her finished crochet work against her knee. "There's more than what you saying."

"I don't want to talk about it," Sandra Lee said.

Her grandmother cleared her throat and spat into her wad of tissue. "Since when do you come to be short of words?"

"Since now," Sandra Lee said.

Her grandmother's little beady black eyes glared at her. "No mocking in my house, miss."

Sandra Lee bit her lip and began stitching furiously.

"How do I got to tell your father?" her mother whispered to the paring knife in her hands.

Norris gave her wheel chair a quick little spin, the boards under the linoleum creaked, and she was at Sandra Lee's side. She pulled the sewing from her hands. "You began out by talking," she said, "now you finish up."

"I told you."

"Don't they eat lunch with you?" her mother asked faintly. "You said they eat with you."

"Sort of. But it isn't just lunch."

"How?" Norris said. "Tell us how."

"Well," Sandra Lee said, "if I go sit at a table that's empty they don't ever come and sit by me. But if I go sit with them, they talk to me and it's all right."

"Lord of mine!" her mother hissed her breath with relief. "What you expect them to do? They been going there for years and you just come. And what's it got to hurt you to go to their table and not them."

"Little jackass," Norris said bitterly.

And for a minute Sandra Lee wondered whether she meant her or her mother.

"We thought about nothing when we was young," her grandmother said suddenly, "beyond the color of our new shoes, and our men, and if there was going to be somebody to play the piano in the evenings."

"You just got to work harder," her mother said, "no reason you can't keep up. You won the scholarship."

"I'm keeping up," Sandra Lee said. "I don't have any trouble keeping up."

"You don't want to be the only one," Norris said softly. "Not the only black face all by yourself in all that white."

"I just don't want to go."

"My God," her mother said, "oh my God."

"Tais-toi!" Norris said, forgetting. "You are more foolish than your child."

Sandra Lee looked down at her empty hands folded across her lap.

"You are fixing to come running back to where you been," Norris asked. "No?"

"I don't belong there," Sandra Lee said, "that's all."

Norris snickered. "Where you belong, *chère?* Tell me."

"I don't know," Sandra Lee said miserably.

Norris snickered again. "You belong in Africa, maybe?" She held up the blue plaid dress. "You going back to Africa wearing this dress?"

Her mother chuckled and dropped the chopped onions into a frying pan.

"I'm just not going," Sandra Lee said.

"I won't, I won't," her grandmother mimicked.

"You going back," Norris said, "because there's no place else for you."

Sandra Lee bent her head and was surprised to see the splotches of water fall on her hands. She had not realized that she was crying.

"We won't say nothing about this," her mother said, "not to your father nor nobody else."

"I been trouble all my life." Norris looked at her withered legs. "From the day I was born, I been troubling others and there wasn't nothing to do about it."

"The Lord in his mercy," the grandmother said.

"But you now, you got two legs and a head on your shoulders, and you got no cause to be a burden."

"There's eight more months of school," Sandra Lee said, and she saw them stretch ahead like the shining curve of a railroad track, endless.

"You going tomorrow," Norris said as if she had not heard, "and all the days after. And when you come home in the evening, you are going to tell us what kind of a day you had, and what you did at lunchtime, and all that you learned."

Sandra Lee had turned her hands over and was studying the insides of them, the lines and hollows. Some people, she thought, they could tell what would happen to you from your hands, that the mark of the future was there, all spelled out, if you could just read it.

"And," Norris said, "you won't tell us no more of what you're thinking."

"No," her grandmother said. "No more."

The silence was thick and heavy until her mother said, "There's no milk for the morning, and I was forgetting about that."

"Yes'm," Sandra Lee said.

"My purse's on top the bureau."

Sandra Lee got up and walked toward the front of the house. She opened the purse and found a fifty-cent piece and, holding it in her hand, she went out the front door, the one that let directly onto the street.

The bricks gave out their gentle sound under her steps, houses passed one after the other, misted and shaded by fear and misery. She felt the pressure of her people behind her, pushing her, cutting off her tears.

She got the milk. For a minute she thought about throwing the bottle down in the gutter and running off in the other direction. Instead she looked at the black and white spotted cat that ambled loose-limbed along the walk, hugging the shelter of the houses. And so the moment passed, and when she looked up again, the other way was gone. The street in front of her had only one opening and one way to it, and her feet put themselves on that path, and she walked home.

"How was school?" her mother asked.

Sandra Lee put the milk in the icebox and closed the door. "It was fine," she said.

The Other Times

by Peter Taylor

Can anybody honestly like having a high-school civics teacher for an uncle? I doubt it. Especially not a young girl who is popular and good-looking and who is going to make her debut some day at the Chatham Golf and Country Club. Nevertheless, that's who the civics teacher was at Westside High School when we were growing up in Chatham. He was the brother of Letitia Ramsey's father, and he had all the failings you would expect of a high-school civics teacher and baseball coach. In the classroom he was a laughing-stock for the way he butchered the King's English, and out of school he was known to be a hard drinker and general hell-raiser. But the worst part of it was that he was a bachelor and that the Ramseys had to have him for dinner practically every Sunday.

If you had a Sunday afternoon date with Letitia, there the civics teacher would be, out on the front lawn, playing catch with one of Letitia's narrow-eyed little brothers. Somehow, what disturbed *me* about this particular spectacle when I was having Sunday dates with Letitia was the uncle's and the little brother's concentration on the ball and the kind of real fondness they seemed to feel for the thing. When either of them held it in his hand for a minute, he seemed to be wanting to make a pet of it. When it went back and forth between them, smacking their gloves, they seemed to hear it saying, yours, mine, yours, mine, as though nobody else had ever thrown or caught a baseball. But of course that's not the point. The point is that it was hard to think of Letitia's having this Lou Ramsey for an uncle. And I used to watch her face when we were leaving her house on a Sunday afternoon to see if she would show anything. But not Letitia!

It may not seem fair to dwell on this unfortunate uncle of a girl like Letitia Ramsey, but it was through him that I got a clearer idea of what she was like, and the whole Ramsey family, as well. They were very well-bred people, and just as well-to-do, even in the Depression. Mr. Ramsey, like my own father, was from the country, but, also like my father, he was from one of the finest country families in the state. And Mrs. Ramsey and my mother had gone through Farleigh Institute together, which was an old-fashioned school where they studied Latin so long that it made a difference in the way they spoke English all the rest of their lives.

Anyway, though I didn't take Latin, fortunately I didn't take civics, either (since I was hoping to go to college if the Depression eased up), and fortunately I didn't go out for the baseball team. This made it not too hard for me to pretend not to notice who Letitia's uncle was. Also, since Letitia didn't go to the high school but went to Miss Jordan's, a school that has more or less replaced Farleigh Institute in Chatham, it could have been as easy for her to pretend not to notice as it was for me.

It could have been, except that Letitia didn't want it that way. When she and I went across the lawn to my father's car on those Sunday afternoons and her uncle and one of her little brothers were carrying on with that baseball, she would call out something like "Have fun, you two!" or "Come see us this week, Uncle Louis!" And her voice never sounded sweeter than it did then. After we were in the car, if I hadn't thought of something else to talk about she would sometimes begin a long spiel like "I always forget you don't really know my uncle. I wish you did. You probably know how mad he is about sports. That's why my little brothers adore him. And he's just as shy as they are. Look at him and Charlie there. When I'm dressed up like this to go out on a date, he and the boys won't even look at me."

The truth is I felt that Letitia Ramsey was just as smart as she could be—not in school, necessarily, but in the way she handled subjects like undesirable relatives. I think she was very unusual in this. There was one of her friends, named Nancy O'Connor, who had a grandmother who had once run a fruit stand at the old curb market, up on the North Side. The grandmother lived with the O'Connors and was a right funny sort of person, if you know what I mean, and Nancy was forever apologizing for her. Naturally, her apologizing did nothing but make you uncomfortable. Also, there was Trudie Hauser, whose brother Horst was a good friend of mine. The Hausers lived out in the German section of town, where my mother hadn't usually gone to parties in her day, and they still lived in the kind of castle-like house that the first one of the Hausers to get rich had built. Poor Trudie and poor Horst! They had not one but three or four peculiar relatives living with them. And they had German servants, to whom their parents were apt to speak in German, right before you, and make Trudie and Horst, who were both very blond, blush to the roots of their hair the way blonds are apt to do. Then there was also a girl named Maria Thomas. She had a much older brother who was a moron—a real one—and if he passed through the room, or even came in and sat down, she would simply pretend that he wasn't there, that he didn't even exist.

This isn't to say, of course, that all the girls in Chatham had something like that in their families. Lots of girls—and lots of the boys, too—had families like mine, with nobody in particular to be ashamed of. Nor is it to say that the girls who did have something of this kind weren't just as popular as the others and didn't have you to their houses to parties just as often. Nancy O'Connor's family, for instance, lived in a most beautiful Spanish-style house, with beamed ceilings and orange-colored tile floors downstairs, and with a huge walled-in sort of lawn out in the back, where Nancy gave a big party every June. But, I will say, at those parties you always felt that everybody was having more fun than Nancy, all because of the old grandmother. The peculiar old woman never came out into the light of the Japanese lanterns at the party, or anywhere near the tennis court, where the dancing was. She kept always in the shadows, close to the walls that enclosed the lawn. And someone said that Nancy said this was because her grandmother was afraid we would steal the green fruit off the trees she had trained to grow like vines up the walls.

Whether or not Nancy had a good time, her June party was always one of the loveliest events of the year in Chatham. Even though it was the Depression, we had many fine and really lovely parties, and Nancy O'Connor's usually surpassed all others. It was there, at one of them, two nights after we had graduated from high school, that Horst Hauser and Bob Southard and I made up our minds to do a thing that we had been considering for some time and that a lot of boys like us must have done at one time or another. We had been seniors that year, you understand, and in Chatham boys are apt to go pretty wild during their senior year in high school. That is the time when you get to know a city as you will never have a chance to again if you come from the kind of people that I do. I have lived away from Chatham quite a long while now, mostly in places which are not too different from it but about which I never kid myself into thinking I know very much. Yet, like a lot of other men, I carry in my head, even today, a sort of detailed map of the city where I first learned to drive a car and first learned to make dates with girls who were not strictly of the kind I was brought up to date. And I don't mean nice girls like Nancy and Trudie, whose parents were different from mine but who were themselves very nice girls indeed. Chatham being only a middle-sized city—that is, without a big-league baseball team, yet with almost a quarter of a million big-league fans—and being not thoroughly Midwestern and yet not thoroughly Southern either, the most definitely complimentary thing I usually find to say about it is that it was a good place to grow up in. By which I don't mean that it is a good place to come *from,* or anything hateful like that.

For I like Chatham. And I remember everything I ever knew about it. Sometimes, when I go back there for a visit, I can direct people who didn't grow up there to a street or a section of town or even to some place out in the country nearby that they wouldn't have guessed I had any knowledge of. And whenever I am there nowadays, the only change I notice and the only thing that gives me a sad feeling is that the whole city is so much more painted up and prosperous-looking than it used to be during the Depression. And in connection with this, there is something I cannot help feeling is true and cannot help saying. My father, who came from a country town thirty-five miles east of Chatham, used to tell us how sad it made him to see the run-down condition of the house where he was born, out there in the country. But my feeling is that there is something even more depressing about going back to Chatham today and finding the house where I lived till I was grown—and the whole city, too—looking in much better shape than it did when

I called it home. There are moments when I almost wish I could buy up the whole town and let it run down just a little.

Of course, that's an entirely selfish feeling, and I realize it. But it shows what wonderful times we had—decent good times, and others not so decent. And it shows that while we were having those fine times we knew exactly what everything around us was like. We didn't like money's being so tight and didn't like it that everything from the schoolhouse to the country club was a little shabby and rundown. We boys certainly *minded* wearing our fathers' cut-down dinner jackets, and the girls certainly *minded* wearing their older sisters' hand-me-down evening dresses; although we knew that our party clothes looked all right, we knew, too, that our older brothers and sisters, five years before, wouldn't have put up with them for five minutes. We didn't like any of this a bit, and yet it was *ours* and the worriers among us worried even then about how it was all bound to change.

Of course, when the change came, it wasn't at all what anyone had expected. For it never occurred to us then that a war would come along and solve all the problems of the future for us, in one way or another. Instead, we heard so much talk of the Depression that we thought that times were bound to get even worse than they had been, and that all the fun would go out of life as soon as we finished high school, or, at the latest, after college. If you were a worrier, as I was, it didn't seem possible that you would ever be able to make a living of the kind your father had always made. And I sat around some nights, when I ought to have been studying, wondering how people would treat me when I showed that I couldn't make the grade and began to go to pieces. It was on those nights that I used to think about Letitia Ramsey's uncle, whom I considered the most dismal failure of my acquaintance, and then think about how he was treated by Letitia. This became a thing of such interest to me that I was never afterward sure of my own innocence in the way matters developed the night of Nancy O'Connor's party.

I don't need to describe the kind of mischief the boys in my crowd were up to that year—that is, on nights when we weren't having movie dates or going to parties with the usual "nice girls" we had always known. Our mischief doesn't need going into here, and besides it is very old hat to anyone who grew up with the freedom boys have in places like Chatham (especially at a time like the Depression, when all the boys' private schools were closed down). Also, I suppose it goes without saying that we were pretty careful not to mix the one kind of wonderful time we were having with the other. To the girls we had known longest, we did make certain jokes and references they couldn't understand, or pretended they couldn't. We would kid each other, in front of them, about jams we had been in when they weren't along, without ever making any of it very clear. But that was as far as we went until, toward the end of the year, some of the girls got so they would beg us, or dare us, to take them with us some night to one of our "points of interest," which was how we referred to the juke joints and road-houses we went to. We talked about the possibility of this off and on for several weeks. (Five years before, it wouldn't have taken our older brothers five minutes to decide to do such a thing.) And finally, on the night of Nancy O'Connor's party, Horst Hauser and Bob Southard and I decided that the time had come.

The three of us, with our dates, slipped away from the party just after midnight, telling Nancy that we would be back in about an hour, which we knew we wouldn't. And we didn't tell her mother we were going at all. We crossed the lawn and went out through a gate in the back wall at one of the corners, just behind a sort of tool house that Nancy called "the dovecote." She had told us how to find the gate, and she told us also to watch for her grandmother. And, sure enough, just as we were unlocking the gate, there came the old grandmother running along the side wall opposite us, and sticking close to it even when she made the turn at the other corner. She was wearing a long black dress, and at the distance from which we saw her I thought she might easily have been mistaken for a Catholic nun.

But we got the gate open and started through it and into the big vacant lot we had to cross to get to Horst Hauser's car. I held the gate for the other couples, and then for my own date. While I was doing this, I kept one eye on the old woman. But I also peered around the dovecote and saw Nancy O'Connor leave the bright lights of the tennis court and head across the grass under the Japanese lanterns, walking fast in order to catch her grandmother before she reached us. And when I shut the gate after me, I could just imagine the hell the old woman was going to catch.

It wasn't very polite, leaving Nancy's party that way and making trouble in the family—for Nancy was sure to blame the old woman for our going, somehow—but the whole point is that the girl who happened to be my date that night and for whom I had stood there holding the gate was none other than Letitia Ramsey.

Now, there is no use in my not saying right here that all through that spring Letitia's uncle, whom the high-school students generally spoke of as "the Ram," had been having the usual things said about him. And there is no use in my denying that by this time I knew those things were so. For we hadn't had our *other* wonderful times all winter long without running into the Ram at a number of our points of interest—him, along with a couple of his star athletes and his and their girl friends. In fact, I knew by this time that the rumors all of us had heard about him every year since we entered high school were true, and I knew, too, that it was the very athletes he coached and trained and disciplined from the day they first reported for practice, after junior high, that he ended by making his running mates when they were seniors.

But all that sort of thing, in my opinion, is pretty much old hat to most people everywhere. The important thing to me is that when we decided to leave Nancy's wonderful party that night and take our dates with us out to a dine-and-dance joint called Aunt Martha's Tavern, something crossed my mind. And I am not sure that it wasn't something I hoped for instead of something I dreaded, as it should have been. It was that this Aunt Martha's Tavern was exactly where we were most likely to run into the Ram on a Saturday night, which this happened to be, with, of course, one of his girl friends and a couple of his athletes with their girl friends, too.

Well, it couldn't have been worse. We all climbed into Horst Hauser's car and drove out west of town to Aunt Martha's. It was the kind of place where you had to ring several times before they would come and let you in. And when we had rung the bell the second time and were standing outside under the light, with its private flock of bugs whirling around it, waiting there for Aunt Martha to have a look at us through some crack somewhere and decide if she would let us in, a rather upsetting thing happened to me. We were all standing on the stoop together, facing the big, barnlike batten door to the place. Letitia was standing right next to me, and I just thought to myself I would steal a quick glance at her while she wasn't noticing. I turned my head only the slightest bit, but I saw at once that *she* was already looking at *me*. When our eyes met, I felt for the first second or two that she didn't realize they *had* met, because she kept right on looking without changing her expression. I couldn't at once tell what the expression meant. Then it came over me that there was something this girl was expecting me to say—or, at least, hoping I would say. I said the first thing that popped into my mind: "They always make you wait like this." And Letitia Ramsey looked grateful, even for that.

At last, the door was pulled open, though only just about six inches, and inside we saw the face of Aunt Martha's old husband. The old fellow gaped at the girls for a couple of seconds with a stupid grin on his face—he was a deaf-mute and a retired taxidermist—and then he threw the door wide open. We went inside—and, of course, there the Ram was, out on the floor dancing.

There weren't any lights on to speak of, except around the sides, in the booths, and the curtains to some of the booths were drawn. But even so, dark as it was, and with six or eight other couples swinging around on the dance floor, right off the bat I spotted the Ram. Maybe I only recognized him because he was doing the old-time snake-hips dancing that he liked to do when he was high. I can't be sure. But I have the feeling that when we walked into that place that night, I would have seen the Ram just as plainly even if he had not been there—seen the freckled hand he pumped with when he danced, seen the white sharkskin suit, seen the head of sandy hair, a little thin on top but with the sweaty curls still thick along his temples and on the back of his neck.

Once we were inside, I glanced at Letitia again. And for some reason I noticed now that either before she left the party or in the car coming out here she had moved the gardenia corsage that I had sent her from the shoulder strap of her dress to the center of its low-cut neckline. When I saw this, I suddenly turned to Bob and Horst and said, "Let's not stay here."

Letitia and the other two girls smiled at each other. "I think he thinks we'll disgrace him," Letitia said after a moment.

I don't know when she first saw her uncle. It may have been when I did, right off the bat. It being Letitia, you couldn't tell. Or *I* couldn't. The one clue I had was that when the old deaf-mute made signs for us to follow him across the floor to an empty booth, I saw her throw her little powder blue evening jacket, which was the same color as her dress, around her shoulders. It was a hot night, and before that she had only been carrying it over her arm.

Yet it wasn't necessarily her uncle's presence that caused Letitia to put the jacket around her bare shoulders. It could have been just the kind of place we were in. It could have been Martha's crazy-looking old husband, with his tufts of white hair sticking out in all directions. It seemed to me at the time that it might be only the sight of the old man's stuffed animal heads, which were hung all around the place. You didn't notice most of these with it so dark, but above the beer counter were the heads of three collie dogs, and as we went across the floor, the bubbly lights of the jukebox would now and again catch a gleam from the glass eyes of those collie dogs. Any other time in the world, I think the effect would have seemed irresistibly funny to me. I would have pointed it out to Horst and Bob, and afterward there would have been cryptic references made to it before girls like Letitia who normally wouldn't ever have been inside such a place.

We went into our booth, which was a big one in a corner, and almost as soon as we sat down, I saw two of the Ram's athletes come out on the dance floor with their girls. The Ram had disappeared, and I didn't see him dancing again. But every so often the two athletes would come out and dance for the length of about half a record and then go back to their booth, pushing the curtains apart just enough to let themselves slip through. None of us said a word about seeing them out there. And, of course, nobody mentioned the Ram. I guess we were all pretty uncomfortable about it, because we made a lot of uncomfortable and silly conversation. All of us except Letitia. We joked and carried on in a very foolish way, trying to cover up. But everything we said or did seemed to make my toes curl under.

For instance: Bob pretended he was going to close the curtains to our booth, and there was a great scramble between him and his date over keeping them open. And all the while, across the way, the curtains to the Ram's booth were never opened wider than it took for one person to slip in or out.

Also: "Where in the world *are* we?" one of the girls asked. That we were way out in the country, of course, they knew, but *where?* And it had to be explained that Aunt Martha's Tavern was across the line in Clark County, about twelve miles due west of Chatham, which is in Pitt County, and this meant we were only about three miles from Thompsonville. Thompsonville, I knew, if some of the others didn't, was where Letitia's uncle and her father grew up. We were in an area that Letitia's Uncle Louis must have known pretty well for a long time.

And finally: There was the business about Aunt Martha. She came herself to take our orders. None of us was hungry, and the girls wouldn't even order Cokes. But she took us boys' orders for mixers, and while she was there, Horst Hauser tried to get her to sing "Temptation" for us. Martha wasn't so very old—you could tell it by her clear, smooth skin and her bright green eyes—and nobody really called her Aunt Martha. But she must have weighed about three hundred pounds and she hadn't a tooth in her head. She wore her hair in what was almost a crew cut. And she was apt to be barefoot about half the time; she was barefoot that night. She wouldn't sing "Temptation" for us, but she talked to the girls and told them how pretty their dresses were and asked them their names—"Just your first names, I'm no good at last names," she said—so she would be sure to remember them next time they came. "You know," she said. "In case you come with some other fellows, and not these jelly beans." And she gave them a big wink.

We three boys pretended to look very hurt, and she said, "They know I'm a tease. These here boys are my honey babes." Then she looked at us awfully close to make sure that we did know. She hung around telling the girls how her old husband had built the tavern singlehanded, as a wedding present for her, and how, after practicing taxidermy "in many parts of the world and for over forty years," he had given it up and settled down in the country with her, and how generally sweet he was. "It mayn't seem likely to you girls," she said, her green eyes getting a damp look, "but they can be just as fine and just as noble without a tongue in their head as with one." Then, from fear of being misunderstood, maybe, or not wanting to depress the customers, she added, "And just as much fun, honey babes!" She gave us boys a wink and went off in a fit of laughter.

When she had gone, we all agreed that Martha was a good soul and that the old deaf-mute was a lucky man. But we couldn't help trying to take her off. And I laughed with the others till, suddenly, it occurred to me that her accent and her little turns of speech sounded, on our lips, just like things the Ram was quoted as saying in his civics class. He said "territory" and "A-rab" and "how come" and "I'm done." I knew that Letitia's own father didn't say things like that; it only showed the kind of low company Lou Ramsey had always kept, even as a boy in Clark County.

Well, when Martha went for the mixers, it was time for Bob and Horst and me to flip a coin to see who was going outside and buy us a pint of whiskey at the back door, which was where you always had to buy it. Unfortunately, I was odd man, and so I began collecting the money from the other two. Letitia didn't understand about the whiskey, and we had to explain to her about local option and Clark County's being a dry county, and about bootleg's being cheaper than the legal whiskey in Chatham. But while we explained, she didn't seem to listen. She only kept looking at me questioningly, and finally she squinted her eyes and said, "Are you sure you know how to buy it, and where?"

I went out the front door and around to the kitchen door, and bought the whiskey from Martha's husband, who had gone back there to meet me. I was glad for a breath of fresh air and to be away from the others for a few minutes. And yet I was eager to get back to them, too. I hurried toward the front, along the footpath between the parking lot and the side wall of the tavern—a dark wall of unpainted vertical planking. The night seemed even hotter and muggier now than it had earlier. The sky, all overcast, with no stars shining through anywhere, was like an old, washed-out gray sweater. On the far side of the parking lot, a few faint streaks of light caught my eye. I knew they came from Aunt Martha's tourist cabins, which were ranged along the edge of the woods over there. The night was so dark it was hard to tell much about the cars in the parking lot, but I could tell that they were mostly broken down jalopies and that the lot looked more like a junkyard than any real parking lot. Everything I saw looked ugly and raw and unreal to me, and when I came round to the front, where the one big light bulb above the entrance still flickered brightly in its swarm of bugs, I could see a field of waist-high corn directly across the road, and somehow it looked rawer and more unreal to me than anything else.

When I rang at the front door to be let in again, the old man had already come through the place. He opened up for me, grinning as though it were a big joke between us—his having got there as soon as I did. But I didn't want any of his dumb-show joking just then. He was making all kinds of silly signs with his hands, but I passed by him and went on back to our booth. And I was struck right away by how happy Letitia looked when she saw me. She didn't seem to be concerned about her uncle at all, which, of course, was what I was watching to see. I was glad, and yet it didn't ease my mind a bit. What were you to make of such a girl? Ever since we got there, I had been watching her in a way that I felt guilty about, because I knew it was more curiosity than sympathy. And I was certain now that she had been watching me, for some kind of sign. I couldn't have been more uncomfortable. It was strange. She was such a marvelously pretty girl, really!—with her pale yellow hair and her almond eyes, with her firm little mouth that you couldn't help looking at when she opened it a little and smiled, no matter how much respect you had for her, and no matter what else you had on your mind. I kept looking at her, and I tried not to seem too self-conscious when I drew the pint of whiskey out of the pocket of my linen jacket and put it on the table.

But I did feel self-conscious about it, and even more so because she continued to sit there just as casually as though we were having a milkshake somewhere after the show and were settling down to enjoy ourselves for the rest of the evening. When I first came back, she had looked at me as though I were a hero because I had gone around to the back door to buy a pint of bootleg whiskey and had got back alive, and now she commenced puttering around with the glasses and the mixers with a happy, helpful attitude. Bob and Horst and their two dates were still jabbering away as much as before, but Letitia made me feel now that they weren't there at all. She had set the three tumblers in front of me, and so I worked away at opening the pint bottle and then began pouring drinks for us three boys. I wasn't sure how much we ought to have right at first, and I decided I had got too much in two of the glasses. I tried to pour some back into the bottle, and made such a mess of it that I cursed under my breath. During this time, the jukebox was playing away, of course, but I do think I was half aware of some other noise somewhere, though it didn't really sink in. It didn't even sink in when Letitia put her hand on my sleeve, or when I looked up at her and saw her looking at me very much as she had outside the door a while before. The others still went on talking, and after a second Letitia drew away her hand. She began fidgeting with her gardenias, and she wasn't looking at me any more. For a moment, I wondered if she hadn't really expected us to have the drinks. But it wasn't that, and now I saw that she had tilted her head to one side to get a better view of something across the floor. I cut my eyes around and saw that the curtains to the Ram's booth had been pulled apart and that there he was, in plain view, with his girl and his star pitcher and outfielder and their two girls. I thought to myself, She's just now realized that they're all here together. Then I took another look over there, wondering why in hell they hadn't kept those curtains drawn, and I saw that something very unusual was up.

This all happened in an instant, of course—much quicker than I can tell it. The Ram was getting up very slowly from his seat and seemed to be giving some kind of orders to his pitcher and his outfielder. His own girl was still sitting at the table, and she stayed there, but the two other girls were climbing on top of the table. Pretty soon, they had opened the little high window above their booth—there was one above each of the booths—and you could see that the next thing they were going to do was to try to climb out that window. I guess they did climb out, and it wasn't long before people in some of the other booths were doing the same thing.

After a minute or so, there was nobody left on the dance floor, and all of a sudden someone unplugged the jukebox. Without the music, we could hear the knocking on the doors of the tourist cabins, and I began to notice lights flashing outside the little window above our booth. I knew now there was a raid on the cabins, but I didn't want to be the first to mention the existence of those cabins to the girls. And though I was sure enough of it, I just couldn't make myself admit that the raid would be happening to the tavern, too, in about three minutes.

I saw the Ram leave his booth, and he seemed to be starting in the direction of ours. Letitia looked relieved now, and actually leaned forward across the table as though she were trying to catch his eye. Both Bob Southard and I got up and started out to meet him, but he held out a stiff arm, motioning us back, and he went off toward the beer counter without ever looking at Letitia.

When Bob and I turned back toward our booth, Horst and the girls were standing up, saying nothing. But Letitia gave me a comforting smile and she opened her mouth to say something that she never did say. I can almost believe she had been about to tell me how shy her uncle was, and to ask if I noticed how he wouldn't look at her when she was dressed up this way.

But now the Ram was headed back toward us with Martha, and Martha had slipped on some brown loafers. There was loud banging now on the front and back doors of the tavern, but apparently she and her husband weren't set to open up yet; I guessed the old man hadn't finished hiding the whiskey. By now, anybody who was going to get away had to chance it through the windows. We could hear people dropping on the ground outside those little high windows, and hear some of them grunting when they landed.

As soon as the Ram and Martha got near us, he said, "We're going to put you out of sight somewhere. They won't want to take too many in. They just want their quota."

Martha wasn't ruffled a bit. I suppose she could see we were, though. She looked at the girls and said, "Chickabiddies, I wouldn't have had this happen for nothing in this world."

The Ram glanced back at his own booth, to make sure that his athletes were still there—and maybe his girl friend. They hadn't moved a muscle. They just sat there very tense, watching the Ram.

You would have thought they were in the bullpen waiting for a signal from him to come in and pitch. But they never got one. The Ram said to Martha, "Just anywhere you stick her and the rest of them is all right, but upstairs in your parlor would be mighty nice." From the way he said it, you would have thought he was speaking to one of the old lady teachers at Westside.

"You know I ain't about to hide nobody upstairs," she said firmly but politely. "Not even for you, honey baby."

"Then put them in the powder room yonder," he said.

"If they'll fit, that's fine," she said. She led the way and we followed.

It was over at the end of the counter—just a little closet, with "SHE" painted on the door and a toilet inside, and not even one of the little high windows. Martha made sure the key was in the lock, inside, and told us to turn off the light and lock ourselves in. We had to squeeze to get in, and one of us would have stood on the toilet except there wasn't a lid. While we were crowding in, the banging on the doors kept getting louder and began to sound more in earnest, and Martha's husband ambled up and stood watching us with his mouth hanging open. Martha looked around at him and burst out laughing. "He can't hear it thunder, bless his heart," she said. And the old fellow laughed, too.

The Ram said, "Get them inside, please, ma'am. They'll *have* to fit."

But Martha merely laughed at him. "You better git yourself *out*side if you expect to git," she said.

"I don't expect to git," he said.

"What'sa matter?"

He looked back over his shoulder at the room, where there were only eight or ten people left, most of them staggering around in the shadows, looking for a window that wasn't so high. "They'll have to have their quota of customers," he said, "or they might make a search."

"Well, it's your funeral you're planning, not mine," Martha said, and she winked at nobody in particular. Then her little green eyes suddenly darted another look at her husband. "O.K.," she said, "and I better take a quick gander to see he left out their quota of whiskey-take." With that, she slipped her feet out of her shoes again and padded along behind the counter and into the kitchen, with the old man following her. The banging on the doors couldn't get any louder, but they could have knocked the doors down by this time if they had really been as earnest about it as they made it sound. And we would long since have been locked inside the toilet except that while the Ram and Martha were having their final words, Letitia had put one foot over the sill again and was waiting to say something to her uncle.

"Uncle Louis," she began very solemnly. The Ram's face turned as red as a beet. Not just his face but the top of his head, too, where his sandy hair had got so thin. And, from the quick way he jerked his head around and fixed his eyes on the front door, it seemed as if he hadn't heard the banging over there till now. The truth was he *didn't* want to look at Letitia. But of course he had to, and it couldn't wait. So he sticks out that square chin, narrows his eyes under those blond eyebrows of his, and gives Letitia the hardest, impatientest look in the world. But it was nothing. The thing that was something was not the expression on *his* face but the one on hers. I won't ever forget it, though I certainly can't describe it. It made me think she was going to thank him from the bottom of her heart or else say how sorry she was about everything, or even ask him if something couldn't be done about hiding those poor athletes of his. I thought most likely it would be something about the athletes, since their being there with him was bound to make a scandal if it got into the newspapers. But in a way what she said was better than any of that. She said, "I don't have any money with me, Uncle Louis. Do you think I ought to have some money?"

"*Good* girl!" he practically shouted. And the guy actually smiled —the very best, most unselfish kind of smile. He reached down in his pocket and pulled out a couple of crumpled-up bills. I saw that one of them was a five. Letitia took the two bills and stuffed them in the pocket of her jacket. "Good girl," he said again, not quite so loud. He was smiling, and seemed nearly bursting with pride because Letitia had thought of something important that he had overlooked.

"It's going to be all right, isn't it?" she said then.

"Why, sure it is," he said. It was as though the whole raid was something that was happening just to them and concerned nobody else. And now she gave him that look again, and what it showed, and what it had shown before, was nothing on earth but the beautiful confidence she had in him—all because he was an uncle of hers. I suppose.

"Good night, darling," she said. She stepped back into the toilet with the rest of us, and it was every bit as exciting to see as if she had been stepping into a lifeboat and leaving him on a sinking ship. My guess, too, is that when the Ram watched her pulling the door to, he wished he *was* about to go down on a real ship, instead of about to be arrested and taken off with his girl friend and his two athletes to the jail in Thompsonville, the town where he grew up, and then to have it all in the Chatham papers and finally lose his job as civics teacher and baseball coach at Westside High. For that, of course, is the way it turned out.

Somebody locked the door and we stood in there in the dark, and then we heard Martha come back and put on her shoes and go to open the front door. But we couldn't hear everything, because at the first sound of the deputies' voices the two other girls began to shake all over and whimper like little sick animals. Bob and Horst managed to hush them up pretty much, however, and before long I heard a man's voice say, "Well, Lou, haven't *you* played hell?" The man sounded surprised and pleased. "This is too bad, Lou," he said. It was a mean, little-town voice, and you could hear the grudge in it against anybody who had got away even as far as Chatham and amounted to even as little as the Ram did. Or that was how I felt it sounded. "That wouldn't be some of your champs over there, would it, Lou?"

Letitia didn't make a sound. She just shivered once, as though a rabbit had run over her grave, or as though, in the awful stink and heat of that airless toilet, she was really cold. It was black as pitch in there, but I was pressed up against Letitia and I felt that shiver go over her. And then, right afterward, I could tell how easily she breathed, how relaxed she was. I wanted to put my arms around her, but I didn't dare—not in a place like that. I didn't dare even think about it twice.

Once our door was shut, we never heard the Ram's voice again. In a very few minutes, the sheriff's men seemed to have got

everybody out of the tavern except Martha and her husband. The
two girls had stopped all their whimpering and teeth-chattering
now, and we heard one of the men—the sheriff himself, I took it—
talking to Martha while the others were carrying away whatever
whiskey had been left out for them to find.

"Kind of sad about Lou Ramsey," he said, with a little snicker.

"I don't know him," Martha said, cutting things short. "I don't
know any of them by their last names. That's your business, not
mine."

The man didn't answer for a minute, but when he did, he
sounded as though she had hurt his feelings. "You ought to be fair,
Mrs. Mayberry," he said, "and not go blaming me for taking in
them that just stands around waiting for it." I thought I could tell
now that they were both sitting on stools at the counter.

"I don't mind, if he don't mind," she said. "It's his funeral, not
mine." And now it sounded as though it was the Ram she was mad
at, even more than the man she was talking to.

After a minute, he said, "I never been so hot as tonight."

"It's growing weather, honey baby," she said, and slapped her
hand down on the counter.

"There's not nobody else around?" he asked her suddenly.

"What are you asking me that for, honey baby?" she said. "You
got as many as your little jail will 'most hold."

We heard him laugh, and then neither of them said anything
more for a minute. The other men seemed to have made their last
trips to the kitchen and back now, and I heard the man with
Martha get down off his stool at the counter.

"Well'm," he said, "which one of you cares to make the ride this
time?"

"Whichever one you favors," she said.

"You know me," he said. "How's them kids?" For a second I
was absolutely sure he meant us. But then he said, "How you
manage to keep 'em quiet enough up there? You put cotton in their
ears?" Martha didn't answer him, and finally he said, "What'sa
matter with you tonight, Mrs. Mayberry?"

"You wouldn't kid me about something like my kids, would you,
Sheriff?" she asked in a hard voice.

"Like what?"

"Like saying nobody's never told you they was born as deaf as their daddy, yonder."

"You don't say, Mrs. Mayberry," he said, sounding out of breath. "Nobody ever told me that, I swear to God. Why, I've seen them two towheads playing around out there in the lot, but nobody said to me they was deaf."

"Can't hear it thunder," she said, and all at once she laughed. Then she let out a long moan, and next thing she was crying.

"Mrs. Mayberry," the sheriff said, "I am sure sorry."

"No," she said, and she stopped crying just as quick as she had begun. "When somebody says they're about it, I say no, it's a blessing. My kids ain't never going to hear the jukebox play all night, and no banging on doors, neither. It's a blessing, I say, all they won't hear, though it's a responsibility to me. But I won't be sitting up wondering where they are, the way you'll likely be doing with your young'uns, Sheriff. It's a blessing the good Lord sends to some people. It's wrong, but it's *something*. It's *something* I got which most people ain't. Till the day they die, they'll be just as true to me as the old man there."

Just then, one of the sheriff's men called him from outside to say they'd better get going, and I couldn't help being glad for the sheriff's sake. "Hell," he said to Martha, "it's too bad, but one of you has to come with me."

I was glad for us, too, because we were about to smother in there and be sick to our stomachs. The sheriff went on out then, taking one of the Mayberrys along. Everything was quiet after that, except for the motor of the sheriff's truck starting up. At first, we couldn't even tell for certain whether it was Martha or the old man who had gone with the sheriff. We waited a couple of minutes, and then, from the way the floor was creaking overhead, we knew it was Martha who had stayed. In the excitement, and after her outburst, she had forgotten all about us and had gone tiptoeing upstairs to see about her little deaf children.

All at once, Bob Southard said, "Let's get out of here," and he turned the key. We burst out onto the dance floor, and the first thing my eyes hit was Martha's two brown loafers on the pine floor at the end of the counter. They were the first thing I saw, and about the only thing for a minute or so, for we stood there nearly blinded by the bright lights, which the sheriff's men had turned on everywhere and which Martha hadn't bothered to turn out.

It was awful seeing everything lit up that way—not just the mess the place was in, which wasn't so bad considering that there had been a raid, but just seeing the place at all in that light. Those stuffed animal heads of the old man's stared at you from everywhere you could turn—dogs, horses, foxes, bulls, even bobcats and some bears, and one lone zebra—leaning out from the walls, so that their glass eyes were shining right down at you. We got out of there just as quick as we could.

The front door was standing wide open. We didn't stop to pull it to after us. We went outside and around the corner toward the parking lot, and when we showed ourselves there it was the signal for about twenty or thirty people to begin coming out of the woods, where they had been hiding. Some of them came running out, and others kind of wandered out, and at least one came crawling on his hands and knees. With the sky still that nasty gray, we couldn't have seen them at first except for the broad shafts of light that came from the open doorways of the cabins. It was a creepy sight, and the sounds these people made were creepy, too. As they came out of the woods, some of them were arguing, some of them laughing and kidding in a hateful way, and here and there a woman was crying and complaining, as though maybe she had got hurt jumping down from one of those high little windows.

We knew that as soon as they climbed into their old jalopies, there would be a terrific hassle to get out of the parking lot, and so we made a dash for Horst's sedan and all piled into it without caring who sat where or who was whose date. And we were out of that lot and tearing down the road before we even heard a single other motor get started.

All the way to Chatham, and then driving around to take everybody home, we just kept quiet except to talk every now and then about Martha and her old husband's children, about how unfair and terrible it seemed for them to be born deaf, and how unfair and terrible it was to bring up children in a place like that. Even then, it seemed to me unnatural for us not to be mentioning what had happened earlier. But I suppose we were thankful at least to have the other thing to talk about. I was sitting in the back seat, and

Letitia was sitting up in the front. I watched her shaking her head or nodding now and then when someone else was talking. There was certainly nothing special I could say to her from the back seat. But when we finally got to her house and I took her up to her door, I did make myself say, "We certainly owe your uncle a lot, Letitia."

"Yes, poor darling," she said. "But it's a good thing he was there, isn't it?" That's all she said. The marvelous thing, I thought, was that she didn't seem to hold anything against me.

I was away from Chatham most of that summer. The first of July, I went down to New Orleans with a friend of mine named Bickford Harris, and he and I got jobs on a freight boat and worked our way over to England and back. We got back on the fourteenth of September, which was only about a week before I had to leave for college. I had seen Letitia at several other parties before we went off to New Orleans, and had called her on the telephone to say goodbye. I sent her a postcard from New Orleans and I sent her three postcards from England. I didn't write her a letter for the same reason that I only telephoned her, instead of asking her for a date or going by to see her, before we left. I didn't want her to think I was trying to make something out of our happening to be put together that night, and didn't want her to think it meant anything special to me. But when we got back in September, I did ask her for a date, and she gave it to me.

And, of course, Letitia hadn't changed a bit—or only a very little bit. I could tell she hadn't, even when I talked with her on the telephone to make the date. She said she loved my postcards, but that's all she said about them, and it was plain they hadn't made any real impression on her. She told me that she was going to be leaving within a couple of weeks, to go to a finishing school in Washington, D.C., and the next summer she was going to Europe herself, before making her debut in the fall. She talked to me about all these plans on the telephone, and I knew that when a girl in Chatham begins talking about her plans to make her debut, she already has her mind on meeting older guys. That's the "very little bit" I mean she had changed. But she did give me the date—on a Monday night, it was. I was awfully glad about it, yet the minute I walked into her house, I began wishing I had left well enough alone.

For right off the bat I heard her uncle's voice. He was back in the dining room, where they were all still sitting around the table. And I had to go in there and tell them how I'd liked working on a freight boat and how I'd liked England. I also had to shake hands all around, even with the Ram, who was already standing up when I came in, speaking rather crossly to Letitia's three little brothers and hurrying them to get through with their dinner. When I shook his hand, I could tell from the indifferent way he looked at me that he didn't know he had ever seen me before. And suddenly I said to myself, "Why, all he knows about me is that I'm not a Ramsey and I'm not a baseball player."

Most of the time I was in the room, he was still hurrying Letitia's little brothers, under his breath, to finish their dinner. Everyone else had finished, and he was waiting to take her brothers somewhere afterward. I knew what he had been doing since June, when he found out he wouldn't be teaching at the high school in the fall. He had landed a soft daytime job with one of the lumber companies in Chatham, which had hired him so it would have him to manage the company's baseball team. As we were getting out through the living room, I heard his voice getting louder and very cross again with the boys, the way it had sounded when I came in. Letitia heard it, too, and only laughed to herself. Outside, when we were walking across the lawn toward my car, she explained that her uncle was taking her little brothers to a night baseball game, in the commercial league, and that there was nothing in the world they loved better.

Letitia and I had a nice time that night, I suppose. It was just like other dates we'd had. We ran into some people at the movie, and we all went for a snack somewhere afterward. The thing is I don't pretend that I ever did get to know Letitia Ramsey awfully well. As I have said, it was only by chance that she and I were put together for Nancy O'Connor's dance that year. We simply ran with the same crowd, and in our crowd the boys all knew that they would be going to college (or hoped so), and the girls that they would be going off to finishing school, up East or in Virginia, for a year or two and then be making their debuts, and so we tended not to get too serious about each other. It wasn't a good idea, that's all, because it could break up your plans and your family's. The most that usually happened was some terrific crushes and, naturally, some pretty heavy necking that went along with the crushes. But there was never even anything like that between Letitia and me. I never felt that I knew her half as well as I did several of her friends that I had even fewer dates with.

Still, I do know certain things from that evening at Aunt Martha's Tavern. I know how Letitia looked at an uncle who never had —and never has yet—amounted to anything. And I know now that while I watched her looking at him, I was really wishing that I knew how to make a girl like her look at me that trusting way, instead of the way she had been looking at me earlier. It almost made me wish that I was one of the big, common fellows at Westside High who slipped off and got married to one of the public-school girls in their class and then told the teachers and the principal about it, like a big joke, after they'd got their diplomas on graduation night. But the point is I *didn't* know how to make a girl like her look at me that way. And the question is why *didn't* I know how?

Usually, I tell myself that I didn't because I was such a worrier and that I wouldn't have been such a worrier if there hadn't been a Depression, or if I had known a war was going to come along and solve everything. But I'm not sure. Once, during the war, I told this to a guy who didn't come from the kind of people that I do. He only laughed at me and said he wanted to hear more about those other times we were having that year. I pointed out that those other good times weren't the point and that a girl like Letitia Ramsey was something else again. "Yeah," he said, looking rather unfriendly. "That's how all you guys like to talk."

But the worst part, really, is what it's like when you see someone like Letitia nowadays. She may be married to a guy whose family money is in downtown real estate and who has never had a doubt in his life, or maybe to some guy working on commission and drinking himself to death. It doesn't matter which. If it is a girl like Letitia who's married to him, he's part of her family now, and all men outside her family are jokes to her. And she and this fellow will have three or four half-grown children, whom nobody can believe she is really the mother of, since she looks so young. Well, the worst part is when you are back home visiting and meet her at a dinner party, and she tells you before the whole table how she was once on the verge of being head over heels in love with you and you wouldn't give her a tumble. It's always said as a big joke, of course, and everyone laughs. But she goes on and on about it, as though it was really something that had been worrying her. And the more everybody laughs, the more she makes of it and strings it out. And what it shows, more than any number of half-grown children could ever do, is how old she is getting to be. She says that you always seemed to have your mind on other things and that she doesn't know yet whether it was higher things or lower things. Everyone keeps on laughing until, finally, she pretends to look very serious and says that it is all right for them to laugh but that it wasn't funny at the time. Her kidding, of course, is a big success, and nobody really minds it. But all I ever want to say—and don't ever say—is that as far as I'm concerned, it isn't one bit funnier now than it was then.

Spring Is Now

by Joan Williams

Sandra heard first in Miss Loma's store about the Negroes. She was buying cornstarch for her mother when Mr. Mal Walker rushed in, leaving his car at the gas pump, without filling it, to tell the news. His hair plastered to his forehead, he was as breathless and hot as if he had been running. "The school bus was loaded and the driver passed up some niggers in De Soto," he said. "They threw rocks at the bus and a brick that broke the driver's arm." That was all he knew about that. "But," he said, pausing until everyone in the store was paying attention. "There's some registered for your high school in Indian Hill."

At that moment Sandra found the cornstarch. The thought of going to school with Negroes leapt at her as confusedly as the box's yellow-and-blue design. Coming slowly around the bread rack, she saw Mal Walker, rapidly swallowing a Dr Pepper he had taken from the cold-drink case. She put the cornstarch on the counter. Miss Loma fitted a sack over the box and said, "Is that all?"

Sandra nodded and signed the credit pad Miss Loma shoved along the counter. In Miss Loma's pierced ears, small gold hoops shook as, turning back to Mal Walker, she said, "How many?"

"Three I heard." Almost smiling, he looked around and announced—as if the store were full of people, though there was only an apologetic-looking country woman, with a dime, waiting for the party line to clear—"If your kids haven't eat with niggers yet, they will have by Friday. I thank the Lord I live in Indian Hill. Mine will walk home to lunch. When it comes to eating with them, I draw the line."

"Sandra, you want something else?" Miss Loma said.

"No ma'am." Sandra went out and slowly up the hill toward her house opposite, thinking how many times she had eaten with Minnie, who worked for her mother, and how often her mother had eaten in the kitchen, while Minnie ironed. Even Grandmomma had said she would sit down with Minnie, Minnie was like one of the family, though Sandra could not remember that her grandmother ever had. For one reason, she was always in the living room looking at television. There now, she was shelling butter beans and Sandra passed behind her chair, saying nothing, because Grandmomma was hard of hearing. In the kitchen, Sandra put down the cornstarch and said, "Mother, Mister Mal Walker says there's Negroes coming to our high school."

"Are you sure?" Her mother, Flo, was frying chicken and stood suddenly motionless, a long-handled fork outstretched over the skillet full of popping meat and grease. She and Sandra had similar pale faces and placid gray-green eyes, which they widened now, in worry. "I guess we knew it was coming," Flo said.

"Three, he thinks."

In bifocals, Grandmomma's eyes looked enormous. She stood in the doorway saying, "Three what?" Having seen Flo motionless, she sensed something had happened and hearing what, she threw her hands to her throat and said, "Oh, you don't mean to tell me." With the fork, Flo stuck chicken pieces, lifting them onto paper toweling. "Now, Momma," she said, "we knew it was coming." Then Grandmomma, resigned to one more thing she had not expected to live to see, let her hands fall to her sides. "I sure do hate to hear it," she said. "Are they girls and boys?"

"I don't know," Sandra said.

"I just hope to goodness it's girls," Grandmomma said, looking at Flo, who said again, "Now, Momma."

At sundown, when her father came from the fields, Sandra was watching television with Grandmomma. The pickup stopped, a door slammed, but the motor continued to run. From the window she saw her father, a sturdy, graying man; he was talking to Willson, a field hand, who backed the truck from the drive as her father came inside. "Daddy," she said, "there's Negroes going to our school."

He stood a moment looking tired from more than work. Then he said, "I guess it had to happen." He frowned and his eyebrows drew together across his forehead. "The schools that don't take them don't get government money. I knew you'd be with them at the university. But I'm sorry you had to start a year earlier."

Grandmomma, looking up from her program, said, "I just hope they're girls."

"Oh, Grandmomma," Sandra said with irritation and followed her father across the hall. "Why'd Willson take the truck, Daddy?"

Having bent over the bathroom basin to wash, he lifted his head. "That boy of his sick in Memphis can come home tonight. I loaned him the truck to go get him," he said, and his splashed face seemed weighted by the drops of water falling away.

"The one that's had all that trouble with his leg swelling?" Flo said. She brought the platter of chicken to the table.

"He's on crutches but will be all right," the father said.

"I declare, that boy's had a time," Grandmomma said, joining them at the table. "When Willson brings the truck, give him some of my grape jelly to carry to the boy."

They bent their heads and Sandra's father said his usual long blessing. Afterward they looked at one another across the centerpiece of zinnias, as if words were left unsaid. But no one said anything and they began to eat. Then the father said, "Guess what happened? Willson and some of his friends asked if I'd run for road supervisor."

"Why, Tate," Flo said. "What'd you say?"

"I said, 'When would I find the time?'" he said.

"It shows the way they're thinking," Flo said.

"How?" Sandra said.

"They know they can't run one of them yet, but they want a man elected they choose," she said. "Still, Tate, it's a compliment."

"I guess it is," he said.

"The time's just going to come," Grandmomma said.

"Of course, it is," he said.

At six-fifteen the next morning, Sandra from her bed heard a repeated knock rattling the side door. There were the smells of coffee and sausage, and Flo, summoned, pushed her chair from the table to answer the door. Air-conditioning so early made the house too cold and Sandra, reaching for her thin blanket, kept her eyes closed.

"Morning, how're you?" It was Johnson, the Negro who cleaned the Methodist church. He had come to get his pay from Flo, the church's treasurer.

"Pretty good, Johnson, how're you?" Flo said.

"Good but not pretty." He and Flo laughed, then were quiet while she wrote the check. Sandra heard him walk off down the gravel drive and it seemed a long time before she fell back to sleep. Then Flo shook her, saying, "Louise wants to drive the car pool today. You have to be at school at ten to register. Hurry, it's after nine."

"Why'd Johnson come so early?" she said.

"Breakfast was the only time he knew he could catch me home," Flo said.

Drinking orange juice, Sandra stood by the refrigerator and Grandmomma called from the living room, "Are you going to school all winter with your hair streaming down your back like that? I wish you'd get it cut today."

"I don't want it cut," Sandra said.

"Well, I wish you'd wear it pretty like this girl on television then. Look, with it held back behind a band like that."

Sandra came into the living room to look. "Her hair's in a pageboy; it's shorter than mine," she said.

"At least comb it," her mother called from the kitchen.

"I combed it!" Sandra said.

"Well you need to comb it again," her mother said. "And eat something."

"I'm not hungry in the mornings," Sandra said and went out into the heat and down the steep driveway to wait for her friend Louise. There was no high school in their town and they went twenty miles away to a larger place. "Cold," Sandra said, getting in Louise's car.

"Turn that valve and the air conditioner won't blow straight on you," Louise said. She pushed back hair that fell, like a mane, over her glasses. "You heard?"

"About the Negroes?"

"Yes. I heard there were thirteen."

"Thirteen! I heard three."

Louise laughed. "Maybe there's none and everybody's excited about nothing."

There had been a drought all summer in northwest Mississippi. They rode looking out at cotton fields nowhere near bloom, corn limp and brown, and soybeans stunted, flat to the ground. Between the fields were stretches of crumbly dirt, enormous and empty, where crops failed from the drought had been plowed under. Nearby, a pickup raced along a gravel road and as far as they could see, dust trailed it, one cloud rising above the flatland. Once, workmen along the road turned to them faces yellowed by dust, with dark holes for eyes, and Sandra thought of the worry that had been on her father's face all summer, as farmers waited for rain. And all summer, wherever they went, her mother had said, "You don't remember what it was like before everybody had air-conditioned cars. All this dust blew in the windows. Whew! I don't know how we stood it."

And, not remembering she had said it before, Grandmomma would say, "You don't remember either what it was like trying to sleep. Sometimes we'd move our mattresses out into the yard and sleep under the trees. We'd wring out towels and put them on the bed wet to cool the sheets." That she had lived then, though she did not remember it, seemed strange to Sandra.

At school, she found out only that some Negroes had already registered. None were there and the teachers would answer no other questions. Standing in long lines all morning, Sandra found she watched for the Negroes anyway. Other students said they had done the same. She thought the Negroes had been paid more attention by being absent than if they had been present. On the way home, Louise said, "If it weren't such a mystery, I don't think I'd think much about them. If there's a few, I just feel I'm not going to bother them and they're not going to bother me, if they're not smart-alecky."

"I know," Sandra said. "What's the difference, three or thirteen, with the rest of us white?" They stopped on the highway at the Mug'n Cone for hot dogs and root beer. Nearing home, Sandra began to dread questions she would be asked, particularly since she knew little more than when she left. At Miss Loma's, she got out to buy shampoo. The old men were gathered on the store porch playing dominoes, and she said only, "Afternoon," though her mother always said they would be glad for conversation. She thought of when her grandfather had been among them and entered the store.

Miss Loma had already heard the news from the Indian Hill school. She and a Memphis salesman were talking about a family nearby, in the Delta, who passed as white, though people steered clear of them, believing they had Negro blood. "I'll tell you how you can always tell a Negro," the salesman said. "By the blue moons on their nails. They can't hide those."

"I've heard," Miss Loma said, her earrings shaking, "they have black streaks at the ends of their spinal cords. Now, that's what men who've been with them in the army say. Of course, I don't know if it's true. I doubt it." She and the salesman could not decide whether she ought to stock up on straight-lined or dotted-lined primary tablets. With a practical finger, Miss Loma twirled the wire school-supply rack. The salesman pushed back a sporty straw hat with a fishing-fly ornament and said, "Wait till school starts and see what the teacher wants. One thing I hate to see is, somebody stuck with primary tablets they can't sell."

An amber container decided Sandra on a shampoo. She brought the bottle to the counter. "I've heard," she said, "they wear makeup on TV that'll make them look whiter."

"Of course they do," Miss Loma said.

Also, Sandra had heard that Negroes never kissed one another. They made love without preliminaries, like animals, or did nothing. But she was afraid to offer that information. Sometimes, even her mother and father did not seem to know she knew people made love.

Miss Loma said, "Honey, take that shampoo on home as a present. Happy birthday."

"How'd you know it was my birthday?"

"A bird told me."

"Grandmomma," Sandra said.

"You heard about the little nigger baby up in Memphis that's two parts animal?" the salesman said.

"No!" Miss Loma said.

"It's got a little dear face and bare feet," the salesman said, and when Sandra went out, he and Miss Loma were laughing.

In his dusty, green pickup, Sandra's father drew up to the gas pump. Willson's wife, along with another Negro woman, stepped from the truck's cab and went into a grocery across the road. "I see you got your nigger women with you today, Tate," said one of the old men playing dominoes.

Lifting the hose, Sandra's father stood putting in gas, laughing. "Yeah, I carried them with me today," he said. "Sandra, I got to go on back to the field. There's a dressed chicken on the front seat Ida sent. Take it on to your momma." Sandra opened the truck's door, thinking how many people made remarks about her father letting Negroes ride up front with him. He always answered that if somebody asked him for a ride, he gave it to them; why should they sit out in the open truck bed covered with dust and hit by gravel? She heard him call into the store, "Four-ninety for gas, Loma," and holding the chicken, Sandra waved as he drove off.

Ida's husband had been a field hand for Sandra's father and now was too old to work. Sandra's father let the old couple stay on, rent free, in the cabin on his land. Ida raised chickens and brought one to Flo whenever she killed them. When Flo went to the bakery in Indian Hill, she brought Ida something sweet. Sandra came into the kitchen now and put the chicken on the sink. "That's a nice plump one," Flo said. "If we hadn't had chicken last night, I'd put it on to cook. I hope your daddy let Ida know how much we appreciate it."

"He says he always thanks her," Sandra said.

"But I don't know whether he thanks her enough," her mother said.

The kitchen smelled of cake baking and Sandra pretended not to notice. "Aren't you going to ask about the Negroes at school?" she said.

"Honey, I couldn't wait for you to come wandering in. I called around till I found out."

"I don't see why they got to register at a special time. Why couldn't they register when we did?" Sandra said.

"I don't understand it myself," Flo said.

"I don't understand why they have to be there at all,"

Grandmomma said, on her way to the bathroom during a commercial. "I declare, I don't."

"Oh Grandmomma," Sandra said.

"I guess they didn't want to take chances on trouble during registration," Flo said. "If the Negroes are just there when school starts, no one can say anything."

"There's plenty of things folks could say if they just would," Grandmomma called.

"I thought she was hard of hearing," Sandra said.

"Not all of the time," Flo said. When Grandmomma came back through the kitchen, Flo said, "We haven't had anything to say about what's happened so far. Everything else has just been shoved down our throats, Mother. I don't know why you think we'd have a chance to say anything now." Sandra, going out and down the hall, wondered why her mother bothered trying to explain to Grandmomma. "What are you going to do?" Flo called.

"Wash my hair," Sandra said.

"Well, for heaven's sake, roll it up as tight as you can and try to keep it curled."

"I wish you'd put it behind a band like that girl on television," Grandmomma called, and Sandra closed the bathroom door.

The candles flickered, then burned, as Flo hesitated in the doorway, smiling, before bringing the decorated cake in to supper. The family sang "Happy Birthday" to Sandra. Her father rolled in a portable television atop brass legs and she jumped up with a squeal. Her hair, waved and tied with a ribbon to please them, loosened and fell toward her shoulders. Now she could see programs without arguing with Grandmomma.

Flo's face was in wrinkles, anxious, as though she feared Ida had not been thanked enough for a chicken, and Sandra knew she was to like her grandmomma's present more than ordinarily. On pink tissue paper, in a tiny box, lay a heavy gold pin twisted like rope into a circle. "Why, Grandmomma!" Sandra said in surprise. Her exclamation was taken for admiration and everyone looked pleased. When she had gone into Grandmomma's room as a small child, to poke among her things, she had been shown the pin. Grandmomma's only heirloom, it had been her own mother's.

"I've been afraid I wouldn't live till you were sixteen," Grandmomma said. "But I wanted to give you the pin when you were old enough to appreciate it."

"She never would give it even to me," Flo said.

"No, it was to be for my first grandchild," Grandmomma said. "I decided that when Momma died and left it to me. It was all in the world she had to leave and it's all I've got. But I want you to enjoy it now, instead of when I'm gone."

Had she made enough fuss over the pin? Sandra asked later. Flo said she had, but to thank her grandmother occasionally again. "Mother, it's not really the kind of pin anyone wears," Sandra said. The pin hung limply, lopsided, on her striped turtleneck jersey.

Flo said, "It is kind of heavy and antique. Maybe you'll like it when you're grown. Wear it a few times anyway."

The morning that school started, Sandra hung the pin on her coat lapel and forgot it. She walked into her class and there sat a Negro boy. His simply sitting there was disappointing; she felt like a child who had waited so long for Christmas that when it came, it had to be a letdown. He was to be the only Negro in school. The others had changed their minds, the students heard. But by then everyone had heard so many rumors, no one knew what to believe. The Negro was tall and light-skinned. Louise said the officials always tried to send light-skinned ones first. He was noticeably quiet and the girls, at lunch, found he had spoken in none of his classes. Everyone wondered if he was smart enough to be in the school. From her table Sandra saw him eating by a window with several other boys. Still, he seemed alone and she felt sorry for him.

In the car pool with her and Louise were two boys, Don and Mark. Don, the younger, was an athlete. Going home that afternoon, he said the Negro was not the type for football but was so tall, maybe he would be good at basketball. Sandra thought how little she knew about the Negro and how many questions she would be asked. He had worn a blue shirt, she remembered, and he was thin. Certainly, he was clean. Grandmomma would ask that. She did not even know the Negro's name until Don said, "He lives off this road."

"Who?" she said.

"The colored boy, Jack Lawrence," he said.

"We could ask him to be in the car pool," Louise said, laughing.

Mark, sandy-haired and serious, said, "You all better watch your talk. I had my interview at the university this summer and ate lunch in the cafeteria. There were lots of Negroes and all kinds of people. Indians. Not with feathers, from India. Exchange students."

Dust drifted like clouds over fields, and kudzu vine, taking over the countryside, filling ditches and climbing trees, was yellowed by it. Young pines, set out along the road banks, shone beneath a sun that was strong, even going down. Sandra looked out at tiny pink flowers just appearing on the cotton and tried to imagine going as far away, to a place as strange, as India. That Indians had come all the way to Mississippi to school made her think about people's lives in a way she never had. She entered the house saying, before Grandmomma could ask questions, "Grandmomma, you know they got Indians from India going to Ole Miss?"

Grandmomma looked up through the lower half of her glasses. "You don't mean to tell me," she said, and it took away some of her curiosity about the Negro too. At supper, Sandra gave all the information she could. The Negro boy was clean, looked nice, and his name was Jack Lawrence. All the information she could give in the next month was that he went his way and she went hers. Finally even Grandmomma stopped asking questions about him. He and Sandra had no reason to speak until one morning, she was working the combination to her locker when a voice, quite deep, said, "Sandra, you left this under your desk."

Her dark hair fell forward. In the moment that she pushed it back, something in the voice's deep tone made her think unaccountably how soft her own hair felt. Jack Lawrence held out the book she had forgotten, his face expressionless. It would have been much more natural for him to smile. She saw for the first time how carefully impersonal he was. Other students had mentioned that he never spoke, even to teachers, unless spoken to first. She smiled and said, "Lord, math. I'm bad enough without losing the book too. Thanks."

"Okay. I just happened to notice you left it." He started down the hall and Sandra joined him, as she would have anyone going the way she was. She held her books against her, as if hugging herself in anticipation, but of what, she did not know. She had a curiously excited feeling to be walking beside anyone so tall. No, she thought, not anyone, a boy. They talked about the afternoon's football game, then Jack Lawrence continued down the hall and Sandra turned into her class. There was certainly nothing to that, she thought. But Louise, leaning from her desk, whispered, "What were you talking *about?*"

"Football," Sandra said, shrugging. She thought of all the Negroes she had talked to in her life, of those she talked to every day, and wondered why it was strange to talk to Jack Lawrence. Her mother complained that at every meal, Sandra's father had to leave the table, answer the door, and talk to some Negro who worked for him. They would stand together a long time, like any two men, her father propping his foot on the truck's bumper, smoking and talking. Now she wondered what they talked about.

Jack Lawrence's eyes, when she looked into them, had been brown. Were the eyes of all Negroes? From now on, she would notice. On her way to the stadium that afternoon, she wondered if her gaiety was over the football game or the possibility of seeing— not the Negro, she thought, but Jack Lawrence? Louise went ahead of her up the steps and turned into the bleachers. "I have to sit higher," Sandra said, "or I can't see," adding, "Lon's up there." Louise was crazy about Lon, the basketball coach's son, and rising obediently, she followed Sandra to a seat below him. Lon was sitting with Jack Lawrence. Looking up, Sandra smiled but Jack Lawrence turned his eyes to the game and his lips made no movement at all. When she stood to cheer, to buy a Coke, popcorn, a hot dog, Sandra wondered if he watched her. After the game, he and Lon leapt from the bleachers and went out a back way. That night, she slept with a sense of disappointment.

At school, she always nodded and spoke to him and he spoke back: but they did not walk together again. Most often, he was alone. Even to football games, he did not bring a friend. There was a Thanksgiving dance in the gym, festooned with balloons and crepe paper, but he did not come. On Wednesday before the holiday, driving the car pool, Sandra had seen Jack Lawrence walking along a stretch of country road, hunched into his coat. The motor throbbed loudly in the cold country stillness as she stopped the car and said, "You want a ride?"

He stood, looking as if he did not want any favors, but with eyes almost sore-looking from the cold, then climbed into the back seat with Don and Mark. The countryside's stillness came again as Sandra stopped at the side road he mentioned. With coat collar turned up, untangling long legs, he got out. She was aware of the way her hair hung, of her grandmother's pin too old and heavy for her coat, of the skirt that did not cover her knees, which Grandmomma said was indecent. And she was aware of him, standing in the road against the melancholy winter sunset, looking down to say, "Thank you."

"You're welcome," she said, looking up.

That night she asked her father whether she should have given Jack Lawrence a ride. Her father said she was not to give a ride to Negroes when she was alone. "Not even to women?" she said.

"Oh well, to women," he said.

"Not even to Willson?" she said.

Her father seemed to look inward to himself a long time, then he answered, "No, not even to Willson."

Thanksgiving gave Sandra an excuse to start a conversation. She saw Jack Lawrence in the hall the first day afterward and said, "Did you have a nice holiday?"

"Yes," he said. "Did you?"

Sandra mentioned, briefly, things she had done. "Listen," she said. "We go your way every day, if you'd like a ride."

"Thanks," he said, "but most of the time I have one." He turned to his locker and put away his books and Sandra, going on down the hall, had the strangest feeling that he knew something she did not. She remained friendly, smiling when she saw him, though he made no attempt to talk. He only nodded and smiled when they met and she thought he seemed hesitant about doing that. She asked the boys in the car pool questions about him. Why hadn't he gone out for basketball, how were his grades, what did he talk about at lunch, did anybody know exactly where he lived, besides down that side road?—until one day, Louise said, "Sandra, you talk about that Negro so much, I think you like him."

"Yes, I like him. I mean, I don't dislike him, do you? What reason would we have."

"No, I don't dislike him," Louise said. "He's not at all smart-alecky."

In winter when they came home from school, it was dark. Flo said, "If you didn't have those boys in your car pool, I'd drive you girls back and forth myself. I don't know what Don and Mark could do if anything happened, but I feel better they're there." Sandra's parents, everyone, lived in fear of something happening. South of them, in the Delta, there was demonstrating, and Negroes tried to integrate restaurants and movies in several larger towns. Friends of Sandra's mother began carrying tear gas and pistols in their pocketbooks. Repeatedly, at the dinner table, in Miss Loma's, Sandra heard grown-ups say, "It's going to get worse before it gets any better. We won't see the end of this in our lifetime." Grandmomma always added, "I just hate to think what Sandra and her children will live to see."

One day after Christmas vacation, those in the car pool again saw Jack Lawrence walking along the road. "Should we stop?" Louise said. She was driving, with Don beside her.

"Of course. Would you just drive past him?" Sandra said. She was sitting in the back seat with Mark, and when Jack Lawrence climbed into the car, she was sitting between them. They spoke of the cold, of the snow that had fallen after Christmas, the deepest they could ever remember, and of how you came across patches of it, still, in unexpected places. Side roads were full of frozen ruts. Jack Lawrence said he hated to think of the mud when a thaw came. There could be one at any time. That was the way their weather was. In the midst of winter, you could suddenly have a stretch of bright, warm, almost spring days. There was a silence and Jack Lawrence, looking down at Sandra, said, "Did you lose that pin you always wear?"

"Oh Lord," Sandra said, her hand going quickly, flat, against her lapel.

"Sandra, your Grandmomma's pin!" Louise said, looking into the rearview mirror.

"Maybe it fell off in the car," Mark said. The three in back put their hands down the cracks around the seat. Sandra felt in her pocket, shook out her skirt. They held their feet up and looked under them. Don, turning, said, "Look up under the front seat."

Bending forward at the same instant, Sandra and Jack Lawrence knocked their heads together sharply. "Ow!" Mark cried out for them, while tears came to Sandra's eyes. They clutched their heads. Their faces were close, and though Sandra saw yellow, dancing dots, she thought, Of course Negroes kiss each other when they make love. She and Jack Lawrence fell back against the seat laughing, and seemed to laugh for miles, until she clutched her stomach in pain.

"Didn't it hurt? How can you laugh so?" Louise said.

"I got a hard head," Jack Lawrence said.

When he stood again in the road thanking them, his eyes, glancing into the car, held no message for Sandra. Tomorrow, he said silently, by ignoring her, they would smile and nod. That they had been for a time two people laughing together was enough. As they rode on, Sandra held tightly the pin he had found, remembering how she had looked at it one moment lying in his dark hand, with the lighter palm, and the next moment, she had touched the hand lightly, taking the pin. Opening her purse, she dropped the pin inside.

"Is the clasp broken?" Mark said.

"No, I guess I didn't have it fastened good," she said.

"Aren't you going to wear it anymore?" Louise said, looking back.

"No," she said.

"What will your grandmomma say?" Louise said.

"Nothing I can worry about," Sandra said.

The Zenner Trophy
by Gore Vidal

"I understand that Sawyer left early this morning, before anyone had a chance to talk with him, before the faculty met." The Principal was appropriately grave.

"That's correct, sir," said Mr Beckman. "And according to his adviser he left most of his clothes behind," he added, as though by a very close examination of all detail he might somehow avoid the crisis. He had been at the School less than a year and although he'd faced any number of trying situations at other schools, he was by no means prepared to handle a disaster as vast as this one.

Fortunately, the Principal was a rock. In twenty years he had become the School or rather the School had been reshaped in his own image, to the delight of everyone except the faculty old guard. When he spoke he was able to do so with total knowledge and total authority; not only could he quote the entire constitution of this century-old academy but he could also make cogent analogies between today and yesterday, this century and the last. Rather like an Arab sage, thought Mr Beckman, as the Principal made a precise and intelligent comparison between the present crisis and an earlier one for, like the Arab philosophers, he assembled the main facts and then produced . . . from memory not from reason . . . a relevant antique text which gave him his solution, shaped by precedent and the cumulative wisdom of an old institution.

Such an efficient man, thought Mr Beckman, nodding intelligently, not listening, too much absorbed by his sincere appreciation of this splendid human being who had saved him the year before from Saint Timothy's where he'd been an underpaid history instructor with nothing to look forward to but a future of dim discomfort, of dining hall dinners (cold tuna fish, brown lettuce, potato chips and canned peas) made edible only by the frequent, the

ritualistic use of a richly carved pepper mill given him by the
parents of a sub-normal pupil he had befriended. But the previous
spring his luck had changed; he was offered a summer job tutoring
a boy at Oyster Bay. He had accepted the assignment, enjoyed the
summer and the company of the boy's uncle, who, by a fortunate
coincidence, was the Principal himself. . . . And here I am,
thought Mr Beckman complacently, crossing his legs and leaning
forward, tuning in again, as it were, on his chief.

"And so, Mr Beckman, you can see that this distasteful business
is not by any means unfamiliar. We have faced it squarely in the
past and no doubt we will have to face it again in the future, as
squarely, alas." He paused, allowing that classical epithet of sorrow, that stylized expression of grief to represent his attitude toward not only this particular instance of viciousness but toward all
moral lapses, in school and out.

"I see what you mean, sir. Even at Saint Timothy's there was a
similar case . . ."

"I know, Mr Beckman, I know," interrupted the Principal. "It is
the specter of all schools and the ruin of some; but not ours, Mr
Beckman, not ours." The Principal smiled proudly up at the portrait of himself over the mock-fireplace. It was a good portrait,
painted in the Sargent manner, idealized but recognizable. The
Principal gazed at his own portrait, as though drawing strength
from this official version of himself, strength from the confident
knowledge that this work would hang for generations in the chapel
of the School, a decorative symbol of the reign of the thirteenth
Principal, a likeness which would impress everyone with the distinguished arrangement of the features: a large, strong nose, a firm,
lipless mouth, white brows and a full head of hair. In every respect
it was the face of a man of power (that the body was small and fat
made no difference for it was hidden by academic robes). Then,
sustained by this vision of his own posterity, the Principal returned
to his vexing problem, or, as it soon developed, Mr Beckman's
vexing problem.

"You have seen, sir, the speed with which the School has acted."
Mr Beckman nodded, wondering if anyone since Dr Johnson had
so achieved the knack of making the ordinarily respectful "sir"
sound a cozy diminutive. "We have always moved quickly in these

matters. The . . . revelation was made last night. By ten o'clock this morning the faculty, a majority of the faculty at least, had met and acted. That's quick action. Even *you* must admit that."

Mr Beckman admitted that it was very quick indeed: the "even you" was the Principal's little joke for he liked to pretend that Mr Beckman was a critical and supercilious outsider, a spy from the church academies, eager to find fault with this sternly Protestant school.

"Now Sawyer, it seems, has preferred to leave before his fate was made known to him. A cowardly flight but on the whole sensible for there could have been no doubt in his mind as to what our decision would be: by leaving, he has saved us a certain embarrassment. I've written his parents already." He paused as though expecting some word of approbation from Mr Beckman; none came for Mr Beckman was now studying the portrait and wondering to himself what future generations would say when they saw it in the chapel: "Who was that ape?" The irreverent thought amused him and he faced the original of the painting with a smile which the Principal interpreted as applause. Nodding abruptly as though both to acknowledge and silence a cheering crowd, the Principal continued. "I believe I have presented the case quite dispassionately. I feel that the facts speak for themselves, as facts will, and that it would be gratuitous of me to make further comments. The responsibility is no longer mine but theirs. *Sawyer is no longer one of us.* Flynn, however, presents a more difficult problem."

"You mean because he *hasn't* left?"

The Principal shook his head and he looked, thought Mr Beckman, somewhat anxious. "No, although I must say it might have helped matters if he'd gone when the other did. But that's not the trouble."

"The Trophy?"

"Exactly. The Carl F. Zenner Award for clean sportsmanship, our highest honor. He was, if you remember, an extremely popular choice."

"I certainly do remember. The boys cheered him for hours in chapel. I thought they'd never stop."

The Principal nodded glumly. "Fortunately, the trophy itself is not presented until Commencement Day; we have at least a week in which to consider what's to be done. Flynn of course can't have it now. I must say I wish we hadn't made the announcement so far in advance . . . but it's done and that's that and we'll have to make the best of it. I favor rewarding it but the Athletics Director tells me Flynn was the only possible choice . . . our finest athlete." He paused. "Do you remember the day he pitched against Exeter? Marvelous! Quite a good-looking boy, too. But I'm afraid I never knew him well." The Principal was, in every way, the modern head of a great school: aloof, majestic, concerned only with the more abstract theories of education as well as the unrelenting, Grail-like quest for endowments. He had met very few of his youthful charges. In any case, after thirty years, one boy tends to be very like another.

"Yes, he was a fine athlete," agreed Mr Beckman and he wondered how he might extricate his chief from this dilemma. The problem was partly his since the boy had been his advisee. Each boy had an official adviser among the faculty. The duties of these advisers, however, were somewhat ill-defined; they were generally thought to be responsible for the academic careers of their advisees but actually they were policemen, commissioned to keep order in the dormitories. The boy, Flynn, had been one of Mr Beckman's charges and until now he had been his dormitory's chief ornament; he was the best athlete the school had produced in over a decade; so celebrated was he, in fact, that Mr Beckman had been somewhat shy with him and consequently had not come to know him well.

"We must keep this from the students," said the Principal, suddenly, looking at Mr Beckman as though he suspected him of giddiness, of tale-bearing.

"I quite agree, sir, but I'm afraid that they'll find out sooner or later. I mean it's not just as if Flynn were an ordinary student. He's one of the heroes of the School. When the boys discover he isn't going to graduate they'll wonder."

"I realize that there will be talk but I see no reason for us to reveal the true cause of the young man's separation from this institution." The operative verb puzzled Mr Beckman until he remembered that the Principal had been, for a year or two during the war, a colonel in Washington and that he could still turn a military phrase with the best of the younger faculty men who had also served in the war.

"But *what* are we to say?" Mr Beckman persisted. "We shall have to give some excuse."

"There is no occasion, Mr Beckman, for us *ever* to give excuses," said the Principal in a cool star-chamber voice. "Besides, Commencement is only a week away and I am sure that if we all maintain a discreet silence the business will soon be forgotten. The only complication, as I've mentioned before, involves the Zenner Trophy. At the moment I'm tempted not to give it at all this year, but of course we'll have to see what our faculty committee digs up. . . . Anyway that has nothing to do with the business at hand which, specifically, concerns the expulsion of Flynn, an unpleasant task traditionally performed by the Dean. In his absence, and he is absent, the sad duty must be performed by the faculty adviser involved."

"Not by the Principal?"

"*Never* by the Principal," said that officer, constructing a pile of papers in front of him as though to barricade himself even more securely against the sordid life of the School.

"I see. I don't suppose there is any chance of keeping him on? I mean of letting him graduate next week?" He felt that it was his duty to make this suggestion.

"Of course not! How could you suggest such a thing after what's happened? There were two witnesses and both were faculty members. Had there been only *one* witness we might perhaps . . ." The Principal paused, contemplating collusion . . . to no avail. He returned quickly to his original position, remarking that the morality of the thing was perfectly clear and that the crime and the punishment were both well-known and that there wouldn't have been this much discussion if it had not been for that damned award. "No, the boy has been expelled and that's that. I've already written to his parents."

"Did you tell them what has happened? In detail?"

"I did," said the Principal firmly. "After all, he's their son and they should know everything. I wouldn't be doing my duty if I did not tell them."

"Rather hard on him, don't you think?"

"Are *you* defending him?" The Principal reduced Mr Beckman's momentary disaffection to total compliance with a single glance from agate eyes, eyes which had so often quelled student revolts, bullied the faculty, extorted endowments from the most brutal of millionaires.

"No, sir . . . I only thought . . ." That was the end of that, thought Mr Beckman gloomily, mumbling himself back into favor again.

"Very good," said the Principal arising, ending the audience. "You'll talk to him. Tell him that the faculty has unanimously expelled him and that the Zenner Trophy will be given to someone else. You might also mention the sorrow with which I personally learned of his . . . activities and that I do not condemn him too much; rather, I pity him. It is a terrible handicap not to know right from wrong in such matters."

"I shall tell him that, sir."

"Good. . . . Just what sort of young man is he? I've seen him play ball many times, of course . . . a real champion . . . but I never got to know him. On the few occasions when we did meet he seemed perfectly . . . well-adjusted. He comes from a good home, too. Odd that he should be such a marvelous athlete, all things considered."

"Yes, a marvelous athlete," repeated Mr Beckman. This was apparently to be Flynn's epitaph; he tried to translate it into Latin but failed, unable to remember the word for athlete.

"You never noticed anything unusual about him, did you? Any clue which might, in retrospect, explain what has happened."

"No, sir. I'm sorry to say that I noticed nothing at all."

"Well, it's no fault of yours, or of the School's. These things will happen." The Principal sighed. Then: "Drop by my office around five . . . if it's convenient."

II

The morning was marvelously clear and bright and Mr Beckman's weak eyes watered as he crossed the lawn of the quadrangle, a vivid area of green in the solemn light of noon.

Students greeted him politely and he responded vaguely, not seeing them, his eyes not yet accustomed to the day. He blundered accurately across the quadrangle to the library where he stood a moment, blinking, until at last he could see that it was indeed a lovely day and that the School looked most handsome.

The main buildings bordered the vast green lawn of the quadrangle, a lawn marked with numerous graveled paths, designed with considerable geometric ingenuity to allow, its architect had mistakenly supposed, for any possible crossing a student might want to make. Of the buildings on the quadrangle, the Administration Hall was the handsomest and the oldest; it was nearly old enough to be in fact what it was in facsimile: a colonial affair of red brick with a clock-tower and bell, a bell which irritated Mr Beckman unreasonably. It rang at five minutes to every hour as well as on the hour from morning chapel until the last evening class. The bell rang now. Eleven o'clock. He had exactly one hour in which to "separate" Flynn from the school he had so brilliantly adorned. A warm wind stirred the lilacs and, suddenly, he was frightened at what he had to do. He was not equipped to deal with mysteries. He had very early chosen the bland familiar for his domain and he had never before ventured into the dangerous interior of another's life: now, in a few moments, he must sack a temple, sow foreign earth with salt and rend a mystery. Half shutting his eyes against the blaze of sun, Mr Beckman made his way to the rose-brick senior dormitory where Flynn and he both lived. Inside the building, he proceeded down the wax-smelling corridor, his tongue dry, his hands cold, panic insecurely leashed. At Flynn's door, he stopped. He knocked softly. Receiving no answer, he turned the knob and opened the door, praying the boy was gone.

Flynn had not gone. He was sitting on the edge of his bed, an open suitcase on the floor in front of him. He stood up when Mr Beckman entered.

"Am I out?" he asked.

"Yes." That was quick. For a moment Mr Beckman considered flight.

"I figured that would happen." The boy sat down on the bed again. Mr Beckman wondered what he should say next. Since nothing occurred to him, he seated himself at the desk by the window and assumed an expression of grave sympathy. The boy continued to pack his suitcase. A long moment of silence stretched taut Mr Beckman's nerves. At last, he broke the silence.

"The Principal wanted me to tell you he is very sorry about what's happened."

"Well, you tell him I'm sorry too," said Flynn, looking up from his packing and, to Mr Beckman's surprise, he was grinning. He seemed not at all shaken, Mr Beckman remarked with wonder, examining him carefully. The eighteen-year-old Flynn was a well-constructed man of middle-height, muscular but not burly like the other athletes; his freckled face was amiable and quite mature, his eyes dark blue; his hair, of no particular color, was worn short, in a crew-cut. During the winter his hair had been longer and Mr Beckman recalled that it had been quite curly, like the head of the young Dionysus.

He looked about the room, at the banners on the walls and at the calendar of partly-dressed girls, one for each month. In a corner was piled athletic equipment: football helmet, shoulder pads, sweat-marked jerseys, shorts, tennis racket . . . the tools of a serious career rather than the playthings of an energetic boy. No, he would never have known, never.

There was another long pause, but this time Mr Beckman was more at ease even as he sensed his own position becoming less and less secure. "I suppose," he said, "that you'll go on to college now."

"Yes, I suppose I will. I got all the credits I need from high school, and the university back home wants me to play ball. I won't have any trouble getting in . . . will I?"

"Oh, no. No trouble at all, I'm sure."

"*They* don't plan to make any trouble for me, do they?"

"Who do you mean by 'they'?"

"The School. They aren't going to write the university or anything like that, are they?"

"Oh, Heavens no!" Mr Beckman was relieved to have some good news, no matter how negative. "Except for expelling you, they are doing nothing at all. Of course . . ." He paused, noticing that the other looked very grim.

"Of course what?"

"They have written your parents."

"Written my parents *what*?"

"The . . . the whole business. It's customary, you understand. The Principal wrote the letter himself, today, this morning, as a matter of fact," he added precisely, addressing his attention, as he always did in a crisis, to the periphery of the situation, to the incidental detail in the hopes that he might yet avoid involvement. But it was no use.

"Well, I'll be damned!" Flynn sat up straight, his large square hands clenched into two useful and dangerous-looking fists. Mr Beckman trembled. "So he went and wrote everything, did he . . ." He stopped and hit the bed with his fist; the springs creaked. It was all very dramatic and Mr Beckman sat up straight in his chair, raising one hand as though to defend himself.

"You must remember," he said, his voice trembling, "that the Principal was only doing his duty. You *were* caught, you know, and you *were* expelled. Don't you feel your parents deserve some sort of explanation?"

"No, I don't. Not like that, anyway. It's bad enough being kicked out without having that dumb bastard go and upset them. It's no way of getting back at me: I earn my own way. I can go to any school I want on a scholarship. Or I can turn pro tomorrow and make ten times the money that fool Principal makes. But why, I want to know, does somebody who doesn't even know me go out of his way to make such a mess for my family?"

"I'm sure it's not a deliberate persecution," said Mr Beckman dryly. "And you should have thought of all that when . . . when you did what you did. There *are* certain rules of conduct, you know, which must be obeyed and you obviously forgot . . ."

"Oh, shut up!"

Mr Beckman had a dizzy sense that he was falling; only with great effort did he get to his feet, saying, shakily, "If you're going to take that tone with me, Flynn, I see no point in . . ."

"I'm sorry. I didn't mean it. Come on, sit down." And Mr Beckman sat down, his authority gone. He could no longer predict the direction this conversation would take and he was actually relieved that the initiative was no longer his.

"You see how I feel, don't you?"

"Yes," said Mr Beckman. "I do." And unhappily he did. Not only was he sympathetic: He was partisan, hopelessly identified with the other. He shuddered at the thought of the meeting between son and parents and he tried to think of what would happen . . . would she have a stroke? would she weep? "If there is anything I might do . . ." he began.

Flynn smiled. "No, I don't think there's anything to be done, thanks. I guess it was probably too much to expect . . . I mean that they'd keep it quiet. But what about the rest of the school? Is the Principal going to get up in chapel and tell the whole story?"

"Oh, no. His plan is to say nothing at all to the students. He's instructed the faculty to keep absolutely quiet."

"Well, that's good news but you know they're going to be wondering why Sawyer and I didn't graduate, why we left just a week before Commencement." He paused; then: "What're they going to do about the Trophy?"

"I don't know. Since they can't give it to you they're in rather a spot: If they reaward it, that will draw attention to the fact you've been expelled. I have a hunch they won't give it at all this year." And Mr Beckman chuckled, totally aligned against the School which until an hour ago he had so much admired and had so sincerely longed to serve.

"I guess that's their worry now," said Flynn. "Were they pretty shocked?"

"Who?"

"The faculty. You know: all the ones who knew me, like the coaches I worked with. What did they say?"

"No one said much of anything. I think they were all surprised. I mean you were just about the last person anyone would have expected to be involved . . . like this. I'm afraid *I* was rather surprised, too," he added shyly, waiting.

But Flynn only snorted and looked out the window at the tower of the Administration Building, red brick against blue sky. At last he said: "I guess there *is* something wrong with me, Mr Beckman, because I can't for the life of me see what business it is of anyone else what I do."

This was not at all what Mr Beckman had anticipated; identified as he was with Flynn, he still found it difficult to accept the curious amorality of this attitude. He took a firm line. "You must realize," he said, as gently as possible, "that we are all guided by a system of conduct formulated and refined by many centuries. Should this system, or any important part of it, be destroyed, the whole complex structure of civilization would collapse." Yet even as he said these familiar words, he realized that they were, in this case at least, irrelevant and he noticed dispassionately that Flynn was not listening to him. He was standing over his athletic equipment, tossing the pieces he didn't want into a far corner of the room. Mr Beckman enjoyed watching him move for he never struck an ugly or a self-conscious attitude. "And so you see," he concluded to the boy's back, "that when you do something as basically wrong as what you've done, you'll have all of organized society down on you and you'll be punished."

"Maybe so." Flynn straightened up, holding his armor, his weapons in his hands. "But I still don't see why what I want to do should ever be anybody's business except my own . . . after all it doesn't affect anybody else, does it?" Noisily, he dumped the equipment into the open suitcase. Then he sat down on the bed again and looked at Mr Beckman. "You know I'd really like to get my hands on those two," he said abruptly, scowling.

"They were only doing their duty. They had to report you."

"I suppose I should have known they were suspicious in the first place . . . when I saw them last night, before I went up to Sawyer's room. They were hanging around the common room, whispering. Sawyer thought there was something going on but I said so what."

"And you were caught."

"Yes," he blushed and looked away. He seemed for the first time very young; Mr Beckman was compassionate.

"I gather," he said slowly, allowing the other to regain his composure, "that Sawyer went home?"

Flynn shook his head. "No, he's over at the Inn, waiting for me. I figured they might want to question us and I thought I'd better be the one who did the talking. He went over there first thing this morning."

"What sort of boy is Sawyer? I don't think I've seen him around."

Flynn looked at him with surprise. "Of course you've seen him. He's on the track team. He's the best sprinter we got."

"Oh yes, of course." Mr Beckman had not gone to any of the track meets. He had found that after he'd attended the football and the baseball games that he didn't very much want to see the swimming team or the track team or even the school's celebrated basketball team.

"He's too small to play football and besides he hasn't got the right temperament for a football player," said Flynn professionally. "He blows up too easily and he doesn't work out on a team . . ."

"I see. And you've been good friends for a long time?"

"Yes," said Flynn and he shut the suitcase with a snap.

"Where do you think you'll go now?" asked Mr Beckman, obscurely anxious to prolong this interview.

"Back home and it's not going to be much fun. I just hope my mother doesn't have a relapse or anything like that."

"Where will Sawyer go?"

"Oh, he's coming on to the university with me. He's got a high school diploma, too. He won't have any trouble getting in."

"So then you aren't really very discouraged by all of this?"

"Why? I don't like what's happened but then I don't see what I can do about it now."

"You're very sensible. I'm afraid that if I'd been in your place I would have been most upset."

"But you *wouldn't* have been in my place, would you, Mr Beckman?" Flynn smiled.

"No, no, I don't suppose so," said Mr Beckman, aware that he had been abandoned long ago and that there was no one he could turn to now, no one he could confide in. He realized that he was quite alone and he hated Flynn for reminding him of the long and tedious journey ahead, down an endless, chalk-smelling corridor where each forward step took him ever farther away from this briefly glimpsed design within a lilac day.

The bell rang. He stood up. It was time to go to class. "I suppose you'll be leaving for Boston on the next train?"

Flynn nodded. "Yes, I've got to take some books back to the library first; after that, I'll pick up Sawyer at the Inn. Then we go."

"Well, good luck." Mr Beckman paused. "I'm not so sure that, after all, any of this matters very much," he said, in a last effort to console himself as well as the other.

"No, I don't suppose it does either." Flynn was gentle. "You've been very nice about this . . ."

"Don't mention it. By the way, if you like, I'll return any library books for you."

"Thanks a lot." Flynn took three books from the top of the desk and handed them to him.

Mr Beckman hesitated. "Do you ever get to Boston? I mean do you think you'll come into town much after you enter the university?"

"Sure, I suppose so. I'll let you know and we might get together some weekend."

"I should like that. Well, good-by." They shook hands and Mr Beckman left the room, already late for class. Outside, he glanced at the titles of the books he was carrying: One was a volume of historical documents (required reading) and one was a mystery story. The third was a volume of Keats. Dazzled by sunlight, he crossed the quadrangle, aware there was nothing left that he could do.

1950

Split Cherry Tree

Jesse Stuart

"I don't mind staying after school," I says to Professor Herbert, "but I'd rather you'd whip me with a switch and let me go home early. Pa will whip me anyway for getting home two hours late."

"You are too big to whip," says Professor Herbert, "and I have to punish you for climbing up that cherry tree. You boys knew better than that! The other five boys have paid their dollar each. You have been the only one who has not helped pay for the tree. Can't you borrow a dollar?"

"I can't," I says. "I'll have to take the punishment. I wish it would be quicker punishment. I wouldn't mind."

Professor Herbert stood and looked at me. He was a big man. He wore a gray suit of clothes. The suit matched his gray hair.

"You don't know my father," I says to Professor Herbert. "He might be called a little old-fashioned. He makes us mind him until we're twenty-one years old. He believes: 'If you spare the rod you spoil the child.' I'll never be able to make him understand about the cherry tree. I'm the first of my people to go to high school."

"You must take the punishment," says Professor Herbert. "You must stay two hours after school today and two hours after school tomorrow. I am allowing you twenty-five cents an hour. That is good money for a high school student. You can sweep the schoolhouse floor, wash the blackboards and clean windows. I'll pay the dollar for you."

I couldn't ask Professor Herbert to loan me a dollar. He never offered to loan it to me. I had to stay and help the janitor and work out my fine at a quarter an hour.

I thought as I swept the floor: "What will Pa do to me? What lie can I tell him when I go home? Why did we ever climb that cherry tree and break it down for anyway? Why did we run crazy over the hills away from the crowd? Why did we do all of this! Six of us climbed up in a little cherry tree after one little lizard! Why did the tree split and fall with us? It should have been a stronger tree! Why did Eif Crabtree just happen to be below us plowing and catch us in his cherry tree? Why wasn't he a better man than to charge us six dollars for the tree?"

It was six o'clock when I left the schoolhouse. I had six miles to walk home. It would be after seven when I got home. I had all my work to do when I got home. It took Pa and me both to do the work. Seven cows to milk. Nineteen head of cattle to feed, four mules, twenty-five hogs, firewood and stovewood to cut and water to draw from the well. He would be doing it when I got home. He would be mad and wondering what was keeping me!

I hurried home. I would run under the dark leafless trees. I would walk fast uphill. I would run down the hill. The ground was freezing. I had to hurry. I had to run and reached the long ridge that led to our cow pasture. I ran along this ridge. The wind dried the sweat on my face. I ran across the pasture to the house.

I threw down my books in the chipyard, I ran to the barn to spread fodder on the ground for the cattle. I didn't take time to change my clean school clothes for my old work clothes. I ran out to the barn. I saw Pa spreading fodder on the ground to the cattle. That was my job. I ran to the fence. I says: "Leave that for me, Pa. I'll do it. I'm just a little late."

"I see you are," says Pa. He turned and looked at me. His eyes danced fire. "What in th' world has kept you so. Why ain't you been here to help me with this work? Make a gentleman out'n one boy in th' family and this is what you get! Send you to high school and you get too onery fer th' buzzards to smell!"

I never said anything. I didn't want to tell why I was late from school. Pa stopped scattering the bundles of fodder. He looked at me. He says: "Why are you gettin' in here this time o' night? You tell me or I'll take a hickory withe to you right here on th' spot."

I says: "Our Biology Class went on a field trip today. Six of us boys broke down a cherry tree. We had to give a dollar apiece to pay for the tree. I didn't have the dollar. Professor Herbert is making me work out my dollar. He gives me twenty-five cents an hour. I had to stay in this afternoon. I'll have to stay in tomorrow afternoon!"

"Are you telling me th' truth?" says Pa.

"I'm telling you the truth," I says. "Go and see for yourself."

"That's just what I'll do in th' morning'," says Pa. "Jist whose cherry tree did you break down?"

"Eif Crabtree's cherry tree!"

"My God," says Pa, "what was you doing clear out in Eif Crabtree's place? He lives four miles from th' County High School. Don't they teach you no books at that high school? Do they jist let you get out and gad over th' hillsides? If that's all they do I'll keep you at home, Dave. I've got work here fer you to do!"

"Pa," I says, "spring is just getting here. We take a subject in school where we have to have bugs, snakes, flowers, lizards, frogs and plants. It is Biology. It was a pretty day today. We went out to find a few of these. Six of us boys saw a lizard at the same time sunning on a cherry tree. We all went up the tree to get it. We broke the tree down. It split at the forks. Eif Crabtree was plowing down below us. He ran up the hill and got our names. The other boys gave their dollar apiece. I didn't have mine. Professor Herbert put mine in for me. I have to work it out at school."

"Poor man's son, huh," says Pa. "I'll attend to that myself in th' mornin'. I'll take keer o' 'im. He ain't from this county nohow. I'll go down there in th' mornin' and see 'im. Lettin' you leave your books and galavant all over th' hills. What kind of a damn school is it nohow! Didn't do that, my son, when I's a little shaver in school. All fared alike too."

"Pa please don't go down there," I says. "Just let me have fifty cents and pay the rest of my fine! I don't want you to go down there! I don't want you to start anything with Professor Herbert!"

"Ashamed of your old Pap are you, Dave," says Pa, "atter th' way I've worked to raise you! Tryin' to send you to school so you can make a better livin' than I've made.

"I'll straighten this thing out myself! I'll take keer o' Professor Herbert myself! He ain't got no right to keep you in and let the other boys off jist because they've got th' money! I'm a poor man. A bullet will go in a Professor same as it will any man. It will go in a rich man same as it will a poor man. Now you get into this work before I take one o' these withes and cut the shirt off'n your back!"

I thought once I'd run through the woods above the barn just as hard as I could go. I thought I'd leave high school and home forever! Pa could not catch me! I'd get away! I couldn't go back to school with him. He'd have a gun and maybe he'd shoot Professor Herbert. It was hard to tell what he would do. I could tell Pa that school had changed in the hills from the way it was when he was a boy but he wouldn't understand. I could tell him we studied frogs, birds, snakes, lizards, flowers, insects. But Pa wouldn't understand. If I did run away from home it wouldn't matter to Pa. He would see Professor Herbert anyway. He would think that high school and Professor Herbert had run me away from home. There was no need to run away. I'd just have to stay, finish foddering the cattle and go to school with Pa the next morning.

I would take a bundle of fodder, remove the hickory witheband from around it and scatter it on rocks, clumps of greenbriars and brush so the cattle wouldn't trample it under their feet. I would lean it up against the oak trees and the rocks in the pasture just above our pigpen on the hill. The fodder was cold and frosty where it had set out in the stacks. I would carry bundles of the fodder from the stack until I had spread out a bundle for each steer. Pa went to the barn to feed the mules and throw corn in the pen to the hogs.

The moon shone bright in the cold March sky. I finished my work by moonlight. Professor Herbert really didn't know how much work I had to do at home. If he had known he would not have kept me after school. He would have loaned me a dollar to have paid my part on the cherry tree. He had never lived in the hills. He didn't know the way the hill boys had to work so that they could go to school. Now he was teaching in a County High School where all the boys who attended were from hill farms.

After I'd finished doing my work I went to the house and ate my supper. Pa and Mom had eaten. My supper was getting cold. I heard Pa and Mom talking in the front room. Pa was telling Mom about me staying after school.

"I had to do all th' milkin' tonight, chop th' wood myself. It's too hard on me after I've turned ground all day. I'm goin' to take a day off tomorrow and see if I can't remedy things a little. I'll go down to that high school tomorrow. I won't be a very good scholar fer Professor Herbert nohow. He won't keep me in atter school. I'll take a different kind of lesson down there and make 'im acquainted with it."

"Now Luster," says Mom, "you jist stay away from there. Don't cause a lot o' trouble. You can be jailed fer a trick like that. You'll get th' Law atter you. You'll jist do down there and show off and plague your own boy Dave to death in front o' all th' scholars!"

"Plague or no plague," says Pa, "he don't take into consideration what all I haf to do here, does he? I'll show 'im it ain't right to keep one boy in and let the rest go scot-free. My boy is good as th' rest, ain't he? A bullet will make a hole in a schoolteacher same as it will anybody else. He can't do me that way and get by with it. I'll plug 'im first. I aim to go down there bright and early in the mornin' and get all this straight! I aim to see about bug larnin' and this runnin' all over God's creation huntin' snakes, lizards, and frogs. Ransackin' th' country and goin' through cherry orchards and breakin' th' trees down atter lizards! Old Eif Crabtree ought to a-poured th' hot lead to 'em instead o' chargin' six dollar fer th' tree! He ought to a-got old Herbert th' first one!"

I ate my supper. I slipped upstairs and lit the lamp. I tried to forget the whole thing. I studied plane geometry. Then I studied my biology lesson. I could hardly study for thinking about Pa. "He'll go to school with me in the morning. He'll take a gun for Professor Herbert! What will Professor Herbert think of me! I'll tell him when Pa leaves that I couldn't help it. But Pa might shoot him. I hate to go with Pa. Maybe he'll cool off about it tonight and not go in the morning."

Pa got up at four o'clock. He built a fire in the stove. Then he built a fire in the fireplace. He got Mom up to get breakfast. Then he got me up to help feed and milk. By the time we had our work done at the barn, Mom had breakfast ready for us. We ate our breakfast. Daylight came and we could see the bare oak trees covered white with frost. The hills were white with frost. A cold wind was blowing. The sky was clear. The sun would soon come out and melt the frost. The afternoon would be warm with sunshine and the frozen ground would thaw. There would be mud on the hills again. Muddy water would then run down the little ditches on the hills.

"Now Dave," says Pa, "Let's get ready fer school. I aim to go with you this mornin' and look into bug larnin', frog larnin', lizard and snake larnin' and breakin' down cherry trees! I don't like no sicha foolish way o' larnin' myself!"

Pa hadn't forgot. I'd have to take him to school with me. He would take me to school with him. We were going early. I was glad we were going early. If Pa pulled a gun on Professor Herbert there wouldn't be so many of my classmates there to see him.

I knew that Pa wouldn't be at home in the high school. He wore overalls, big boots, a blue shirt and a sheepskin coat and a slouched black hat gone to seed at the top. He put his gun in its holster. We started trudging toward the high school across the hill.

It was early when we got to the County High School. Professor Herbert had just got there. I just thought as we walked up the steps into the schoolhouse: "Maybe Pa will find out Professor Herbert is a good man. He just doesn't know him. Just like I felt toward the Lambert boys across the hill. I didn't like them until I'd seen them and talked to them. After I went to school with them and talked to them, I liked them and we were friends. It's a lot in knowing the other fellow."

"You're th' Professor here, ain't you?" says Pa.

"Yes," says Professor Herbert, "and you're Dave's father."

"Yes," says Pa, pulling out his gun and laying it on the seat in Professor Herbert's office. Professor Herbert's eyes got big behind his black-rimmed glasses when he saw Pa's gun. Color came into his pale cheeks.

"Jist a few things about this school I want to know," says Pa. "I'm tryin' to make a scholar out'n Dave. He's the only one out'n eleven youngins I've sent to high school. Here he comes in late and leaves me all th' work to do! He said you's all out bug huntin' yesterday and broke a cherry tree down. He had to stay two hours after school yesterday and work out money to pay on that cherry tree! Is that right?"

"Wwwwy," said Professor Herbert, "I guess it is."

He looked at Pa's gun.

"Well," says Pa, "this ain't no high school. It's a damn bug school, a lizard school, a snake school! It ain't no damn school nohow!"

"Why did you bring that gun," says Professor Herbert to Pa.

"You see that little hole," says Pa as he picked up the long blue forty-four and put his finger on the end of the barrel, "a bullet can come out'n that hole that will kill a schoolteacher same as it will kill any other man. It will kill a rich man same as a poor man. It will kill a man. But atter I come in and saw you, I know'd I wouldn't need it. This maul o' mine could do you up in a few minutes."

Pa stood there, big, hard, brown-skinned and mighty beside of Professor Herbert. I didn't know Pa was so much bigger and harder. I'd never seen Pa in a schoolhouse before. I'd seen Professor Herbert. He always looked big before to me. He didn't look big standing beside of Pa.

"I was only doing my duty," says Professor Herbert, "Mr. Sexton, and following the course of study the state provided us with."

"Course o' study," says Pa, "what study, bug study? Varmit study? Takin' youngins to th' woods. Boys and girls all out there together a-galavantin' in the brush and kickin' up their heels and their poor old Ma's and Pa's at home a-slavin' to keep 'em in school and give 'em a education! You know that's dangerous too puttin' a lot o' boys and girls out together like that! Some o' us Paps is liable to add a few to our families!"

Students are coming into the schoolhouse now.

Professor Herbert says: "Close the door, Dave, so others won't hear."

I walked over and closed the door. I was shaking like a leaf in the wind. I thought Pa was going to hit Professor Herbert every minute. He was doing all the talking. His face was getting red. The red color was coming through the brown weather-beaten skin on Pa's face.

"I was right with these students," says Professor Herbert. "I know what they got into and what they didn't. I didn't send one of the other teachers with them on this field trip. I went myself. Yes, I took the boys and girls together. Why not?"

"It jist don't look good to me," says Pa, "a-takin' all this swarm of youngins out to pilage th' whole deestrict. Breakin' down cherry trees. Keepin' boys in atter school."

"What else could I have done with Dave, Mr. Sexton?" says Professor Herbert. "The boys didn't have any business all climbing that cherry tree after one lizard. One boy could have gone up in the tree and got it. The farmer charged us six dollars. It was a little steep I think but we had it to pay. Must I make five boys pay and let your boy off? He said he didn't have the dollar and couldn't get it. So I put it in for him. I'm letting him work it out. He's not working for me. He's working for the school!"

"I jist don't know what you could a-done with 'im," says Pa, "only a-larruped 'im with a withe! That's what he needed!"

"He's too big to whip," says Professor Herbert pointing to me. "He's a man in size."

"He's not too big fer me to whip," says Pa. "They ain't too big until they're over twenty-one! It jist don't look fair to me! Work one and let th' rest out because they got th' money. I don't see what bugs has got to do with a high school! It don't look good to me nohow!"

Pa picked up his gun and put it back in its holster. The red color left Professor Herbert's face. He talked more to Pa. Pa softened a little. It looked funny to see Pa in the high school building. It was the first time he'd ever been there.

"We were not only hunting snakes, toads, flowers, butterflies, lizards," says Professor Herbert, "but, Mr. Sexton, I was hunting dry timothy grass to put in an incubator and raise some protozoa."

"I don't know what that is," says Pa. "Th' incubator is th' new-fangled way o' cheatin' th' hens and raisin' chickens. I ain't so sure about th' breed o' chickens you mentioned."

"You've heard of germs, Mr. Sexton, haven't you," says Professor Herbert.

"Jist call me Luster if you don't mind," says Pa, very casual like.

"All right, Luster, you've heard of germs, haven't you?"

"Yes," says Pa, "but I don't believe in germs. I'm sixty-five years old and I ain't seen one yet!"

"You can't see them with your naked eye," says Professor Herbert. "Just keep that gun in the holster and stay with me in the

high school today. I have a few things I want to show you. That
scum on your teeth has germs on it."

"What," says Pa, "you mean to tell me I've got germs on my
teeth!"

"Yes," says Professor Herbert. "The same kind as we might be
able to find in a living black snake if we dissect it!"

"I don't mean to dispute your word," says Pa, "but damned if I
believe it. I don't believe I have germs on my teeth!"

"Stay with me today and I'll show you. I want to take you
through the school anyway! School has changed a lot in the hills
since you went to school. I don't guess we had high schools in this
county when you went to school!"

"No," says Pa, "jist readin', writin' and cipherin'. We didn't
have all this bug larnin', frog larnin', and findin' germs on your
teeth and in the middle o' black snakes! Th' world's changin'."

"It is," says Professor Herbert, "and we hope all for the better.
Boys like your own there are going to help change it. He's your
boy. He knows all of what I've told you. You stay with me today."

"I'll shore stay with you," says Pa. "I want to see th' germs off'n
my teeth. I jist want to see a germ. I've never seen one in my life.
'Seein' is believin',' Pap allus told me."

Pa walks out of the office with Professor Herbert. I just hoped
Professor Herbert didn't have Pa arrested for pulling his gun. Pa's
gun has always been a friend to him when he goes to settle dis-
putes.

The bell rang. School took up. I saw the students when they
marched in the schoolhouse look at Pa. They would grin and
punch each other. Pa just stood and watched them pass in at the
schoolhouse door. Two long lines marched in the house. The boys
and girls were clean and well-dressed. Pa stood over in the school
yard under a leafless elm, in his sheepskin coat, his big boots laced
in front with buckskin and his heavy socks stuck above his boot
tops. Pa's overalls legs were baggy and wrinkled between his coat
and boot tops. His blue work shirt showed at the collar. His big
black hat showed his gray-streaked black hair. His face was hard
and weather-tanned to the color of a ripe fodder blade. His hands
were big and gnarled like the roots of the elm tree he stood beside.

When I went to my first class I saw Pa and Professor Herbert going around over the schoolhouse. Professor Herbert and Pa just quietly came in and sat down for awhile. I heard Fred Wurts whisper to Glenn Armstrong: "Who is that old man? Lord, he's a rough looking scamp." Glenn whispered back: "I think he's Dave's Pap." The students in geometry looked at Pa. They must have wondered what he was doing in school. Before the class was over, Pa and Professor Herbert got up and went out. I saw them together down on the playground. Professor Herbert was explaining to Pa. I could see the prints of Pa's gun under his coat when he'd walk around.

At noon in the high school cafeteria Pa and Professor Herbert sat together at the little table where Professor Herbert always ate by himself. They ate together. The students watched the way Pa ate. He ate with his knife instead of his fork. A lot of the students felt sorry for me after they found out he was my father. They didn't have to feel sorry for me. I wasn't ashamed of Pa after I found out he wasn't going to shoot Professor Herbert. I was glad they had made friends. I wasn't ashamed of Pa. I wouldn't be as long as he behaved. He would find out about the high school as I had found out about the Lambert boys across the hill.

In the afternoon when we went to biology Pa was in the class. He was sitting on one of the high stools beside the microscope. We went ahead with our work just as if Pa wasn't in the class. I saw Pa take his knife and scrape tartar from one of his teeth. Professor Herbert put it on the lens and adjusted the microscope for Pa. He adjusted it and worked awhile. Then he says: "Now Luster, look! Put your eye right down to the light. Squint the other eye!"

Pa put his head down and did as Professor Herbert said: "I see 'im," says Pa. "I'll be damned. Who'd a ever thought that? Right on a body's teeth! Right in a body's mouth. You're right certain they ain't no fake to this, Professor Herbert?"

"No, Luster," says Professor Herbert. "It's there. That's the germ. Germs live in a world we cannot see with the naked eye. We must use the microscope. There are millions of them in our bodies. Some are harmful. Others are helpful."

Pa holds his face down and looks through the microscope. We stop and watch Pa. He sits upon the tall stool. His knees are against the table. His legs are long. His coat slips up behind when he bends over. The handle of his gun shows. Professor Herbert pulls his coat down quickly.

"Oh, yes," says Pa. He gets up and pulls his coat down. Pa's face gets a little red. He knows about his gun and he knows he doesn't have any use for it in high school.

"We have a big black snake over here we caught yesterday," says Professor Herbert. "We'll chloroform him and dissect him and show you he has germs in his body too."

"Don't do it," says Pa. "I believe you. I jist don't want to see you kill the black snake. I never kill one. They are good mousers and a lot o' help to us on the farm. I like black snakes. I jist hate to see people kill 'em. I don't allow 'em killed on my place."

The students look at Pa. They seem to like him better after he said that. Pa with a gun in his pocket but a tender heart beneath his ribs for snakes, but not for man! Pa won't whip a mule at home. He won't whip his cattle.

"Man can defend hisself," says Pa, "but cattle and mules can't. We have the drop on 'em. Ain't nothin' to a man that'll beat a good pullin' mule. He ain't got th' right kind o' a heart!"

Professor Herbert took Pa through the laboratory. He showed him the different kinds of work we were doing. He showed him our equipment. They stood and talked while we worked. Then they walked out together. They talked louder when they got out in the hall.

When our biology class was over I walked out of the room. It was our last class for the day. I would have to take my broom and sweep two hours to finish paying for the split cherry tree. I just wondered if Pa would want me to stay. He was standing in the hallway watching the students march out. He looked lost among us. He looked like a leaf turned brown on the tree among the treetop filled with growing leaves.

I got my broom and started to sweep. Professor Herbert walked up and says: "I'm going to let you do that some other time. You can go home with your father. He is waiting out there."

I laid my broom down, got my books, and went down the steps.

Pa says: "Ain't you got two hours o' sweepin' yet to do?"

I says: "Professor Herbert said I could do it some other time. He said for me to go home with you."

"No," says Pa. "You are goin' to do as he says. He's a good man. School has changed from my day and time. I'm a dead leaf, Dave. I'm behind. I don't belong here. If he'll let me I'll get a broom and we'll both sweep one hour. That pays your debt. I'll hep you pay it. I'll ast 'im and see if he won't let me hep you."

"I'm going to cancel the debt," says Professor Herbert. "I just wanted you to understand, Luster."

"I understand," says Pa, "and since I understand he must pay his debt fer th' tree and I'm goin' to hep 'im."

"Don't do that," says Professor Herbert. "It's all on me."

"We don't do things like that," says Pa. "We're just and honest people. We don't want somethin' fer nothin'. Professor Herbert, you're wrong now and I'm right. You'll haf to listen to me. I've larned a lot from you. My boy must go on. Th' world has left me. It changed while I've raised my family and plowed th' hills. I'm a just and honest man. I don't skip debts. I ain't larned 'em to do that. I ain't got much larnin' myself but I do know right from wrong atter I see through a thing."

Professor Herbert went home. Pa and I stayed and swept one hour. It looked funny to see Pa use a broom. He never used one at home. Mom used the broom. Pa used the plow. Pa did hard work. Pa says: "I can't sweep. Durned if I can. Look at th's streaks o' dirt I leave on th' floor! Seems like no work a-tall fer me. Brooms is too light 'r somethin'. I'll jist do th' best I can, Dave. I've been wrong about th' school."

I says: "Did you know Professor Herbert can get a warrant out for you for bringing your pistol to school and showing it in his office! They can railroad you for that!"

"That's all right," says Pa. "I've made that right. Professor Herbert ain't goin' to take it to court. He likes me. I like 'im. We jist had to get together. He had the remedies. He showed me. You must go on to school. I am as strong a man as ever come out'n th' hills fer my years and th' hard work I've done. But I'm behind, Dave. I'm a little man. Your hands will be softer than mine. Your clothes will be better. You'll allus look cleaner than your old Pap. Jist remember, Dave, to pay your debts and be honest. Jist be kind to animals and don't bother th' snakes. That's all I got agin th' school. Puttin' black snakes to sleep and cuttin' 'em open."

It was late when we got home. Stars were in the sky. The moon was up. The ground was frozen. Pa took his time going home. I couldn't run like I did the night before. It was ten o'clock before we got the work finished, our suppers eaten. Pa sat before the fire and told Mom he was going to take her and show her a germ some time. Mom hadn't seen one either. Pa told her about the high school and the fine man Professor Herbert was. He told Mom about the strange school across the hill and how different it was from the school in their day and time.

Ten Indians
by Ernest Hemingway

After one Fourth of July, Nick, driving home late from town in the big wagon with Joe Garner and his family, passed nine drunken Indians along the road. He remembered there were nine because Joe Garner, driving along in the dusk, pulled up the horses, jumped down into the road and dragged an Indian out of the wheel rut. The Indian had been asleep, face down in the sand. Joe dragged him into the bushes and got back up on the wagon box.

"That makes nine of them," Joe said, "just between here and the edge of town."

"Them Indians," said Mrs. Garner.

Nick was on the back seat with the two Garner boys. He was looking out from the back seat to see the Indian where Joe had dragged him alongside of the road.

"Was it Billy Tabeshaw?" Carl asked.

"No."

"His pants looked mighty like Billy."

"All Indians wear the same kind of pants."

"I didn't see him at all," Frank said. "Pa was down into the road and back up again before I seen a thing. I thought he was killing a snake."

"Plenty of Indians'll kill snakes tonight, I guess," Joe Garner said.

"Them Indians," said Mrs. Garner.

They drove along. The road turned off from the main highway and went up into the hills. It was hard pulling for the horses and the boys got down and walked. The road was sandy. Nick looked back from the top of the hill by the schoolhouse. He saw the lights of Petoskey and, off across Little Traverse Bay, the lights of Harbor Springs. They climbed back in the wagon again.

"They ought to put some gravel on that stretch," Joe Garner said. The wagon went along the road through the woods. Joe and Mrs. Garner sat close together on the front seat. Nick sat between the two boys. The road came out into a clearing.

"Right here was where Pa ran over the skunk."

"It was further on."

"It don't make no difference where it was," Joe said without turning his head. "One place is just as good as another to run over a skunk."

"I saw two skunks last night," Nick said.

"Where?"

"Down by the lake. They were looking for dead fish along the beach."

"They were coons probably," Carl said.

"They were skunks. I guess I know skunks."

"You ought to," Carl said. "You got an Indian girl."

"Stop talking that way, Carl," said Mrs. Garner.

"Well, they smell about the same."

Joe Garner laughed.

"You stop laughing, Joe," Mrs. Garner said. "I won't have Carl talk that way."

"Have you got an Indian girl, Nickie?" Joe asked.

"No."

"He has too, Pa," Frank said. "Prudence Mitchell's his girl."

"She's not."

"He goes to see her every day."

"I don't." Nick, sitting between the two boys in the dark, felt hollow and happy inside himself to be teased about Prudence Mitchell. "She ain't my girl," he said.

"Listen to him," said Carl. "I see them together every day."

"Carl can't get a girl," his mother said, "not even a squaw."

Carl was quiet.

"Carl ain't no good with girls," Frank said.

"You shut up."

"You're all right, Carl," Joe Garner said. "Girls never got a man anywhere. Look at your pa."

"Yes, that's what you would say," Mrs. Garner moved close to

Joe as the wagon jolted. "Well, you had plenty of girls in your time."

"I'll bet Pa wouldn't ever have had a squaw for a girl."

"Don't you think it," Joe said. "You better watch out to keep Prudie, Nick."

His wife whispered to him and Joe laughed.

"What you laughing at?" asked Frank.

"Don't you say it, Garner," his wife warned. Joe laughed again.

"Nickie can have Prudence," Joe Garner said. "I got a good girl."

"That's the way to talk," Mrs. Garner said.

The horses were pulling heavily in the sand. Joe reached out in the dark with the whip.

"Come on, pull into it. You'll have to pull harder than this tomorrow."

They trotted down the long hill, the wagon jolting. At the farm-house everybody got down. Mrs. Garner unlocked the door, went inside, and came out with a lamp in her hand. Carl and Nick unloaded the things from the back of the wagon. Frank sat on the front seat to drive to the barn and put up the horses. Nick went up the steps and opened the kitchen door. Mrs. Garner was building a fire in the stove. She turned from pouring kerosene on the wood.

"Good-by, Mrs. Garner," Nick said. "Thanks for taking me."

"Oh, shucks, Nickie."

"I had a wonderful time."

"We like to have you. Won't you stay and eat some supper?"

"I better go. I think Dad probably waited for me."

"Well, get along then. Send Carl up to the house, will you?"

"All right."

"Good night, Nickie."

"Good night, Mrs. Garner."

Nick went out the farmyard and down to the barn. Joe and Frank were milking.

"Good night," Nick said. "I had a swell time."

"Good night, Nick," Joe Garner called. "Aren't you going to stay and eat?"

"No, I can't. Will you tell Carl his mother wants him?"

"All right. Good night, Nickie."

Nick walked barefoot along the path through the meadow below the barn. The path was smooth and the dew was cool on his bare feet. He climbed a fence at the end of the meadow, went down through a ravine, his feet wet in the swamp mud, and then climbed up through the dry beech woods until he saw the lights of the cottage. He climbed over the fence and walked around to the front porch. Through the window he saw his father sitting by the table, reading in the light from the big lamp. Nick opened the door and went in.

"Well, Nickie," his father said, "was it a good day?"

"I had a swell time, Dad. It was a swell Fourth of July."

"Are you hungry?"

"You bet."

"What did you do with your shoes?"

"I left them in the wagon at Garner's."

"Come on out to the kitchen."

Nick's father went ahead with the lamp. He stopped and lifted the lid of the icebox. Nick went on into the kitchen. His father brought in a piece of cold chicken on a plate and a pitcher of milk and put them on the table before Nick. He put down the lamp.

"There's some pie, too," he said. "Will that hold you?"

"It's grand."

His father sat down in a chair beside the oilcloth-covered table. He made a big shadow on the kitchen wall.

"Who won the ball game?"

"Petoskey. Five to three."

His father sat watching him eat and filled his glass from the milk pitcher. Nick drank and wiped his mouth on his napkin. His father reached over to the shelf for the pie. He cut Nick a big piece. It was huckleberry pie.

"What did you do, Dad?"

"I went out fishing in the morning."

"What did you get?"

"Only perch."

His father sat watching Nick eat the pie.

"What did you do this afternoon?" Nick asked.

"I went for a walk up by the Indian camp."

"Did you see anybody?"

"The Indians were all in town getting drunk."

"Didn't you see anybody at all?"

"I saw your friend, Prudie."

"Where was she?"

"She was in the woods with Frank Washburn. I ran into them. They were having quite a time."

His father was not looking at him.

"What were they doing?"

"I didn't stay to find out."

"Tell me what they were doing."

"I don't know," his father said. "I just heard them threshing around."

"How did you know it was them?"

"I saw them."

"I thought you said you didn't see them."

"Oh, yes, I saw them."

"Who was it with her?" Nick asked.

"Frank Washburn."

"Were they—were they——"

"Were they what?"

"Were they happy?"

"I guess so."

His father got up from the table and went out the kitchen screen door. When he came back Nick was looking at his plate. He had been crying.

"Have some more?" His father picked up the knife to cut the pie.

"No," said Nick.

"You better have another piece."

"No, I don't want any."

His father cleared off the table.

"Where were they in the woods?" Nick asked.

"Up back of the camp." Nick looked at his plate. His father said, "You better go to bed, Nick."

"All right."

Nick went into his room, undressed, and got into bed. He heard his father moving around in the living room. Nick lay in the bed with his face in the pillow.

"My heart's broken," he thought. "If I feel this way my heart must be broken."

After a while he heard his father blow out the lamp and go into his own room. He heard a wind come up in the trees outside and felt it come in cool through the screen. He lay for a long time with his face in the pillow, and after a while he forgot to think about Prudence and finally he went to sleep. When he awoke in the night he heard the wind in the hemlock tree outside the cottage and the waves of the lake coming in on the shore, and he went back to sleep. In the morning there was a big wind blowing and the waves were running high up on the beach and he was awake a long time before he remembered that his heart was broken.

First Love and
Other Sorrows

by Harold Brodkey

Toward the end of March, in St. Louis, slush fills the gutters, and
dirty snow lies heaped alongside porch steps, and everything seems
to be suffocating in the embrace of a season that lasts too long.
Radiators hiss mournfully, no one manages to be patient, the wind
draws tears from your eyes, the clouds are filled with sadness.
Women with scarves around their heads and their feet encased in
fur-lined boots pick their way carefully over patches of melting ice.
It seems that winter will last forever, that this is the decision of
nature and nothing can be done about it.

At the age when I was always being warned by my mother not to
get overheated, spring began on that evening when I was first allowed to go outside after dinner and play kick-the-can. The ground
would be moist, I'd manage to get muddy in spite of what seemed
to me extreme precautions, my mother would call me home in the
darkness, and when she saw me she would ask, "What *have* you
done to yourself?" "Nothing," I'd say hopefully. But by the time I
was sixteen, the moment when the year passed into spring, like so
many other things, was less clear. In March and early April, track
began, but indoors; mid-term exams came and went; the buds appeared on the maples, staining all their branches red; but it was
still winter, and I found myself having feelings in class that were
like long petitions for spring and all its works. And then one evening I was sitting at my desk doing my trigonometry and I heard
my sister coming home from her office; I heard her high heels
tapping on the sidewalk, and realized that, for the first time since
fall, all the windows in the house were open. My sister was coming
up the front walk. I looked down through a web of budding tree
branches and called out to her that it was spring, by God. She
shrugged—she was very handsome and she didn't approve of me—

and then she started up the front steps and vanished under the roof of the porch.

I ran downstairs. "The bus was crowded tonight," my sister said, hanging up her coat. "I could hardly breathe. This is such a warm dress."

"You need a new spring dress," my mother said, her face lighting up. She was sitting in the living room with the evening paper on her lap.

She and my sister spread the newspaper on the dining-room table to look at the ads.

"We'll just have to settle for sandwiches tonight," my mother said to me. My father was dead, and my mother pretended that now all the cooking was done for my masculine benefit. "Look! That suit's awfully smart!" she cried, peering at the paper. "Montaldo's always has such nice suits." She sighed and went out to the kitchen, leaving the swinging door open so she could talk to my sister. "Ninety dollars isn't too much for a good suit, do you think?"

"No," my sister said. "I don't think it's too much. But I don't really want a suit this spring. I'd much rather have a sort of sky-blue dress—with a round neck that shows my shoulders a little bit. I don't look good in suits. I'm not old enough." She was twenty-two. "My face is too round," she added, in a low voice.

My mother said, "You're not too young for a suit." She also meant my sister was not too young to get married.

My sister looked at me and said, "Mother, do you think he shaves often enough? How often *do* you shave?"

"Every three days," I said, flushing up my neck and cheeks.

"Well, try it every other day."

"Yes, try to be neater," my mother said. "I'm sure girls don't like boys with fuzz on their chin."

"I think he's too proud of his beard to shave it," my sister said, and giggled.

"I feel sorry for the man who marries you," I said. "Because everybody thinks you're sweet and you're not."

She smiled pityingly at me, and then she looked down over the newspaper again.

* * *

Until I was four, we lived in a large white frame house overlooking the Mississippi River, south of St. Louis. This house had, among other riches, a porte-cochere, an iron deer on the lawn, and a pond with goldfish swimming in it. Once, I asked my mother why we had left that earlier house, and she said, "We lost the money—that's why. Your father was a very trusting man," she said. "He was always getting swindled."

She was not a mercenary woman, nor was she mean about money—except in spells that didn't come often—but she believed that what we lost with the money was much of our dignity and much of our happiness. She did not want to see life in a grain of sand; she wanted to see it from the shores of the Riviera, wearing a white sharkskin dress.

I will never forget her astonishment when she took us—she was dressed in her best furs, as a gesture, I suppose—to see the house that was to be our home from then on and I told her I liked it. It had nine rooms, a stained-glass window in the hall, and neighbors all up and down the block. She detested that house.

As she grew older, she changed, she grew less imperious. She put her hair into a roll, wore dark-colored clothes, said often, "I'm not a young woman any more," and began to take pride in being practical. But she remained determined; she had seen a world we didn't remember too clearly, and she wanted us to make our way back to it. "I had it all," she said once to my sister. "I was good-looking. We were rich. You have no idea what it was like. If I had died when I was thirty, I would have died completely happy. . . ."

But being practical did not come easy to her. She was not practical in her bones, and every spring brings back the memory of my mother peering nearsightedly, with surprise, at the tulip shoots in her flower border. And it brings back her look of distraught efficiency during spring housecleaning. "You'd better clear your closet shelves tonight," she would warn me, "because tomorrow Tillie and I are going in there with a vacuum cleaner, and we'll throw out everything we find." Year after year, I would run upstairs to save my treasures—even when I was sixteen and on the verge of a great embarkation, the nature of which I could not even begin to guess. My treasures consisted of my postcard collection—twenty-five hundred cards in all, arranged alphabetically by states of the Union and countries of the world (the wonder was that *I* lived in St. Louis)—an old baseball glove, my leaf collection, two obscene comic books I had won in a poker game at a Boy Scout jamboree, my marble collection, and thirty-five pages of secret thoughts written out in longhand. All these had to be taken out to the garage and hidden among the tools until the frenzy of cleaning was over and I could smuggle them back upstairs.

After supper, as the season grew warmer, my mother and sister and I would sit on the screened porch in the rear of the house, marooned among the shadows and the new leaves and the odor of insect spray, the light from our lamps sticking to the trees like bits of yellow paper. Usually the radio was on, and my mother, a book on her lap, her face abstracted (she was usually bored; her life was moved mainly by the burning urge to rise once more along the thin edge of social distinction), would listen to the comedians and laugh. When the phone rang, she would get up and go into the house with long strides, and if the call was for my sister, my mother would call her to the phone in a voice mottled with triumph.

Sometimes in the evening my mother would wash my sister's hair. My sister would sit in front of the basin in Mother's bathroom, a towel around her shoulders, smiling. From my room across the hall I would hear my sister chattering about the men she knew—the ones she dated, the ones she wanted to date, the ones she wouldn't touch with a ten-foot pole. My mother would interrupt with accounts of her own cleverness, her sorties and successes when young, sometimes laughingly, but sometimes gloomily, because she regretted a lot of things. Then she and my sister would label my sister's suitors: one or two had family, one had money, one—a poor boy—had a brilliant future, and there were a few docile, sweet ones who were simply fillers, who represented the additional number of dates that raised my sister to the rank of a very popular girl.

In these conversations, my mother would often bring up matters of propriety. Late dates were improper, flirting with boys other than one's date, breaking dates. Then, too, she would try to instruct my sister in other matters, which had to do with keeping passion in its place and so preventing embarrassment for the boy and disaster for the girl. My sister would grow irritated. "I don't know why you talk like that—I behave very well," she would tell my mother. "Better than the other girls I know." Her irritation would please my mother, who would smile and say that only good-looking girls could afford to be good, and then they would both laugh.

I used to wonder why my mother didn't take my sister's success for granted. My sister was lovely, she had plenty of dates, the phone rang incessantly. Where was the danger? Why did she always lecture my sister?

Once, my mother said my sister ought not to dance with too many boys or she would frighten off the more serious ones. My sister was getting dressed for the spring dance at the country club. Arrogant and slender, she glistened like a water nymph, among her froth of bottles and jars and filmy clothes. She became furious; she screamed that she *liked* to dance. I closed the door to my room, but I could still hear the two of them. "Don't be so foolish," my mother kept saying, over and over again. "Please don't be foolish. . . ." Then my sister, on the verge of tears, said she just wanted to have a good time. My sister's date arrived, and I went downstairs to let him in, and by the time I came back upstairs, the two of them were laughing. My mother said she was just trying to be helpful; after all, my sister was impractical and her looks wouldn't last forever. My sister, as she opened the door of her room, said, under her breath, "They'll last a lot longer yet."

I'll never forget the wild rustling of her voluminous white skirt as she came down the hallway toward me. Her face was strangely still, as if seen by moonlight. Her hair was smooth and shining, her hands bent outward at the wrist, as if they were flowers. "How beautiful you look!" I cried. My sister smiled and then solemnly turned all the way around, and her huge skirt rose and fell like a splash of surf. She was so beautiful I could hardly bear it. I hugged her, and she laughed.

Later that night I asked my mother why she got so distraught. Wasn't my sister popular enough? My mother was sitting in the kitchen, in an old, faded yellow housecoat, drinking a glass of warm milk. "You don't know anything about it," she said, with such sadness that I rose from the table and fled to my room.

"I know what I'm saying!" my mother would cry when she argued with my sister. "You must listen to me. People talk. . . . You don't know who you'll meet on a date; it's good to accept even if you don't like the boy. . . . Girls have to be very careful. You're thoughtless. Don't you think in fifty years I've learned what makes the world go around? Now, listen to me. I know what I'm saying. . . ." But my sister's face was so radiant, her charm was so intense, she pushed her blond hair back from her face with a gesture so quick, so certain, so arrogant and filled with vanity, that no one, I thought, could doubt that whatever she did would be right.

I wanted to be arrogant, too. I didn't want to wear glasses and be one of the humorless, heavy-handed boys my sister despised. I was on her side as much as she'd let me be. She was the elder, and she often grew impatient with me. I didn't seem to understand all the things involved in being on her side.

Night after night I saw her come home from work tired—she had a secretarial job in a hospital and she hated it—and two hours later she would descend the stairs, to greet her date, her face alight with seriousness or with a large, bright smile, depending on her mood or on where her escort was taking her that evening. A concert or an art movie made her serious; one of the hotel supper clubs brought the smile to her face. She would trip down the stairs in her high heels, a light, flimsy coat thrown over one arm, one hand clutching a purse and gloves, her other hand on the banister. In the queer yellow light of the hall chandelier, her necklace or her earrings would shine dully, and sometimes, especially if she was all dressed up, in a black dress, say, with a low neck, because they were going out to a supper club, there would be an air, in spite of her gaiety, of the captive about her. It was part of her intense charm. In her voluminous white skirt, she went to the spring dance at the country club and brought back to my mother the news that she had captured the interest of Sonny Bruster, the oldest son of M. F. Bruster, a banker and a very rich man—more than interest, it turned out, because he started calling my sister up almost every day at work and taking her out almost every night. My mother was on the phone much of the afternoon explaining to her friends that my sister wasn't engaged. It was criminal the way some people gossiped, she said. My sister had only gone out with the boy ten or twelve times. They were just getting to know each other. Then my mother began to *receive* calls; someone had heard from a friend of Mrs. Bruster's that Mrs. Bruster had said her son was very serious about my sister, who was a very charming, very pretty girl, of good family. . . . My mother rubbed her hands with glee. She borrowed money from her brothers, and every week my sister had new clothes.

My sister would come home from work and run upstairs to change. Sonny would be due by seven, to take her out to dinner. My sister would kick her shoes off, struggle out of her dress, and dash around the upstairs in her slip.

"Mother, I can't find my earrings."

"Which earrings, dear?"

"The little pearls—the little tiny pearl ones that I got two Easters ago, to go with my black . . ."

My sister was delighted with herself. She loved being talked about, being envied.

"Mother, do you know what Ceil Johnson said to me today? She said that Beryl Feringhaus—you know, the real-estate people—was heartbroken because she thought Sonny Bruster was going to get engaged to her." My sister giggled. Her long hair was tangled, and my mother yanked a comb through it.

"Maybe you ought to cut your hair," my mother said, trying to hide her own excitement and to stay practical. During this period, my mother was living in the imminence of wealth. Whenever she stopped what she was doing and looked up, her face would be bright with visions.

That spring when I was sixteen, more than anything else in the world I wanted to be a success when I grew up. I did not know there was any other way of being lovable. My best friend was a boy named Preston, who already had a heavy beard. He was shy, and unfortunate in his dealings with other people, and he wanted to be a physicist. He had very little imagination, and he pitied anyone who did have it. "You and the word 'beautiful'!" he would say disdainfully, holding his nose and imitating my voice. "Tell me—what does 'beautiful' mean?"

"It's something you want," I would say.

"You're an aesthete," Preston would say. "I'm a scientist. That's the difference."

He and I used to call each other almost every night and have long, profound talks on the telephone.

On a date, Preston would sit beside his girl and stolidly eye her. Occasionally, toward the end of the evening, he would begin to breathe heavily, and he would make a few labored, daring jokes. He might catch the girl's hand and stare at her with inflamed and wistful eyes, or he might mutter incoherent compliments. Girls liked him, and escaped easily from his clumsy longing. They slipped their hands from his grasp and asked him to call them up again, but after a few dates with a girl Preston would say disgustedly, "All she does is talk. She's frigid or something. . . ." But the truth was, he was afraid of hurting them, of doing something wrong to them, and he never really courted them at all.

At school, Preston and I had afternoon study hall together. Study hall was in the library, which was filled with the breathing of a hundred and fifty students, and with the dim, half-fainting breezes of high spring, and with books: it was the crossroads of the world. Preston and I would sign out separately, and meet in the lavatory. There we would lean up against the stalls and talk. Preston was full of thoughts; he was tormented by all his ideas. "Do you know what relativity means?" he would ask me. "Do you realize how it affects every little detail of everyday life?" Or it might be Spinoza that moved him: "Eighteenth-century, but by God *there* was a rational man." I would pace up and down, half listening, half daydreaming, wishing *my* name would appear on Preston's list of people who had elements of greatness.

Or we talked about our problems. "I'm not popular," I would say. "I'm too gloomy."

"Why is that, do you think?" Preston would ask.

"I don't know," I would say. "I'm a virgin. That has a lot to do with everything."

"Listen," Preston said one day, "you may not be popular but you're likable. Your trouble is you're a snob." He walked up and down the white-tiled floor, mimicking me. He slouched, and cast his eyes down, and jutted his chin out, and pulled a foolish, serious look over his face.

"Is that me?" I cried, heartbroken.

"Well, almost," Preston said.

Or, leaning on the window sill, sticking our heads out into the golden afternoon air and watching a girl's gym class doing archery under the trees, we talked about sex.

"It starts in the infant," Preston said. "And it lasts forever."

"Saints escape it," I said mournfully.

"The hell they do," Preston said. The girls beneath us on the hillside drew their bows. Their thin green gym suits fluttered against their bodies. "Aren't they nice?" Preston asked longingly. "Aren't they wonderful?"

After school, Preston and I went out for track. The outdoor track was a cinder oval surrounding the football field. A steep, grassy hill led up to the entrance of the school locker room. "Run up that hill every night, boys," the coach pleaded—Old Mackyz, with his paunch and his iron-gray wavy hair—at the end of the practice period. "Run, boys, because when you're abso-lootly exhausted, that's when you got to give *more*. It's the *more,* boys, that makes champions." And then he'd stand there, humble, and touched by his own speech.

During our warmup sessions, we used to jog-trot the length of the field and back again, keeping our knees high. The grand inutility of this movement filled me with something like exaltation; and on every side of me, in irregular lines, my fellow-males jogged, keeping their knees high. What happiness!

"The turf's too springy," Preston would mumble. "Bad for the muscles." Preston was a miler. He was thickset and without natural grace; Mackyz said he had no talent, but he ran doggedly, and he became a good miler. I ran the 440. I was tall and thin, and even Mackyz said I ought to be good at it, but I wasn't. Mackyz said I didn't have the spirit. "All you smart boys are alike," he said. "You haven't got the *heart* for it. You always hold back. You're all a bunch of goldbricks." I tried to cure my maimed enthusiasm. As I ran, Mackyz would bawl desperately, "Hit the ground harder. Hit with your toes! Spring, boy! SPRING! Don't coddle yourself, for

Christ's sake. . . ." After a race, I'd throw myself down on a knoll near the finish line, under a sycamore tree, where the track manager dug a new hole every day for us to puke in. Three or four others would join me, and we'd lie there wearily, our chests burning, too weak to move.

Among my other problems was that I was reduced nearly to a state of tears over my own looks whenever I looked at a boy named Joel Bush. Joel was so incredibly good-looking that none of the boys could quite bear the fact of his existence; his looks weren't particularly masculine or clean-cut, and he wasn't a fine figure of a boy—he was merely beautiful. He looked like a statue that had been rubbed with honey and warm wax, to get a golden tone, and he carried at all times, in the neatness of his features and the secret proportions of his face and body that made him so handsome in that particular way, the threat of seduction. Displease me, he seemed to say, and I'll get you. I'll make you fall in love with me and I'll get you. I'll make you fall in love with me and I'll turn you into a donkey. Everyone either avoided him or gave in to him; teachers refused to catch him cheating, boys never teased him, and no one ever told him off. One day I saw him saying goodbye to a girl after school, and as he left her to join me, walking toward the locker room, he said to her, "Meet you here at five-thirty." Track wasn't over until six, and I could tell that he had no intention of meeting her, and yet, when he asked me about some experiments we had done in physics, instead of treating him like someone who had just behaved like a heel, I told him everything I knew.

He never joined us under the sycamore tree, and he ran effortlessly. He would pass the finish line, his chest heaving under his sweat-stained track shirt, and climb into the stands and sit in the sunlight. I was watching him, one afternoon, as he sat there wiping his face and turning his head from side to side. At one moment it was all silver except for the charred hollows of his eyes, and the next it was young and perfect, the head we all recognized as his.

Mackyz saw him and called out to him to put his sweatshirt on before he caught a cold. As he slipped the sweatshirt on, Joel shouted, "Aw, go fry your head!" Mackyz laughed good-naturedly.

Sprinkled here and there on the football field were boys lifting their arms high and then sweeping them down to touch their toes, or lying on their backs and bicycling their legs in the air. I got up and walked toward them, to do a little jog-trotting and high-knee prancing. I looked at Joel. "I'm cooling off," he said to me. I walked on, and just then a flock of crows wheeled up behind the oak tree on the hill and filled the sky with their vibrant motion. Everyone—even Preston—paused and looked up. The birds rose in a half circle and then glided, scythelike, with wings outspread, on a down current of air until they were only twenty feet or so above the ground; then they flapped their wings with a noise like sheets being shaken out, and soared aloft, dragging their shadows up the stepped concrete geometry of the stands, past Joel's handsome, rigid figure, off into the sky.

"Whaddya know about that?" Mackyz said. "Biggest flock of crows I ever saw."

"Why didn't you get your gun and shoot a couple?" Joel called out. Everyone turned. "Then you'd have some crow handy when-ever you had to eat some," Joel said.

"Take a lap," Mackyz bawled, his leathery face turning red up to the roots of his iron-gray hair.

"He was only kidding," I said, appalled at Mackyz' hurt.

Mackyz looked at me and scowled, "You can take a lap too, and don't talk so much."

I took off my sweatshirt and dropped it on the grass and set off around the track. As soon as I started running, the world changed. The bodies sprawled out across the green of the football field were parts of a scene remembered, not one real at this moment. The whole secret of effort is to keep on, I told myself. Not for the world would I have stopped then, and yet nothing—not even if I had been turned handsome as a reward for finishing—could have made up for the curious pain of the effort.

About halfway around the track, Joel caught up to me, and then he slowed down and ran alongside. "Mackyz isn't watching," he said. "Let's sneak up the hill." I looked and saw that Mackyz was lining up the team for high-jump practice. Joel sailed up over the crest of the hill, and I followed him.

"He's getting senile," Joel said, sighting down the crest of the hill at Mackyz, and then lying down. "Come on, jerk, lie down. You want Mackyz to see you?"

I was uneasy; this sort of fooling was all right for Joel, because he "made the effort," but if Mackyz caught me, he'd kick me off the team. I pointed this out to Joel.

"Aw, Mackyz takes everything too seriously. That's his problem," Joel said. "He's always up in the air about something. I don't see why he makes so much fuss. You ever notice how old men make a big fuss over everything?"

"Mackyz' not so old."

"All right, you ever notice how *middle-aged* men make a big fuss over everything?" A few seconds later, he said casually, his gaze resting on the underside of the leaves of the oak tree, "I got laid last night."

"No kidding?" I said.

He spread his fingers over his face, no doubt to see them turn orange in the sunlight, as children do. "Yeah," he said.

From the football field came the sounds of high-jump practice starting. Mackyz was shouting, "Now, start with your left foot—one, two, three—take off! TAKE OFF, GODDAMN IT! Spread your Goddamned legs, spread 'em. You won't get ruptured. There's sand to catch you, for Christ's sake." The jumper's footsteps made a series of thuds, there was a pause, and then the sound of the landing in the sand. Lifting my head, I could see the line of boys waiting to jump, the lead boy breaking into a run, leaping from the ground, and spreading his arms in athletic entreaty.

"It was disappointing," Joel said.

"How?" I asked.

"It's nothing very special."

I was aroused by this exposé. "You mean the books—"

"It's not like that at all." He turned sullenly and scrabbled with his fingers in the dirt. "It's like masturbation, kind of with bells."

"Maybe the girl didn't know how to do it."

"She was a grown woman!"

"Yeah, but—"

"She was a fully grown woman! She knew what she was doing!"

"Oh," I said. Then, after a minute, "Look, would you mind telling me what you said to her? If I ever had a chance, I wouldn't know what to say. I . . ."

"I don't remember," Joel said. "We just looked at each other, and then she got all tearful, and she told me to take my clothes off."

We lay there a moment, in the late afternoon sunshine, and then I said we'd better be getting back. We walked around behind the hill, and waited until Mackyz wasn't looking before we sprinted out onto the track.

The jumping went on for fifteen or twenty minutes more; then Mackyz raised his arms in a gesture of benediction. "All right, you squirts—all out on the track for a fast lap. And that includes you, goldbrick," he said to me, wagging his finger.

All the boys straightened up and started toward the track. The sun's light poured in long low rays over the roof of the school. Jostling and joking, we started to run. "Faster!" Mackyz yelled. "Faster! Whatsa matter—you all a bunch of girls! Faster! For Christ's sake, faster!"

Since Preston, in his dogged effort to become a good miler, ran three laps to everyone else's one, he was usually in last in the locker room. He would come in, worn out and breathing heavily; sometimes he even had to hold himself up with one hand on his locker while he undressed. Everyone else would long since have showered and would be almost ready to leave. They might make one or two remarks about Preston's running his legs down to stumps or trying to kill himself for Mackyz' sake. Preston would smile numbly while he tried to get his breath back, and somehow, I was always surprised by how little attention was paid to Preston, how cut off and how alone he was.

More often than not, Joel would be showing off in the locker room—walking around on his hands, singing dirty songs, or engaged in some argument or other. Preston would go into the shower. I would talk to Joel, dressing slowly, because I usually waited for Preston. By the time I was all dressed, the locker room would be empty and Preston would still be towelling himself off. Then, instead of hurrying to put his clothes on, he would run his hand over his chest, to curl the few limp hairs. "Oh come on!" I would say, disgustedly.

"Hold your horses," he would say, with his maddening physicist's serenity. "Just you hold your horses."

It took him half an hour to get dressed. He'd stand in front of the mirror and flex his muscles endlessly and admire the line his pectorals made across his broad rib cage, and he always left his shirt until last, even until after he had combed his hair. I found his vanity confusing; he was far from handsome, with his heavy mouth and bushy eyebrows and thick, sloping shoulders, but he loved his reflection and he'd turn and gaze at himself in the mirror from all sorts of angles while he buttoned his shirt. He hated Joel. "There's a guy who'll never amount to much," Preston would say. "He's chicken. And he's not very smart. I don't see why you want him to like you—except that you're a sucker. You let your eyes run away with your judgment." I put up with all this because I wanted Preston to walk me part way home. It seemed shameful somehow to have to walk home alone.

Finally, he would finish, and we would emerge from the now deserted school into the dying afternoon. As we walked, Preston harangued me about my lack of standards and judgment. The hunger I had for holding school office and for being well thought of he dismissed as a streak of lousy bourgeois cowardice. I agreed with him (I didn't like myself anyway); but what was to be done about it? "We might run away," Preston said, squinting up at the sky. "Hitchhike. Work in factories. Go to a whorehouse. . . ." I leaned against a tree trunk, and Preston stood with one foot on the curb and one foot in the street, and we lobbed pebbles back and forth. "We're doomed," Preston said. "Doom" was one of his favorite words, along with "culture," "kinetic," and "the Absolute." "We come from a dying culture," he said.

"I suppose you're right," I said. "It certainly looks that way." But then I cheered up. "After all, it's not as if we were insane or anything."

"It wouldn't show yet," Preston said gloomily. "It's still in the latent stage. It'll come out later. You'll see. After all, you're still living at home, and you've got your half-assed charm—"

I broke in; I'd never had a compliment from him before.

"I didn't say you were charming," he said. "I said you have a half-assed charm. You behave well in public. That's all I meant."

At the corner where we separated, Preston stood a moment or two. "It's hopeless," he said.

"God, do you really think so?" I asked.

"That's my honest opinion," he said.

He turned toward his house. I jogged a block or two, and then felt my stomach muscles. When I came to a maple with a low, straight branch, I ran and jumped up and swung from the branch, while a big green diesel bus rolled ponderously past, all its windows filled with tired faces that looked out at the street going by and at me hanging from the branch and smiling. I was doomed, but I was very likely charming.

I ran in the front door of my house and called out, "Mother! Mother!"

"What is it?" she answered. She was sitting on the screened porch, and I could see a little plume of cigarette smoke in the doorway. There was the faint mutter of a radio news program turned on low.

"Nothing," I said. "I'm home, that's all."

At the dinner table, I would try to disguise myself by slouching in my chair and thinking about my homework, but my mother and my sister always recognized me. "How was track today?" my sister would ask in a slightly amused way.

"Fine," I would say in a low voice.

My mother and my sister would exchange glances. I must have seemed comic to them, stilted, and slightly absurd, like all males.

Almost every evening, Sonny Bruster used to drive up to our house in his yellow convertible. The large car would glide to a stop at the curb, and Sonny would glance quickly at himself in the rearview mirror, running his hand over his hair. Then he'd climb out and brush his pants off, too occupied with his own shyness to notice the children playing on the block. But they would stop what they were doing and watch him.

I would wait for him at the front door and let him in and lead him into the living room. I walked ahead of Sonny because I had noticed that he could not keep himself from looking up the stairs as we passed through the hallway, as if to conjure up my sister then and there with the intensity of his longing, and I hated to see him do this. I would sit in the high-backed yellow chair, and Sonny would settle himself on the couch and ask me about track, or if I'd picked a college yet. "You ought to think carefully about college," he would say. "I think Princeton is more civilized than Yale." His gentle, well-bred voice was carefully inexpressive. In his manner there was a touch of stiffness to remind you, and himself, that he was rich and if some disrespect was intended for him he wouldn't necessarily put up with it. But I liked him. He treated me with great politeness, and I liked the idea of his being my brother-in-law, and I sometimes thought of the benefits that would fall to me if my sister married him.

Then my sister would appear at the head of the stairs, dressed to go out, and Sonny would leap to his feet. "Are you ready?" he'd cry, as if he had never dared hope she would be. My sister would hand him her coat, and with elaborate care he'd hold it for her. It would be perhaps eight o'clock or a little later. The street lamps would be on, but looking pallid because it wasn't quite dark. Usually, Sonny would open the car door for my sister, but sometimes, with a quick maneuver, she would forestall him; she would hurry the last few steps, open the door, and slip inside before he could lift his hand.

Sonny was not the first rich boy who had loved my sister; he was the fourth or fifth. And in the other cases there had been scenes between my mother and sister in which my mother extolled the boy's eligibility and my sister argued that she was too young to marry and didn't want to stop having a good time yet. Each time she had won, and each time the boy had been sent packing, while my mother looked heartbroken and said my sister was throwing her chances away.

With Sonny, the same thing seemed about to happen. My sister missed going out with a lot of boys instead of with just one. She complained once or twice that Sonny was jealous and spoiled. There were times when she seemed to like him very much, but there were other times when she would greet him blankly in the evening when she came downstairs, and he would be apologetic and fearful, and I could see that her disapproval was the thing he feared most in the world.

My mother didn't seem to notice, or if she did, she hid her feelings. Then one night I was sitting in my room doing my homework and I heard my mother and sister come upstairs. They went into my sister's room.

"I think Sonny's becoming very serious," my mother said.

"Sonny's so short," I heard my sister say. "He's not really interesting, either, Mother."

"He seems to be very fond of you," my mother said.

"He's no fun," my sister said. "Mother, be careful! You're brushing too hard! You're hurting me!"

I stopped trying to work, and listened.

"Sonny's a very intelligent boy," my mother said. "He comes from a good family."

"I don't care," my sister said. "I don't want to waste myself on him."

"Waste yourself?" My mother laughed derisively. I got up and went to the door of my sister's room. My sister was sitting at her dressing table, her hair shining like glass and her eyes closed. My mother was walking back and forth, gesturing with the hairbrush. "He's the one who's throwing himself away," she said. "Who do you think we are, anyway? We're nobodies."

"I'm pretty!" my sister objected angrily.

My mother shrugged. "The woods are full of pretty girls. What's more, they're full of pretty, rich girls. Now, Sonny's a very *nice* boy—"

"Leave me alone!" My sister pulled her hair up from her shoulders and held it in a soft mop on the top of her head. "Sonny's a jerk! A jerk!"

"He's nice-looking!" my mother cried.

"Oh, what do *you* know about it?" my sister cried. "You're old, for God's sake!"

The air vibrated. My sister rose and looked at my mother, horrified at what she said. She took her hands from her hair, and it fell tumbling to her shoulders, dry and pale and soft. "I don't care," she said suddenly, and brushed past me, and fled into the bathroom and locked the door. There was no further sound from her. The only trace of her in the house at that moment was the faint odor in her room of the flowery perfume she used that spring.

"Oh, she's so foolish," my mother said, and I saw that she was crying. "She doesn't know what she's doing. . . . Why is she so foolish?" Then she put the hairbrush down and raised her hands to her cheeks and begin to pinch them.

I went back to my room and closed the door.

When I came out again, an hour later, my mother was in bed reading a magazine; she looked as if she had been wounded in a dozen places. My sister sat in her room, in front of the mirror. Her hair streamed down the back of her neck and lay in touching, defenseless little curls on the towel she had over her shoulders. She was studying her reflection thoughtfully. (Are flowers vain? Are trees? Are they consumed with vanity during those days when they are in bloom?) She raised her finger and pressed it against her lower lip to see, I think, if she would be prettier if her lip, instead of being so smooth, had a slight break in the center as some girls' did.

Shortly after this, my mother, who was neither stupid nor cruel, suggested that my sister stop seeing Sonny for a while. "Until you make up your mind," she said. "Otherwise you might break his heart, you know. Tell him you need some time to think. He'll understand. He'll think you're grown-up and responsible."

Sonny vanished from our house. In the evenings now, after dinner, the three of us would sit on the screened porch. My sister would look up eagerly when the phone rang, but the calls were never for her. None of her old boy friends knew she had stopped dating Sonny, and after a while, when the phone rang, she would compose her face and pretend she wasn't interested, or she would say irritably, "Who can that be?" She began to answer the phone herself (she never had before, because it wasn't good for a girl to seem too eager) and she would look sadly at herself in the hall mirror while she said, "Yes, Preston, he's here." She tried to read. She'd skim a few pages and then put the book down and gaze out through the screens at the night and the patches of light on the trees. She would listen with my mother to the comedians on the radio and laugh vaguely when my mother laughed. She picked on me. "Your posture's no good," she'd say. Or "Where do you learn your manners? Mother, he behaves like a zoot-suiter or something." Another time, she said, "If I don't make a good marriage, you'll be in trouble. You're too lazy to do anything on your own." She grew more and more restless. Toying with her necklace, she broke the string, and the beads rolled all over the floor, and there was something frantic in the way she went about retrieving the small rolling bits of glitter. It occurred to me that she didn't know what she was doing; she was not really as sure of everything as she seemed. It was a painfully difficult thought to arrive at, and it clung to me. Why hadn't I realized it before? Also, she sort of hated me, it seemed to me. I had never noticed that before, either. How could I have been so wrong, I wondered. Knowing how wrong I had been about this, I felt that no idea I had ever held was safe. For instance, we were not necessarily a happy family, with the most wonderful destinies waiting for my sister and me. We might make mistakes and choose wrong. Unhappiness was real. It was even likely. . . . How tired I became of studying my sister's face. I got so I would do anything to keep from joining the two women on the porch.

After three weeks of this, Sonny returned. I was never told whether he came of his own accord or whether he was summoned; but one night the yellow convertible drove up in front of our house and he was back. Now when my mother would watch my sister and Sonny getting into Sonny's car in the evenings, she would turn away from the window smiling. "I think your sister has found a boy she can respect," she would say, or "They'll be very happy together," or some such hopeful observation, which I could see no basis for, but which my mother believed with all the years and memories at her disposal, with all the weight of her past and her love for my sister. And I would go and call Preston.

I used to lie under the dining-room table, sheltered and private like that, looking up at the way the pieces of mahogany were joined together, while we talked. I would cup the telephone to my ear with my shoulder and hold my textbook up in the air, over my head, as we went over physics, which was a hard subject for me. "Preston," I asked one night, "what in God's name makes a siphon work?" They did work—everyone knew that—and I groaned as I asked it. Preston explained the theory to me, and I frowned, breathed heavily through my nose, squinted at the incomprehensible diagrams in the book, and thought of sex, of the dignity of man, of the wonders of the mind, as he talked. Every few minutes, he asked "Do you see" and I would sigh. It was spring, and there was

meaning all around me, if only I were free—free of school, free of
my mother, free of duties and inhibitions—if only I were mounted
on a horse. . . . Where was the world? Not here, not near me, not
under the dining-room table. . . . "Not quite," I'd say, untruth-
fully, afraid that I might discourage him. "But I almost get it. Just
tell me once more." And on and on he went, while I frowned,
breathed hard, and squinted. And then it happened! "I see!" I
cried. "I see! I see!" It was air pressure! How in the world had I
failed to visualize air pressure? I could see it now. I would never
again not see it; it was there in my mind, solid and indestructible, a
whitish column sitting on the water. "God damn but science is
wonderful!" I said, and heaved my physics book into the living
room. "Really wonderful!"

"It's natural law," Preston said reprovingly. "Don't get emotion
mixed up with it."

One evening when my sister and Sonny didn't have a date to go
out, my mother tapped lightly on my foot, which protruded from
under the dining-room table. "I have a feeling Sonny may call,"
she whispered. I told Preston I had to hang up, and crawled out
from beneath the table. "I have a feeling that they're getting to the
point," my mother said. "Your sister's nervous."

I put the phone back on the telephone table. "But Mother—" I
said, and the phone rang.

"Sh-h-h," she said.

The phone rang three times. My sister, on the extension upstairs,
said, "Hello. . . . Oh, Sonny. . . ."

My mother looked at me and smiled. Then she pulled at my
sleeve until I bent my head down, and she whispered in my ear,
"They'll be so happy. . . ." She went into the hall, to the foot of
the stairs. "Tell him he can come over," she whispered passionately.

"Sure," my sister was saying on the phone. "I'd like that.
. . . If you want. . . . Sure. . . ."

My mother went on listening, her head tilted to one side, the
light falling on her aging face, and then she began to pantomime
the answers my sister ought to be making—sweet yesses, dignified
noes, and little bursts of alluring laughter.

I plunged down the hall and out the screen door. The street

lamps were on, and there was a moon. I could hear the children: "I see Digger. One-two-three, you're caught, Digger. . . ." Two blocks away, the clock on the Presbyterian church was striking the hour. Just then a little girl left her hiding place in our hedge and ran shrieking for the tree trunk that was home-free base: "I'm home safe! I'm home safe! Everybody free!" All the prisoners, who had been sitting disconsolately on the bumpers of Mr. Karmgut's Oldsmobile, jumped up with joyful cries and scattered abruptly in the darkness.

I lifted my face—that exasperating factor, my face—and stared entranced at the night, at the waving tops of the trees, and the branches blowing back and forth, and the round moon embedded in the night sky, turning the nearby streamers of cloud into mother-of-pearl. It was all very rare and eternal-seeming. What a dreadful unhappiness I felt.

I walked along the curb, balancing with my arms outspread. Leaves hung over the sidewalk. The air was filled with their rustling, and they caught the light of the street lamps. I looked into the lighted houses. There was Mrs. Kearns, tucked girlishly into a corner of the living-room couch, reading a book. Next door, through the leaves of a tall plant, I saw the Lewises all standing in the middle of the floor. When I reached the corner, I put one arm around the post that held the street sign, and leaned there, above the sewer grating, where my friends and I had lost perhaps a hundred tennis balls, over the years. In numberless dusks, we had abandoned our games of catch and handball and gathered around the grating and stared into it at our ball, floating down in the darkness.

The Cullens' porch light was on, in the next block, and I saw Mr. and Mrs. Cullen getting into their car. Eleanor Cullen was in my class at school, and she had been dating Joel. Her parents were going out, and that meant she'd be home alone—if she was home. She might have gone to the library, I thought as the car started up; or to a sorority meeting. While I stood there looking at the Cullens' house, the porch light went off. A minute later, out of breath from running, I stood on the dark porch and rang the doorbell. There was no light on in the front hall, but the front door was open, and I could hear something coming. It was Eleanor. "Who is it?" she asked.

"Me," I said. "Are you busy? Would you like to come out for a little while and talk?"

She drifted closer to the screen door and pressed her nose against it. She looked pale without makeup.

"Sure," she said. "I'll have to go put my shoes on. I'm not in a good mood or anything."

"That's all right," I said. "Neither am I. I just want to talk to somebody."

While I waited for Eleanor to come out, Mattie Seaton appeared, striding along the sidewalk. He was on the track team. "Hey, Mattie," I called out to him.

"Hi," he said.

"What's new?"

"Nothing much," he said. "You got your trig done?"

"No, not yet."

"You going with *her*?" he asked, pointing to the house.

"Naw," I said.

"Well, I got to get my homework done," he said.

"See you later," I called after him. I knew where he was going: Nancy Ellis's house, two blocks down.

"Who was that?" Eleanor asked. She stepped out on the porch. She had combed her hair and put on lipstick.

"Mattie Seaton," I said.

"He's pinned to Nancy," Eleanor said. "He likes her a lot. . . ." She sat down in a white metal chair. I sat on the porch railing, facing her. She fumbled in her pocket and pulled out a pack of cigarettes. "You want a cigarette?" she asked.

"No. I'm in training."

We looked at each other, and then she looked away, and I looked down at my shoes. I sat there liking her more and more.

"How come you're in a bad mood?" I asked her.

"Me? Oh, I don't know. How did you know I was in a bad mood?"

"You told me." I could barely make out her face and the dull color of her hands in the darkness.

"You know, I think I'm not basically a happy person," Eleanor said suddenly. "I always thought I was. . . . People expect you to be, especially if you're a girl."

"It doesn't surprise *me,*" I said.

A breeze set all the leaves in motion again. "It's going to rain," I said.

Eleanor stood up, smoothing her yellow skirt, and threw her cigarette off the porch; the glowing tip landed on the grass. She realized I was staring at her. She lifted her hand and pressed it against her hair. "You may have noticed I look unusually plain tonight," she said. She leaned over the porch railing beside me, supporting herself on her hands. "I was trying to do my geometry," she said in a low voice. "I couldn't do it. I felt stupid," she said. "So I cried. That's why I look so awful."

"I think you look all right," I said. "I think you look fine." I leaned forward and laid my cheek on her shoulder. Then I sat up quickly, flushing. "I don't like to hear you being so dissatisfied with yourself," I mumbled. "You could undermine your self-confidence that way."

Eleanor straightened and faced me, in the moonlight. "You're beautiful," I burst out longingly. "I never noticed before. But you are."

"Wait," Eleanor said. Tears gathered in her eyes. "Don't like me yet. I have to tell you something first. It's about Joel."

"You don't have to tell me," I said. "I know you're going with him. I understand."

"Listen to me!" she said impatiently, stamping her foot. "I'm *not* going with him. He—" She suddenly pressed her hands against her eyes. "Oh, it's awful!" she cried.

A little shudder of interest passed through me. "O.K.," I said. "But I don't care if you don't tell me."

"I want to!" she cried. "I'm just a little embarrassed. I'll be all right in a minute—

"We went out Sunday night . . ." she began after a few seconds. They had gone to Medart's, in Clayton, for a hamburger. Joel had talked her into drinking a bottle of beer, and it had made her so drowsy that she had put her head on the back of the seat and closed her eyes. "What kind of car does Joel have?" I asked.

"A Buick," Eleanor said, surprised at my question.

"I see," I said. I pictured the dashboard of a Buick, and Joel's handsome face, and then, daringly, I added Eleanor's hand, with its bitten fingernails, holding Joel's hand. I was only half listening, because I felt the preliminary stirrings of an envy so deep it would make me miserable for weeks. I looked up at the sky over my shoulder; clouds had blotted out the moon, and everything had got darker. From the next block, in the sudden stillness, I heard the children shouting, uttering their Babylonian cries as they played kick-the-can. Their voices were growing tired and fretful.

"And then I felt his hand on my—" Eleanor, half-drowned in shadow was showing me, on her breast, where Joel had touched her.

"Is that all?" I said, suddenly smiling. Now I would not have to die of envy. "That's nothing!"

"I—I slapped his face!" She exclaimed. Her lip trembled. "Oh, I didn't mean—I sort of wanted— Oh, it's all so terrible!" she burst out. She ran down the front steps and onto the lawn, and leaned against the trunk of an oak tree. I followed her. The pre-storm stillness filled the sky, the air between the trees, the dark spaces among the shrubbery. "Oh, God!" Eleanor cried. "How I hate everything!"

My heart was pounding, and I didn't know why. I hadn't known I could feel like this—that I could pause on the edge of such feeling, which lay stretched like an enormous meadow all in shadow inside me. It seemed to me a miracle that human beings could be so elaborate. "Listen, Eleanor," I said, "you're all right! I've *always* liked you." I swallowed and moved closer to her; there were two moist streaks running down her face. I raised my arm and, with the sleeve of my shirt, I wiped away her tears. "I think you're wonderful! I think you're really something!"

"You look down on me," she said. "I know you do. I can tell."

"How can I, Eleanor. How *can* I?" I cried. "I'm nobody. I've been damaged by my heredity."

"You, too!" she exclaimed happily. "Oh, that's what's wrong with me!"

A sudden hiss swept through the air and then the first raindrops struck the street. "Quick!" Eleanor cried, and we ran up on her porch. Two bursts of lightning lit up the dark sky, and the rain streamed down. I held Eleanor's hand, and we stood watching the rain. "It's a real thundershower," she said.

"Do you feel bad because we only started being friends tonight? I mean, do you feel you're on the rebound and settling on the second-best?" I asked. There was a long silence and all around it was the sound of the rain.

"I don't think so," Eleanor said at last. "How about you?"

I raised my eyebrows and said, "Oh, no, it doesn't bother me at all."

"That's good," she said.

We were standing very close to one another. We talked industriously. "I don't like geometry," Eleanor said. "I don't see what use it is. It's supposed to train your mind, but I don't believe it. . . ."

I took my glasses off. "Eleanor—" I said. I kissed her, passionately, and then I turned away, pounding my fists on top of each other. "Excuse me," I whispered hoarsely. That kiss had lasted a long time, and I thought I would die.

Eleanor was watching the long, slanting lines of rain falling just outside the porch, gray in the darkness; she was breathing very rapidly. "You know what?" she said. "I could make you scrambled eggs. I'm a good cook." I leaned my head against the brick wall of the house and said I'd like some.

In the kitchen, she put on an apron and bustled about, rattling pans and silverware, and talking in spurts. "I think a girl should know how to cook, don't you?" She let me break the eggs into a bowl—three eggs, which I cracked with a flourish. "Oh, you're good at it," she said, and began to beat them with a fork while I sat on the kitchen table and watched her. "Did you know most eggs *aren't* baby chickens?" she asked me. She passed so close to me on her way to the stove that, because her cheeks were flushed and her eyes bright, I couldn't help leaning forward and kissing her. She turned pink and hurried to the stove. I sat on the kitchen table, swinging my legs and smiling to myself. Suddenly we heard a noise just outside the back door. I leaped off the table and took up a polite position by the sink. Eleanor froze. But no one opened the door; no one appeared.

"Maybe it was a branch falling," I said.

Eleanor nodded. Then she made a face and looked down at her

hands. "I don't know why we got so nervous. We aren't doing anything wrong."

"It's the way they look at you," I said.

"Yes, that's it," she said. "You know, I think my parents are ashamed of me. But someday I'll show them. I'll do something wonderful, and they'll be amazed." She went back to the stove.

"When are your parents coming home?" I asked.

"They went to a double feature. They can't possibly be out before eleven."

"They might walk out on it," I said.

"Oh no!" Eleanor said. "Not if they pay for it . . ."

We ate our scrambled eggs and washed the dishes, and watched the rain from the dining-room windows without turning the light on. We kissed for a while, and then we both grew restless and uncomfortable. Her lips were swollen, and she went into the kitchen, and I heard her running the water; when she returned, her hair was combed and she had put on fresh lipstick. "I don't like being in the house," she said, and led me out on the porch. We stood with our arms around each other. The rain was slackening. "Good-bye, rain," Eleanor said sadly. It was as if we were watching a curtain slowly being lifted from around the house. The trees gleamed wetly near the street lamps.

When I started home, the rain had stopped. Water dripped on the leaves of the trees. Little plumes of mist hung over the wet macadam of the street. I walked very gently in order not to disturb anything.

I didn't want to run into anybody, and so I went home the back way, through the alley. At the entrance to the alley there was a tall cast-iron pseudo-Victorian lamppost, with an urn-shaped head and panes of frosted glass; the milky light it shed trickled part way down the alley, illuminating a few curiously still garage fronts and, here and there, the wet leaves of the bushes and vines that bordered the back yards and spilled in such profusion over the fences, hiding the ashpits and making the alley so pretty a place in spring. When I was younger, I had climbed on those ashpits, those brick squares nearly smothered under the intricacies of growing things, and I had searched in the debris for old, broken mirrors, discarded scarves with fringes, bits of torn decorated wrapping paper, and such treasures. But now I drifted down the alley, walking absently on the wet asphalt. I was having a sort of daydream where I was lying with my head on Eleanor's shoulder—which was bare—and I could hear the slow, even sound of her breathing as I began to fall asleep. I was now in the darkest part of the alley, the very center where no light reached, and in my daydream I turned over and kissed Eleanor's hands, her throat—and then I broke into a sprint down the alley, slipping and sliding on the puddles and wet places. I came out the other end of the alley and stood underneath the lamppost. I was breathing with difficulty.

Across the street from me, two women stood, one on the sidewalk, the other on the front steps of a house, hugging her arms. "It's not a bad pain," the woman on the sidewalk said, "but it persists."

"My dear, my dear," said the other. "Don't take any chances—not at our age . . ."

And a couple, a boy and a girl, were walking up the street, coming home from the Tivoli Theatre. The girl was slouching in order not to seem taller than the boy, who was very short and who sprang up and down on the balls of his feet as he walked.

I picked a spray of lilac and smelled it, but then I didn't know what to do with it—I didn't want to throw it away—and finally I put it in my pants pocket.

I vaulted our back fence and landed in our back yard, frightening a cat, who leaped out of the hedge and ran in zigzags across the dark lawn. It startled me so much I felt weak. I tucked my shirt in carefully and smoothed my hair. Suddenly, I looked down at my fingertips; they were blurred in the darkness and moist from the lilac, and I swept them to my mouth and kissed them.

The kitchen was dark. There was no sound in the house, no sound at all, and a tremor passed through me. I turned the kitchen light on and hurriedly examined myself for marks of what had happened to me. I peered at my shirt, my pants. I rubbed my face with both hands. Then I turned the light off and slipped into the dining room, which was dark, too, and so was the hallway. The porch light was on. I ran up the front stairs and stopped short at the top; there was a light on in my mother's room. She was sitting up in bed, with pillows at her back, a magazine across her lap, and a pad of paper on the magazine.

"Hello," I said.

I expected her to bawl me out for being late, but she just looked at me solemnly for a moment, and then she said, "Sonny proposed to your sister."

Because I hadn't had a chance to wash my face, I raised one hand and held it over my cheek and chin, to hide whatever traces of lipstick there might be.

She said. "They're going to be married in June. They went over to the Brusters' to get the ring. He proposed practically the first thing when he came. They were both so—they were *both* so *happy!*" she said. "They make such a lovely couple. . . . Oh, if you could have seen them."

She was in a very emotional state.

I started to back out the door.

"Where are you going?" my mother asked.

"To bed," I said, surprised. "I'm in training—"

"Oh, you ought to wait up for your sister."

"I'll leave her a note," I said.

I went to my room and took the white lilac out of my pocket and put it on my desk. I wrote, "I heard the news and think it's swell. Congratulations. Wake me up when you come in." I stuck the note in the mirror of her dressing table. Then I went back to my room and got undressed. Usually I slept raw, but I decided I'd better wear pajamas if my sister was going to come in and wake me up. I don't know how much later it was that I heard a noise and sat bolt upright in bed. I had been asleep. My sister was standing in the door of my room. She was wearing a blue dress that had little white buttons all the way down the front and she had white gloves on. "Are you awake?" she whispered.

"Yes," I said. "Where's Mother?"

"Downstairs," my sister said, coming into the room. "Sending telegrams. Do you want to see my ring?" She took her gloves off.

I turned the bedside-table lamp on, and she held her hand out. The ring was gold, and there was an emerald and four diamonds around it.

"It was his grandmother's," my sister said. I nodded. "It's not what I—" she said, and sat down on the edge of the bed, and forgot to finish her sentence. "Tell me," she said, "do you think he's really rich?" Then she turned a sad gaze on me, through her lashes. "Do you want to know something awful? I don't like my ring. . . ."

"Are you unhappy?" I asked.

"No, just upset. It's scary getting married. You have no idea. I kept getting chills all evening. I may get pneumonia. Do you have a cigarette?"

I said I'd get her one downstairs.

"No, there's some in my room," she said. "I'll get them. You know, Sonny and I talked about you. We're going to send you to college and everything. We planned it all out tonight." She played with her gloves for a while, and then she said, looking at the toes of her shoes, "I'm scared. What if Sonny's not good at business?" She turned to me. "You know what I mean? He's so young. . . ."

"You don't have to marry him," I said. "After all, you're—"

"You don't understand," my sister said hurriedly, warding off advice she didn't want. "You're too young yet." She laughed. "You know what he said to me?"

Just then, my mother called out from the bottom of the stairs, "Listen, how does this sound to you? 'Dear Greta—' It's a night letter, and we get a lot of words, and I thought Greta would like it better if I started that way. Greta's so touchy, you know. Can you hear me?"

"I have to go," my sister whispered. She looked at me, and then suddenly she leaned over and kissed me on the forehead. "Go to sleep," she said. "Have nice dreams." She got up and went out into the hall.

" '—Dodie got engaged tonight,' " my mother read. "Is 'got engaged' the right way to say it?"

"Became engaged," my sister said, in a distant voice.

I put on my bathrobe and slippers and went out into the hall. My sister was leaning over the banister, talking to my mother at the bottom of the stairs about the night letter. I slipped past her and down the back stairs and into the kitchen. I found a cold chicken in the icebox, put the platter on the kitchen table, and tore off a leg and began to eat.

The door to the back stairs swung open, and my sister appeared. "I'm hungry, too," she said. "I don't know why." She drifted over to the table, and bent over the chicken. "I guess emotion makes people hungry."

My mother pushed open the swinging door, from the dining-room side. "There you are," she said. She looked flustered. "I'll have to think some more, and then I'll write the whole thing over," she said to my sister. To me she said, "Are you *eating* at this time of night?"

My sister said that she was hungry, too.

"There's some soup," my mother said. "Why don't I heat it up." And suddenly her eyes filled with tears, and all at once we fell to kissing one another—to embracing and smiling and making cheerful predictions about one another—there in the white, brightly lighted kitchen. We had known each other for so long, and there were so many things that we all three remembered. . . . Our smiles, our approving glances, wandered from face to face. There was a feeling of politeness in the air. We were behaving the way we would in railway stations, at my sister's wedding, at the birth of her first child, at my graduation from college. This was the first of our reunions.

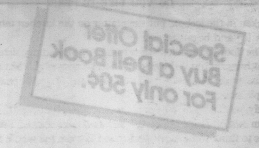

DATE DUE

DEMCO,